NO CURTAIN CALL

When the naked, blood-encrusted body of a well known property developer is discovered on a graveyard slab, there's overwhelming media frenzy. Investigative journalist Emma Boylan is assigned to the case — only to play second fiddle to a rival male reporter. Peeved at being sidelined, Emma pursues a line of inquiries deep in the dark side of London's West End. Dead bodies turn up amid elaborately theatrical settings. Undeterred, she probes further into disturbing deeds that have long remained hidden. Now she must peel away layer after layer of deception, until events collide and spiral into a terrifying, spectacular climax . . .

Books by K. T. McCaffrey
Published by The House of Ulverscroft:

BISHOP'S PAWN

K. T. McCAFFREY

NO CURTAIN CALL

Complete and Unabridged

ULVERSCROFT
Leicester

First published in Great Britain in 2010 by
Robert Hale Limited
London

First Large Print Edition
published 2011
by arrangement with
Robert Hale Limited
London

British Library CIP Data

McCaffrey, K. T.
   No curtain call.
   1. Boylan, Emma (Fictitious character)- -Fiction.
   2. Women journalists- -Fiction.
   3. West End (London, England)- -Fiction.
   4. Detective and mystery stories. 5. Large type books.
   I. Title
   823.9′14–dc22

   ISBN 978–1–44480–522–2

Published by
F. A. Thorpe (Publishing)
Anstey, Leicestershire

Set by Words & Graphics Ltd.
Anstey, Leicestershire
Printed and bound in Great Britain by
T. J. International Ltd., Padstow, Cornwall

For
Margaret Dolan
A wonderful writer and a constant
inspiration to me.

All the world's a stage,
And all men and women merely players:
They have their exits and their entrances;
And one man in his time plays many parts . . .

William Shakespeare

1

The faithful departed slept the eternal sleep, deep in their subterranean beds, undisturbed by the late-night deposit of a blood-encrusted corpse on the earth above them. Unlike the permanent inhabitants of St James's grave-yard, the interloper, a naked male, lay sprawled, face upwards, on top of a horizontal granite slab erected some 185 years earlier. A timber spike protruded from the cadaver's chest. A shroud of low-lying mist enveloped the old churchyard, partially obliterating the nearby abbey ruins. Morning sunlight struggled to penetrate the surreal scene, putrid light bathing the dead body in a silvery sheen. Alien-like figures, clad in white masks, caps, overshoes and surgical gloves, created ghostly patterns, appearing to float within an area delineated by crime-scene tape.

Detective Inspector Jim Connolly, his profile picked out in the defused glare, stood apart from the white suits. He spoke softly to John McCarthy, the uniformed sergeant by his side. 'What d'you think we're dealing with here?' he asked. Connolly had rushed from his apartment as soon as he'd got word of the find. He had just finished his shower and was about to join his partner for breakfast when the call came. Wasn't the first time he'd missed breakfast, but it was the first time he'd taken charge of a crime scene while feeling decidedly hung over.

'I'd say someone took last night's Halloween high jinx a bit too far,' McCarthy said, shaking his head, perplexed.

'Jesus, if this is trick or treat, we're in deeper shit than I thought. Who discovered the body?'

'The old guy over there,' the sergeant said, pointing to a man and a dog standing by the door of the abbey ruin. The man, who Connolly estimated to be in his late seventies, clutched the dog's lead tightly, a disdainful expression on his face.

'How did he happen to find it?'

'Lives around the corner in number 8, Marino Lane,' McCarthy said, referring to his notebook. 'Name's Dick Burke, says he had to keep the mutt in last night because of the fireworks; took him for a walk this morning instead. They were passing this place when the dog began to kick up a racket. Burke noticed the unlocked gate, thought it a bit odd. The dog pulled on the lead, dragged him to the body. He got an awful shock but

2

managed to call 999 on his mobile.'

'I see,' Connolly said, looking towards Burke, struck by the incongruity of modern technology in the shape of the man, his mobile phone, and the contrasting Gothic surroundings. 'Sergeant, could you take Mr Burke to his house and tell him I'd like a word with him later. I need to stick around here for a while, see if I can sort out what the hell's going on.'

Connolly's attention returned to the corpse. A shiver travelled the length of his spine, more from the effects of the chill in the air than the grisly sight on the algae-coated slab. A covering of frost blanched the earth in spite of the previous night's bonfires. Wisps of mist clung to the ground, making it look as though the headstones were levitating.

Garda Technical Bureau personnel busied themselves setting up their equipment while Connolly concentrated his attention on the wooden stake wedged in the cadaver's chest. An A4-size paper notice had been attached to the top of the spike. Laminated in clear plastic, it contained a standard application seeking planning permission to build an apartment block and a series of street-level shop units. Frost had partially distorted the text but the applicant's name at the base of the notice was just about decipherable: Scott

Mansfield. This was a name that had come to prominence in recent months on account of the opposition his proposed development had generated.

Connolly's gaze shifted back to the body. Could it be Mansfield? He'd seen photographs of the property tycoon in recent newspaper coverage. Didn't help him now. The look of abject terror on the face, with its protruding tongue and bulging eyes, would have made identification difficult even for someone who'd known the deceased on a daily basis. Connolly wondered if the victim had been conscious when the stake penetrated his chest.

State Pathologist, Dr Mary McElree nodded to Connolly. 'What a way to die,' she said, easing her mouth mask down. 'Haven't seen anything quite like this before.'

'Was he alive when the stake was pushed through?'

'Unlikely. Haven't examined the body yet but the marks on the throat suggest strangulation.'

'And what, the stake is just for window dressing?'

'Too early to say. It's not something I've encountered before.'

'Me neither,' Connolly said, shaking his head. He'd worked with McElree on a few previous occasions and liked her matter-of-fact approach to procedures. Only a few months into the job, McElree looked too young, too attractive, to fit his preconceived notion of what a pathologist ought to look like but seeing her in work mode left no doubts about her competency.

'Place gives me the creeps,' she said, slipping on a second pair of surgical gloves and acknowledging the photographer's signal that he'd got everything.

'Thought you'd feel right at home in a graveyard,' Connolly commented, 'dead bodies all around you.'

McElree gave him the benefit of a smile before remasking her mouth and adjusting the hood on her head. Her disposable suit did nothing to hide her figure or the ease with which she moved, giving Connolly a stab of guilt for taking note of her femininity in the first place. As she issued orders to the forensic team, he moved outside the cordon tape to observe the surrounding area. McElree was right: it was a creepy place. Overrun with weeds, briars and nettles, the previous night's frost had hardened the ground, eliminating the possibility of finding worthwhile footprints. Headstones had been neglected for decades; those remaining upright leaned every which way while the inscriptions on the horizontal slabs were all but obliterated by fungus and grey and yellow algae. Wasn't a whole lot Connolly could do at the crime scene until he got McElree's report. In the interim he needed to talk to Dick Burke. A short interview, he had no doubt, would suffice, one unlikely to provide any great insight into the grizzly murder.

★ ★ ★

'Would you like a cuppa . . . sausage and black pudding, maybe?' Burke offered, busy brewing a pot of tea and greasing a blackened frying pan.

'Thanks, I'm fine,' Connolly said, his stomach in no state to digest food after the abuse he'd inflicted on it the previous night.

'A drop of the hard stuff in your tea?' Burke pressed, teasingly. 'Help get you over the shock of seeing what's out there.'

Connolly was tempted. He could do with a hair of the dog. Resisted. 'No, not while on duty, thanks all the same.' He decided to wait for Burke to organize the fry-up before asking questions. Burke was tall. No sign of the stooped features one associates with the elderly: his face, angular and sharp, his hair, what was left of it, steel grey. The house, a small terraced two-storey, was situated

6

towards the end of a well-maintained cul-de-sac known as Marino Lane. Nipper, his dog, a black and white mutt, touch of bull terrier, resembled the HMV dog. Explained the name. The dog barked initially, attempting to snap at the back of Connolly's legs, but Burke bribed the animal with a dish of Pal. Quietened him down.

While Nipper devoured the treat, Connolly and Burke sat in a small kitchen that faced on to a neat garden at the rear of the house. Connolly's nostrils detected the lingering whiff of cigarettes and port wine in the room. A picture on the wall showed Burke in teacher's garb. Beside it, encased in a silver-finished frame, a study of a much younger, virile Burke had him standing proudly next to a pretty bride. The absence of family group pictures suggested that the Burke marriage had remained childless. Scatterings of books lay on every conceivable shelf, bench, windowsill and table. Before drinking from his cup of tea, Burke fortified the brew with a generous helping of Irish Mist liqueur.

'I'm not going to pretend,' he said, tipping a wink to Connolly, 'that this is medicinal . . . because it's not. Along with my books and Nipper, this drop of whiskey represents one of the few pleasures left to me since I gave up the classroom. Never could get away with it when my good woman was around, God be good to her.' Burke smiled and shook his head as though remembering. 'Tell us this,' he said, still smiling, 'did you ever see that film where the wife of the character played by Jack Nicholson gets him to squat on the toilet like a woman every time he needs to take a leak?'

'Can't say I ever saw that one.'

'Well, the thing is, the wife didn't want him to wet the seat. After she dies, Nicholson is on the verge of hunkering down to pee when it occurs to him that he doesn't have to do that any more. So, he stands upright, pees with gusto into the bowl, and then, delighted with the new-found sense of freedom, allows his aim to zigzag left and right, purposely splashing the seat and the floor, grinning inanely because there's no one to rebuke him. Well, that's how I feel about my little weakness, so these past few years I've made amends by taking a drop whenever the fancy takes me.'

'Sounds good to me,' Connolly said, taking a liking to the man. 'So, tell me, Mr Burke, how did you happen to come upon the body?'

Burke ran through the events leading up to his finding the body exactly as Sergeant McCarthy had outlined, adding that he recognized the victim as Scott Mansfield.

'You knew Mansfield?'

'Knew him to see, yes. He attended a residents' meeting last week. Tried to explain why it was necessary to uproot the graves.'

'How was that received?'

'Huh, like the proverbial lead balloon. Lucky he wasn't lynched; everyone had objections.'

'Why so?'

'Well, you know what people are like; they don't take kindly to having graves desecrated. Mind you, nobody bothered their bollocks to look after the place for as long as I can remember, so you have to wonder why they're so hot and bothered now, I mean, now that the dead are being offered a change of scenery.' Burke smiled at his little joke and poured another tot of Irish Mist. 'But that's people for you, huh?'

'Tell me something, Mr Burke, in your opinion, did anyone in particular feel strongly enough to . . . well, to take the sort of action — '

'You mean, would one of the residents *kill* Mansfield.'

'Well, yes, what do you think?'

Burke ran his fingers over the white stubbly growth on his jaws, giving the question serious consideration. His deep-set eyes, partially shadowed beneath bushy eyebrows, appeared to disengage from reality. 'Let me think about that for a moment,' he said in a strong classroom voice, one used to having an audience. 'Trouble with that is this: it's not just the locals who object. The lunatic fringe have jumped on the bandwagon.'

'The lunatic fringe? Who do you have in mind?'

'Well, God knows, we've got more than a few queer buggers here in the community but I can't see any of them going to such lengths to save a derelict abbey and a bunch of overgrown graves. And then there's the acid heads; last night being Halloween, it's conceivable that some of them, out of their minds on crack cocaine or whatever it is they're on these days, joined in the festivities and went totally berserk . . . though I don't think so.'

'You don't. So who?'

'It's the outside pressure groups you need to look at: the tree huggers, the heritage and ancient monument contingent, the do-gooder environment activists, the agitators, the rent-a-crowd-publicity-seeking-beard-and-sandal brigade. They're always searching for a cause, any cause at all; helps them justify their existence.'

Connolly nodded, thinking to himself, this is a waste of time, but he found Burke's little rant entertaining. 'Which of these groups in particular do you think I should take a closer look at?'

'Well, they're all gobshites, that's for sure, but if it's my opinion you want, there's one bunch that stands out. Considering how Mansfield met his death, I'd say you could do worse than talk to Stoker's Lair.'

'Stoker's Lair?'

'Yes, Stoker's Lair. An appreciation society that honours the memory of Abraham Stoker, the author of *Dracula*, better known to you and me as Bram Stoker. They refer to St James's Abbey and graveyard as Stoker's Yard.' Burke got up from the table, walked briskly to the window, his head held high, determined not to allow age to diminish him in any way. 'Com'ere till I show you,' he said, gesturing for Connolly to join him. Connolly obliged. He followed Burke's gaze across the small back garden and red-brick wall to a row of houses whose gardens backed on to Burke's plot. Steely light had replaced the earlier fog, revealing a harshly delineated landscape.

'What we're looking at,' Burke said, pointing to the houses, 'is Marino Crescent. Stoker lived in No. 15, back in the mid-1800s; *Dracula*, the character he created has long since eclipsed poor old Bram.'

11

'And he lived here . . . created all that stuff about vampires?'

'Hard to credit, isn't it? What is it about the Irish psyche and their obsession with vampires, hey? Stoker wasn't the first Irishman to take a serious interest in the undead. Bet you didn't know that.'

'I didn't,' Connolly admitted, cloaking his disinterest.

'There you are now; 'tisn't well known but a fellow named Sheridan LeFanu got there before him; wrote about a lesbian vampire in a book called *Carmilla*. Erotic stuff, I'm led to believe. Have you read any vampire books?'

'Can't say I have; seen a few films, though.'

'Good, well then you'll know they're all a load of codswallop. You know the sort of thing: skulking around in the dark, sucking blood from the necks of young nubile women, warding off evil with garlands of garlic and hammering stakes through vampire's hearts. Awful shite, but there's people out there who get off on that kind of stuff. So, giving that this is Stoker's back yard, so to speak, and given that his followers are barking, could be there's a link between what's happened to Mansfield and Stoker's writings.'

'Would ya go on outta that,' Connolly said,

smiling dismissively. 'You're pulling my leg. Next you'll tell me that Mansfield was a vampire?'

Burke scrunching up the wrinkles at the corners of his eyes, said, 'Just because I've reached a certain age doesn't mean I've lost my marbles; no, I'm suggesting that the eejits in Stoker's Lair who, incidentally are the most vociferous opponents of Mansfield's scheme, feel they have a valid reason to preserve St James's. See, the thing is, they claim Stoker attended the abbey as a youth and, according to them, allowed its dark interior to influence his writing.'

'And you think they killed Mansfield in the same way as described by Stoker in order to stop the building project?'

'Hard not to see the symbolism. Makes as much sense as anything else.'

Connolly was never going to buy into the *Dracula* theory but knew that, however daft it sounded, he would have to follow up on it sooner or later. He had no doubt that something far less fanciful lay behind the killing. 'Tell me, Mr Burke, who organized the residents meeting?'

Burke seemed disappointed by Connolly's lack of interest in his *Dracula* theory. 'Well,' he said after a short pause, 'there's a resident's committee who've been meeting quite regularly in the old schoolhouse. I happen to know the chairman; decent enough fellow, works for a government department, can't remember which one exactly.'

'Don't suppose you have his number?'

'Matter of fact I do,' Burke said, going to the telephone on a sideboard and picking up a well-worn notebook. 'Ah yes, here we are.' He handed the book to Connolly, pointing to a name and number.

Connolly copied the information into his notebook and asked Burke if he wouldn't mind accompanying Sergeant McCarthy to the station later in the day.

'We need to get a formal statement from you.'

Burke readily agreed and Connolly took his leave, anxious to get back to talk with the pathologist.

2

Emma Boylan watched Connolly weave a zigzag course between tables. 'You're late,' she said, indicating her watch in mock chastisement. She'd only arrived two minutes earlier herself. The city's newest restaurant, The Wicklow Hills, its name a misnomer, was a mishmash of chrome, mirror and water features. Part of the latest mall development to spring up in the Wicklow Street area, smack bang in the middle of Dublin's city centre, a full hour's drive from Wicklow, and ne'er a hill in sight.

'Sorry, Emma,' he said, pecking her on the cheek before easing his big frame into the chair opposite her. 'Bitch of a job getting away.'

'Yeah, heard about Mansfield's murder,' Emma said, holding on to Connolly's hand. He looked tired. Still the most attractive policeman on the planet, in her opinion, though that opinion she readily conceded might be biased. Recently, while making love, she'd closed her eyes and allowed her finger tips to explore his face, same way a blind person might do it. 'You've got the most exquisite nose,' she'd told him. 'Same shape as the nose on Michelangelo's statue of David.'

His response had made her giggle at the time. 'Glad it's just my nose and not the statue's dick.'

'No fear of that,' she'd said, playfully reaching for his manhood, 'Would've needed extra marble were that the case.'

They'd giggled uncontrollably at that one, wrestling beneath the sheets, grabbing and teasing each other like frisky honeymooners. That was what was so wonderful about their relationship, they could be serious when it was called for but they could laugh with each other too, something that had been missing from both their previous relationships.

He did look tired now, though. The previous night had been a late one. She'd inveigled him to accompany her to the annual media awards bash in The Four Seasons. It was the kind of event he hated. Her name had found its way on to the nominations for Best Investigative Journalist of the Year. On two previous occasions she'd won the award but her luck was out this time. Hadn't stopped her enjoying the celebration. Willie Thompson, a younger, combative, rival reporter at the *Post* couldn't let the occasion pass without getting a dig in: 'Can't win 'em all,

Ms Boylan,' he jeered, 'time you passed on the baton to younger blood.' Emma had responded by raising her glass, giving him her best bogus smile, silently mouthing the words — *piss off.*

Connolly, who'd been at his grumpiest setting out for the do, enjoyed the antagonistic exchange and began to melt into the swing of things, letting his hair down and thoroughly enjoying himself. The economy may have been in free-fall but the supply of wine never flowed more freely. There had been a downside; both felt the worse for wear when the alarm roused them from their alcohol-induced sleep this morning. Aspirin and cold water were the order of the day. She'd felt sorry for Connolly when he'd been called away before having had time for breakfast. She, herself, had felt way too ill to even look at food.

I'm never, never going to drink that much ever again.

The aspirin had taken its own sweet time to kick in. Putting on her face had been quite a trial, requiring more skill than usual. Maintaining a rigorous beauty routine throughout the winter had become an ever-increasing challenge. At thirty-eight and counting, she was combating age with all the willpower and cosmetic arsenal available to her. Bought the best night creams. Supposed to maximize the skins ability to repair itself, but the face in the mirror still looked tired. Her hair, supposedly her crowning glory, had died during the night. She wanted to believe that this morning represented a once-off blip but somehow she doubted it.

Hard not to feel envious of Connolly; he had no need of makeup, hung over or not. Almost a decade older than her, it just didn't seem fair. For a big man, he carried no excess poundage and, thanks to impeccable grooming, looked more like a top corporate executive in some multinational corporation than an overworked, underpaid policeman. Radiant eyes, a full head of black hair, silver flecks at the temple, conferred on him the mantle of suave sophistication. The whole demeanour achieved without any great effort, it seemed to Emma. She truly believed he became more attractive, more debonair, with every passing year, proof, were proof needed, that God must surely be a man.

'The red tops are calling it a vampire slaying,' she said. 'Any chance of an exclusive angle from the man I'm living in sin with?' Her question was half serious, half tongue-in-cheek. She and Connolly had an agreement whereby their respective roles — journalist and detective — did not intrude on each other's patch or encumber their relationship. Didn't always work. But the principle held firm. For the past eighteen months they'd been cohabitants, eighteen months that she regarded as the best time of her life. The fact that they were partners, not husband and wife, didn't bother her unduly. One failed marriage had made her reluctant to venture down that particular path again; it was enough that she'd been given a second shot at happiness.

'What's your take on the murder?' she asked.

Before he could answer, a hovering maître d' handed them lunch menus. After little more than a cursory glance, Connolly signalled a waiter and ordered the roast sirloin of prime beef with Yorkshire pudding, foregoing the starter selection. Emma, not tempted by the main courses on offer, settled for the salad frisée starter.

'Been a crazy morning,' Connolly said, 'Had the unenviable duty of delivering the news to Mansfield's widow. Her two children were at home when I called — midterm break. Didn't make the job any easier. After that, I met the technical bureau crew and the state pathologist; they found fragments of paper in the victim's mouth and gullet. Highly unlikely that he was eating it before he was murdered so we have to presume someone, most likely the killer, forced him to swallow it. We'll know a bit more when the toxicology team examine the fragments in more detail. What we do know for certain is that the victim's thyroid cartilage was broken, the cricoid cartilage shattered, indications of strangulation before the killer hammered home the stake.'

'A revenge killing?'

'Could be. Just imagine the kind of all-consuming hate a person would need to do something like that. He — if it was a he — had to have planned the killing well in advance and must have known the victim, known his movements, known how to get to him. Pure savage.'

Emma shivered. 'Any idea who's behind it?'

'Christ only knows! A freak, certainly, a sociopath with attitude. It's all speculation and hot air at this stage, nothing concrete. We're holding a media briefing in a few hours so anything I tell you will be in the public domain by the time you get anything to the *Post.*'

'I'm free to report what you say?'

'Yes, just don't name me as your source.'

'As if I would,' Emma replied, a mischievous smirk on her face. 'As it happens, Willie

Thompson has been given the assignment.'

'Oh?'

'Yeah. He's been working on a series of articles dealing with the scams associated with the building trade and the exploitation of foreign nationals. My esteemed editor, Bob Crosby, decided that, as Mansfield was in the construction business, Thompson should lead on this one.'

'Does that bother you?'

'Not really. Got quite a lot on my plate as it is. Besides, Crosby has asked me to probe the murder from a peripheral point of view, you know, examine the ripple effects, see if there's a supplementary angle to bolster the main story.'

'Can't see you playing second fiddle,' Connolly said, the smile on his face hiding the tired lines temporarily.

Connolly had come closer to the truth than he'd known but, right now, Emma didn't feel like discussing the row she'd had with her boss. Instead, she returned to the subject of Mansfield, asked, 'Any indications at this stage what direction the investigation will take?'

'Too early to say. There's strong opposition to Mansfield's proposed development which means, potentially, every member of the local residents association has a motive. We'll have to interview the whole bloody lot of them.'

'That should be a load of laughs.'

'Tell me about it; sheer drudgery. We're also looking at all the pressure groups opposed to the development. We'll have to check out all Mansfield's business partners and rivals, examine what sort of deals he was involved in, see whose nose he might have put out of joint.'

Conversation halted as food appeared in front of them. They declined the waiter's entreaty to order wine, settling for mineral water instead.

They dined in silence for a few minutes, content to enjoy their food. Emma was first to get back to the topic uppermost on her mind. 'I've done some research on Mansfield this morning,' she said, 'and from what I've unearthed, he appears to have been an all-round good egg. He's one of the few big property developers not bogged down in the tribunals of enquiry. One of the people I spoke to described him as being the kind of man who's likely to have a daughter who plays the piano.'

'That supposed to be complimentary?'

'It's meant to convey a sense of old-world decency. Mind you, it might have something to do with the fact that Scott Mansfield played the church organ for his local choir. Doesn't sound like your typical property developer, does it?'

'That's for sure,' Connolly agreed. 'He's not a member of 'the natural party of government' — almost unheard of in his line of business. And yet, someone out there hated him enough to stick a stake in his heart.'

'That's the bit that's caught the public's imagination and provided a field day for the tabloids; they really get off on that kind of stuff.'

'I talked to the man who discovered Mansfield's body this morning — a retired school teacher — bit of a character actually; he thinks there's a connection between what happened to Mansfield and the killing of vampires . . . as depicted in *Dracula*.'

'You're having me on?' Emma said, a quizzical gleam in her eyes. 'You saying he thinks it's some sort of ritual sacrifice?'

'Well no, at least I don't think that's what he had in mind.' Connolly related what he'd been told about the link between the scene of the crime and Bram Stoker. 'Bloody waste of time, I know, but I'll have to send one of my officers to check out those people in Stoker's Lair.'

Before Emma could tease the question of Mansfield's death any further, Connolly's mobile signalled a premature end to their lunch break.

3

The man at reception looked away from his paperback, glanced over the rims of his glasses, said, 'How's it goin' there! You're welcome to Stoker's Lair.' Friendly voice, pronounced cadences of Dublin's inner city. 'Anything in particular you'd like to look at?'

'No, not really,' Emma replied, 'Just the exhibits. Is there a charge?'

'No, it's free, gratis and for nothing. We run the Lair as a labour of love . . . but if you feel like purchasing a book from our collection or contributing a few euro to the Bram Stoker Appreciation Society, we'll not object.' He indicated a few sorry-looking bookshelves that were divided into sections under the headings, UNDEAD, SUPERNATURAL, GOTHIC, HORROR, GHOST STORIES, SATANIC, BRAM STOKER and CRIME.

A collection box stood to one side of the door.

Emma made her way past him and entered a darkened room, fitted out to resemble a vault. Fibre optics and pinpoints of light picked out skulls, skeletons and several clusters of fake cobwebs. The Gothic trappings reminded her of The Intrepid Fox, a pub she'd visited in Soho back in the 90s with her then husband. The pub featured heavy metal music at the time, very different from the atmosphere-laden film-track score now seeping from hidden speakers in this make-believe vault. Glass cases contained editions of *Dracula* alongside other Stoker titles, none of which Emma had heard of before. Movie posters, advertising some of the better-known productions of Stoker's creation, rotated on a back-lit screen. A large portrait of Christopher Lee in the role of Count Dracula had drops of blood dripping from his teeth. Emma thought the effect more comical than scary. She used her Cannon 40D to capture the atmosphere of the place; images she would later use to help with her written descriptions. She focused tight on the text of a number of framed certificates and clicked. Exquisite calligraphy proclaimed that Stoker had once been a member of The Golden Dawn Society and The Societas Rosicruciana in Anglia.

Meant nothing to Emma.

Several prints showed the author in London's Lyceum Theatre in the company of Henry Irving and Irving's leading lady, Ellen Terry. Text explained how Stoker had worked with Irving for twenty-seven years, how the great actor had provided inspiration for the aristocratic bearing that the writer bestowed on *Dracula*. A somewhat contradictory caption, beneath a picture of Stoker and Oscar Wilde, claimed that *Dracula* had been inspired by Wilde's conviction for sodomy. The basis for this assertion was not provided. Another print showed Stoker's wife, Florence Balcombe, the caption claiming she'd been a celebrated beauty in her day, and the mother of Noel, their only son. Emma clicked on a separate sepia print that showed Florence on the arm of Oscar Wilde, the blurb beneath claiming that Wilde had been Florence's suitor before she'd pledged her troth to Stoker.

A sudden movement from behind Emma caught her unaware, forcing her to yelp involuntarily.

'It's only me,' the man who'd been at reception said. 'Hugh Foley, at your service.'

Emma suspected he did this to visitors on a regular basis, a ploy to infuse extra scariness to the macabre setting. Not that she thought him in the least bit scary, far from it. In his mid-thirties, he was tall, athletic, had guileful eyes that sparkled in the strange surrounding lights.

'Cool place,' Emma said. 'Nice to see Stoker get the recognition he deserves.'

'We do our best,' Foley said, his face too close to her for comfort. 'Stoker never got the recognition that was his due, even when he was alive back at the end of the nineteenth century. Shame really; he wrote the definitive vampire story but died in poverty, a broken man, imagine that?'

'Really!' Emma said, moving back a step. 'You'd think that someone who'd shown such originality would have had the world at his feet.'

'Indeed you would, but as you know, we Irish have a bad habit of pulling our own down. The literati back then were, as they still are, riddled with snobbery. They didn't approve of his subject matter so they shunned him. Not a whole lot has changed in the interim; this country still ignores Stoker's contribution to literature. I've just come back from the town of Bistrita in Transylvania where they've honoured him with a fine statue. Unlike our shower of philistines, the Romanian tourist board is proud and delighted with how the novel entices count-less visitors to their country.'

'Yes, seems a bit peculiar that we make no effort to honour him. Maybe if he'd based the story in Ireland instead of Transylvania things might have worked out differently for him.'

'Well, funny you should say that because

there is a school of thought that ties the *Dracula* story to events that took place in this country. Bear in mind, he was born in 1847 — height of the potato famine — and was greatly influenced by his mother's stories about the disastrous cholera epidemic of 1832. There's a theory that Stoker was really depicting the behaviour of landlords in Ireland back then. He felt they'd sucked the life's blood out of the peasants by evicting them and leaving them and their families to die of starvation.'

'Never heard that one,' Emma said. 'I thought . . . at least I read somewhere that the character, Count Dracula, was based on an evil ruler who lived in Romania back in the middle ages.'

'Ah yes, that'd be Vlad the Impaler; killed his enemies by impaling them on poles. Of course, the current Romanian government dismiss all that stuff as pure myth. Vlad really did exist, though; there's evidence that he put 20,000 Turkish Muslims to death during his reign. Stoker studied the history of that region so it's possible that this period of bloodshed could have had a bearing on his thinking. Might explain the blood lust element in his writing. Mind you, according to Stoker's son, the whole concept for *Dracula* came to his father in a nightmare after eating too much dressed crab. And then, there's another theory that claims, wrongly I believe, that Bram was a closet homosexual and used his fiction as an outlet for the frustrations of concealing his true sexuality.'

'I read the book back in my student days,' Emma said, 'saw Coppala's movie version more recently, the one with Gary Oldham; I'm not big into that kind of thing but I felt it was, well . . . really *about* sexual menace.'

'Well, there's no end to the theories but, you know, Stoker would have been very familiar with the role of women in Victorian culture and with the sexual repression of that period. I don't think any film to date has captured the erotic nature of Stoker's original text . . . but I'd say the 1979 film with Frank Langella as the Count came closest to depicting the obvious sexual pathology. My favourite adaptation has to be *Nosferatu*, a masterpiece that was filmed shortly after Stoker's death. It catapulted the book into a worldwide best seller — the *DaVinci Code* of its day — a bit late for poor old Bram. His widow sued the film-makers because they made it without her permission, and because they'd refused to pay her any royalties. Won the case, she did, insisted that all prints be destroyed. Luckily, a few copies survived. We have one of those rare prints here. We show it once a month; would you like me to book you in for a screening?'

'No thanks, I'm not much of a horror buff,' Emma admitted, deciding it was time to come clean, explain why she'd really visited Stoker's Lair.

She'd had some difficulty herself in coming to terms with what exactly her role was in the Mansfield murder. Connolly had hit the nail on the head when he'd jokingly likened her assignment to that of second fiddle. There was, she could see, a degree of irony about the situation she found herself in. For ten of the past eleven years, her ex-husband, Vinny, had wanted her to steer clear of the more dangerous crime assignments. They'd rowed over it constantly. His entreaties to her to avoid involvement in the investigation of hardened criminals provoked a stubborn determination on her part to carry on regardless. Throughout this difficult period, Bob Crosby, aware of her husband's objection, allowed her to take on the high-risk assignments.

But in more recent times, Crosby had begun to protect her from some of the more perilous beats. That didn't bother her; it was nice to take a breather from time to time. The thing that really pissed her off was the thought that Connolly, who was a lifelong friend of Crosby, might have had some influence in this regard. Could history be repeating itself? She hoped this latest directive from Crosby — to pursue an off-beat, but safe parallel story on the Mansfield slaying — was a genuine brief, with no undue influences coming from anyone on the outside.

'Have you heard about the death of Scott Mansfield?' she asked.

Hugh Foley looked startled. 'What? Damn! You're not here to look at any of this,' he said, gesturing to the displays, disappointment on his face. 'And the photographs . . . what's that about? Don't tell me . . . you're a reporter, yes?'

'Name's Emma Boylan, and yes, I'm an investigative journalist with the *Post*. I've come here because I'm told Stoker's Lair are outspoken opponents of what Mansfield intended to do with the site at St James's Abbey.'

'I knew it! I bloody well knew it! You couldn't give a toss about *Dracula*. Why couldn't you have told me that when you came in and not let me prattle on about Stoker . . . when, clearly — '

'Actually, I found what you had to say fascinating, honestly.'

Foley smiled and shook his head as he

guided Emma back to the reception desk. 'So, Miss sneaky-boots, how can I *really* help you?'

'Thought you might have an opinion about who's responsible for Mansfield's death.'

'What? You think that one of my lot — I mean Stoker's Lair — might have something to do with his demise?'

'Well, yes! When you consider how he died — '

'How he died? What do you mean, *how he died*? The radio said his body had been found in the grounds of St James's. I presumed he'd had a heart attack or stroke, something like that. You saying there's suspicious circumstances?'

'Umm,' Emma said, scepticism in her voice. 'For sure, there are suspicious circumstances, *very* suspicious circumstances. I would have thought some of your fellow travellers would've been on the blower to you by now to discuss developments.'

'Well, as you've probably noticed, the telephone on my desk is silent. That's because Eircom have cut us off. Happens when there's not enough money to pay the bloody bill. I do have a mobile but, wouldn't you know it, I forgot to charge it. So, tell me, what is it about Mansfield's death that constitutes suspicious circumstances?'

'How about finding a body with a stake through its heart? I'd say that counts as suspicious, wouldn't you?'

Foley groped for words that refused to come.

'You didn't know?' Emma asked, unsure whether Foley's over-the-top facial reaction was for real or a put-on.

'You cannot be serious?' he said at last. 'You're telling me that . . . that Mansfield was . . . Jesus H Christ, this is fantastic, utterly fan-fucking-tastic.'

'I'm surprised that the boys in blue haven't been round already. I mean, with your connection to St James's churchyard . . . your opposition to what Mansfield was planning.'

'Oh, I imagine they'll be on to me soon enough,' Foley said, his cunning face pushing closer to Emma's again. 'Bram must be laughing his head off in his grave . . . this is just too fantastic to be true. Hey listen, great idea, take my picture. If you're going to write about Stoker's Lair, I'd like my mug shot in the frame; we need all the publicity we can get, might unearth a benefactor out there . . . one with a few bob to throw our way.'

Emma aimed the lens in his direction, not bothering to inform him that her pictures were not intended for publication. The *Post* sent professional photographers when pictures were required.

'Don't get me wrong,' Foley said, intertwining his fingers, squeezing his palms together as though in prayer. 'I think it's awful that Mansfield was killed.' He was no longer looking at the camera, his eyes staring vacantly into the middle distance. 'It's just that, well, so . . . so appropriate that he should be . . . you know, killed like a vampire . . . because, in a way, that's what he was; that's what property speculators are; modern-day vampires, no better than the monsters Bram wrote about . . . bloody hell. I'm still having difficult — '

Foley was interrupted by the arrival of two men. Emma knew one of them, Detective Sergeant Mike Dorsett. The lanky, craggy-faced, Donegal bachelor of few words and idiosyncratic dress sense was part of Connolly's team. In the course of past investigations, he'd come in contact with Emma. Dorsett nodded his hello to her without speaking or introducing his younger, more conventionally dressed, sidekick. They'd come to interview Foley, so she made her exit, certain in her own mind that Foley had played no part in the death of Mansfield.

4

Emma missed the rumble that used to come from the huge Roland web machine in the basement. The *Post*, like most national dailies, had ceased in-house printing and for the past six months all editions, as well as numerous supplements, had been outsourced. Old printer trades and skills, so long part and fabric of the *Post*, had been brushed aside in favour of new technology. Over the years Emma had got to know and like many of the print room staff. She'd sympathized with those who'd been forced to accept 'voluntary' redundancy or take on work at the new printing plant in Maynooth. The price of progress had been hard to swallow; Emma just hoped that, as an investigative journalist, her job would remain viable for the foreseeable future.

Right now, she was finishing the article she'd spent hours researching. Her interview with Hugh Foley in Stoker's Lair had provided a smattering of colourful verbiage. She'd used, and embellished, background facts about Bram Stoker and his connections to the location where Scott Mansfield's body had been found, playing up comparisons between the deaths as depicted in the *Dracula* story and the copycat execution of Mansfield. She had visited Dick Burke, the man who'd found the body, taken an immediate liking to the retired teacher, and used one or two quotes from him to add an offbeat slant to what was an already bizarre affair.

Her attempts to get a few quotable quotes from Rev Reginald Steel, vicar of St Andrew's, had met with failure. Mansfield had been the unofficial, unpaid, musical director and choir master at the church so it was natural to expect the vicar, whose flock had gained from Mansfield's beneficence, to offer laudatory comment on his passing but the cleric was uncooperative.

'It is not my practice to talk to the press,' he informed Emma, rather haughtily. 'Any comment I have to offer will be given to the proper authority.'

Too bad. Her article would just have to survive without the aid of the Rev Reginald Steel. Not everyone, Emma had discovered over the years, was as well disposed to the press as she'd like them to be.

She was about to submit the article to editorial, satisfied that she had written an interesting, if quirky, report when Bob

Crosby approached her work station. 'Haven't you heard?' he asked, his bushy eyebrows elevated halfway up his forehead.

'Heard what?' she asked.

'There's been a breakthrough,' he said, leaning his ample posterior against the side of her desk, and taking a sideways glance at the text on her monitor. 'There's been an arrest; well, not an arrest exactly,' he corrected. 'The Mansfield killer has turned himself in, confessed.'

'Oh, when did this happen? Do we have a name?'

'Just happened in the last few minutes and, yes, we have a name. We also have an interview with the killer.'

'We do?'

'Yes, Emma, *you* interviewed him already. Hugh Foley has turned himself in, confessed to the murder.'

'You're serious? Got to be a mistake. When I spoke to Foley, I swear he knew nothing about how Mansfield met his end.'

'No mistake,' Crosby assured her. 'Have it on good authority that he's given himself up, pleaded guilty.'

Emma shook her head, doing a quick mental rerun on the interview she'd had with Foley. *Did I miss something? I doubt it.* There had been no inklings, no vibes, no gut feelings, to suggest that he had anything to do with the killing.

Crosby took her silence as an acceptance. 'I want you to rework your interview. I need your material to tie in with the main lead story.'

'What?' Emma asked, visibly annoyed. 'You saying I should hand over my notes to Willie Thompson, give *wonder-boy* what I — ?'

'Whoa! Hold on to your knickers. I want the two of you to work the piece *together*, OK? Both names on the by-lines, OK? Story's too important to piss around with. You think you can manage that?'

'Yes, boss,' Emma said with a shrug of the shoulders. She accepted his decision but wanted him to know she wasn't happy. The fact that she liked Bob Crosby stopped her from further protest. At fifty-three and a tad shy of six feet tall, he was overweight, had a heavy, intelligent face, kind eyes and a high domed head that struggled for cover beneath a thin scattering of grey hair. As news editors went, Emma placed him in the top league. For more than a decade she'd worked under his supervision and for the most part it had been a fruitful partnership. He could be demanding and difficult at times but, until now, he'd always been even-handed when it came to handing out assignments. Forcing her to cooperate with Willie Thompson was, she grudgingly accepted, the most practical way to handle the Mansfield story.

Doesn't mean I have to like it.

'Did you manage to get any photos when you talked to Foley?'

'Yes,' Emma answered. 'I've downloaded them on to my hard disc but the quality isn't great. Foley's place — it's called Stoker's Lair — is a bit spooky and dark, fitted out like a crypt. Not ideal light for photography.'

Crosby's craggy face lit up. 'We can get our IT guys to work on them. I've seen them perform miracles with the Photoshop pro-gramme. Don't suppose you got a shot of the man himself?'

'But of course I did,' Emma said, her tongue placed firmly in her cheek. 'How do you think I won those two 'Journalist of the Year' awards.' She had no intention of admitting that snapping Foley had not been her idea. Why spoil a winning roll with unnecessary detail? 'Foley is keen on publicity,' she said, sounding a warning note. 'If you ask me, I'd say he's confessed for an ulterior motive.'

Crosby frowned. 'Don't be daft; no one's that stupid.'

'Maybe *not* so stupid. As far as I could see, Stoker's Lair is in deep doo-dah, financially speaking. Foley admitted he hadn't been able to pay the telephone bill. It's possible he sees Mansfield's death as an opportunity to whip up interest in Stoker. Could be he's jumping on the bandwagon, hoping to generate funds by gaining notoriety.'

Crosby considered this. 'Yes, it could be opportunistic as far as Foley's concerned . . . but let's stick to what we have; Foley *admits* he killed Mansfield. If he is as desperate as you suggest, isn't it just possible that he set up the whole theatrical killing, knowing exactly the kind of press and television coverage he'd get?'

'Fair point,' Emma admitted, 'but if he really did commit the murder, why would he confess? I mean, what good would it do to attract publicity and money if he ends up doing time? Doesn't add up.'

'Let's not get too hung up on what his motives are; that's for tomorrow's headlines. What I need right now is for you and Willie Thompson to pool resources, come up with a front page exclusive for the morning's edition, OK?'

'Yes, Boss, three bags full, Boss,' Emma said, unsmiling.

5

Mansfield's murder dominated news reports. Saturation coverage. Bulletins on radio and television, headlines on newspapers. World affairs consigned to minor status. Emma sat at the kitchen counter anxiously reading the front-page report that carried her and Willie Thompson's shared by-line. The digital pictures she'd shot in Stoker's Lair had reproduced surprisingly well. The text owed significantly more to her investigative efforts than that of Thompson. His name appeared first: that annoyed her. Sitting next to her, enjoying breakfast, Connolly reached and prised the newspaper from her hands. 'Hey,' he said frowning, 'not having breakfast?'

'Can't be bothered! I'm cheesed off with Thompson . . . and Crosby.'

'Wouldn't get too bothered if I were you; story's moved on.'

Emma, poured a second coffee. 'You're letting Hugh Foley go?'

'Yep! Best we can charge him with is wasting police time. He had nothing to do with the murder.'

'You're one hundred per cent sure?'

'Absolutely. He hadn't a clue about the key details. We fed him a few false details and he ran with them as though they were fact. His sole purpose was to seek publicity for Stoker's Lair. So happens, he got his fifteen minutes of fame.'

'Yes, and I was the one who unintentionally got it for him.'

'True, but you weren't to know he was spoofing.'

'That's where you're wrong. I told Crosby, I told him he wasn't the killer. Would he listen? Course not! He had his contact in the cops; someone on the inside track . . . except, of course, his contact got it wrong. Just tell me one thing, Jim; tell me you weren't his 'deep throat'?'

'Not guilty. I'd say he got it from his golfing buddy, Superintendent Smith.'

'Just as well, because if you'd been the one to tip off Crosby without telling me first, I'd punch your lights out.' Emma could say things like that to Connolly knowing he wouldn't take offence. Since moving in together, an unspoken understanding had evolved. They'd become what Emma considered true soulmates. Since separating from their respective partners, their new-found relationship had strengthened and solidified into bonds of mutual understanding, love, respect and affection.

Before her marital upheaval, Emma had got to know the detective through cooperating with him on a number of criminal cases. One such case had been pivotal in forging their trust and friendship. She'd been pregnant at the time with her first (and only) baby. To gain banner headlines, she'd exposed herself to a number of foolhardy risks. In one such encounter with a bunch of hardened villains, she'd been pushed head over heels down an escalator. Lost the baby. In the aftermath she'd drifted into a state of depression. Connolly, not her husband, had been the one to help her pull out of her melancholy.

A spark had ignited.

'Tell me something,' Connolly said, suppressing a smile. 'When self-proclaimed hotshot reporting ace, Willie Thompson, discovers your 'scoop' on the Hugh Foley/ Dracula theory is nonsense, won't he be miffed.'

'Damn right, he will! I'll never hear the end of it. I'll get the blame even though Crosby was the one who set that particular ball in motion.' Emma was reluctant to let Connolly know the true extent of her aversion to her rival. In recent weeks Thompson had begun throwing his weight about after being the recipient of kudos from Crosby for having successfully exposed a sex-for-sale scandal among a group of so-called respectable women. This singular success in what had, until then, been a lacklustre career prompted Thompson to ask Crosby to move his work station to one of the more desirable desk-by-the-window locations . . . similar to the one Emma currently enjoyed. Crosby refused, but gave him the lead on the Mansfield murder as a sort of consolation award. Should he prove a success in the assignment, something Emma very much doubted, her cosy window position, with its view to the outside world, might well be in jeopardy.

'Well, at least we can now concentrate on some real suspects,' Connolly said. 'Today, we delve into Mansfield's building contracts, examine his books, discover who his business associates are. Bound to have made enemies on his rise to the top.'

'This mean you're dismissing the protest groups opposed to his plans for St James's churchyard?'

'No, not at all. We'll continue to probe their activities, but I have a gut feeling that Mansfield's killing has a different significance, something far more serious than local opposition. The brutality involved suggests a more personal motive. To go to such elaborate lengths, the killer must have held one hell of a grudge against the victim.'

'Sounds like you have something in mind.'

'Well, yes, but it's not something I can talk about . . . at least not yet.'

'Oh, come on, Jim, I'm not the lead reporter on this assignment, give me something, even something peripheral; help me out here, I'm looking for a different angle.'

'OK, but this is information we're holding back, something you cannot divulge under any circumstances.'

'My lips are sealed; now tell me.'

'OK, OK, all right. We think this could be significant. You remember I mentioned about forensic finding paper fragments shoved down Mansfield's throat? Well, they've now had some time to examine what they retrieved and they've begun to piece the bits together, jigsaw style. Initial results seem to suggest that what we have is a musical score. Giving the fact that Mansfield played the organ in his local church, it could point to there being a musical connection to what's happened.'

Emma was about to tell Connolly about her unproductive interview with the Rev Reginald Steel when she was interrupted by the sound of the phone. 'That'll be for me,' she said getting up from the counter. 'Probably Crosby on the warpath; what's the betting

45

he's going to blame me for everything.

'Hello!' she said pressing the receiver to her ear.

'Put Detective Inspector Connolly on please,' the caller ordered, a male voice, sounding vaguely familiar to Emma, but deliberately disguised to mask its owner.

'Hold on a sec; I'll put him on.'

Connolly took the phone and spent the next three minutes saying little more than *no* several times before hanging up. 'You're never going to believe who that was,' he said to Emma.

'I know that voice, just can't put a name to it.'

'Well, you ought to know him; he's your fellow reporter, Willie Thompson. Thought I would talk to him about the case now that — to use his words — you've been sidelined.'

'Bloody hell! That slimy prick has the cheek of the Devil. I do hope you told him where to get off.'

'Of course I did; said no to him . . . same as I'd say to any reporter looking to get on the inside track.'

'And that includes me, does it?'

Connolly smiled. 'Especially you,' he said, ducking to avoid the playful punch Emma aimed at his gob.

6

By her own admission, Oonagh Kavanagh was a compulsive collector, a habitual hoarder. Born with a magpie gene, her father once remarked. She held on to items that most people chucked in the bin without a second thought. Living alone in a compact dormer bungalow, she used the garage and the upstairs area to store the spoils of her addiction. If pushed on the subject, she would admit that much of the stockpile was of no earthly value and ought really to be disposed of. There was, however, one segment of the amassed cache that represented something special: her newspaper clippings. Spanning two decades, these cuttings represented, at least in part, a record of her family history. Alongside this preserved assortment of newsprint, she'd saved letters, postcards, receipts, notes and documents, all of them with one thing in common: their relevance to her family's turbulent saga.

Newspaper reports on the murder of Mansfield represented her most recent additions to the collection. As far as she was concerned the dead man — she refused to think of him as *victim* — represented the latest chapter in the chronicle of her life. Putting aside her scissors she carefully pasted the articles on to a fresh scrapbook page, giving way to a deep body-felt shudder, wondered when the mayhem bedevilling her life would ever come to an end. One thing she counted on: more deaths would occur before events fully ran their course. She would never reclaim the contented life she once enjoyed, that was out of the question, but she hoped that a measure of peace was not beyond the bounds of possibility. She'd carried the baggage from the past for so long that it took quite an effort to remember there was a time when she hadn't a care in the world.

Happier times.

She had just begun her first year in Dublin City University; had a boyfriend, lots of friends, male and female and, at home, she got on reasonably well with her father and two brothers, less so with her mother. It had never occurred to her then that the idyllic world she inhabited could implode, but that's exactly what happened.

Her father, Trevor Kavanagh, a professor of music in the Metropolitan School of Music, became embroiled in a scandal when one of his students accused him of conducting an improper relationship. The school authorities attempted to keep a lid on the predicament but somehow the media got hold of the story. Back then, newspapers were not as intrusive as today's shameless tabloids. Even so, new revelations were presented to the public on a daily basis, albeit cloaked in a code of inoffensive prose.

When it transpired that the young woman in question was pregnant, there was no way to placate sensibilities, or lessen the shock value. Trevor Kavanagh was suspended from duties pending an internal inquiry. Public opinion on the affair had been split down the middle, half believing her father a philandering cad, the other half convinced the student was to blame. When it transpired that Kavanagh had, on more than one occasion, visited the student's flat, all bets were off. Sympathy for the professor plummeted. He remained defiant, however, claiming that his accuser had persuaded him to give her extra violin tuition to help achieve a higher grade in an upcoming exam. Norma Somers, the student involved, admitted that the tutor had helped with her violin practice but insisted he had been the one to suggest the visits to her flat, claiming further that he demanded sex as payment. The board of governors had heard enough; they sought his immediate resignation. He had little choice but to accede.

For Oonagh Kavanagh, this represented the start of the bad times. The loss of her father's salary meant having to quit university. Her brothers, Fintan and Owen, both older than her, were by then in employment, but neither earned enough, or felt obliged, to supplement her education. She applied to the civil service and got a job in the Department of Social Welfare, a dead-end position that offered little challenge and even less opportunity for promotion. Working nine-to-five did have one benefit; it spared her having to listen to the continuous bickering that had become the norm in her parents' lives. Her father chose to dull the pain of injustice and rejection by taking to the bottle. Stella, her mother, remained less than sympathetic to his plight, her preoccupation being concerned with status in the community. She'd never fully subscribed to the notion of her husband's innocence.

Two months before Norma Somers gave birth to a baby boy, she withdrew the accusation she'd levelled against Trevor Kavanagh, admitting that she had lied. In an amazing turnabout, she confessed that their relationship had been concerned solely with tutoring, and that nothing improper had taken place. She apologized for the distress caused and announced that she was marrying

50

the young man she now claimed to be the real father. The exoneration, though belated, should have brought vindication to the Kavanagh household but that wasn't what happened. The Metropolitan School of Music refused to reinstate the professor, stating, that his transgression — visiting a student's flat — had brought the school's name into disrepute.

This devastating news had been the catalyst that marked her father's descent into hell. It also brought to the surface a merciless side to her mother's personality. The atmosphere in the house deteriorated to such an extent that Oonagh decided to move out. She found a flat in Rathmines and forced herself to look in on her parents from time to time. Within six months, Stella Kavanagh walked out on Trevor and moved to London where an older sister lived. Oonagh made strenuous efforts to contact her but she refused to answer her pleas to come home.

Her father, meanwhile, had begun to give music lessons in the house. He had failed in his efforts to secure a position in any of the city's music institutions, his application in each instance turned down with blunt dismissal. When he enquired why, it was made abundantly clear that his reputation preceded him. Fortunately, he still retained his skills as a tutor and had no difficulty attracting pupils. As a child, Oonagh, along with her brothers, had been taught the piano and violin by him. He'd shown her how to listen, how to discern structure and form in music, how to choose between what was good, what was bad, what she liked, what she didn't. Yes, she could testify to his talent as a teacher; he allowed her and her brothers to experiment with contemporary music while at the same time introducing classical pieces to their exercises. His perseverance and tolerance helped her gain a rounded appreciation of the many different musical disciplines. But unlike her brothers, she'd had to abandon music as a career; her father told her she didn't have the 'neural structures or the requisite ancillary factors' necessary to take it up professionally. His words cut deep. In spite of this disappointment she retained a fondness for the classics and the more melodic offerings in contemporary music.

Abandoned by Stella, Trevor Kavanagh needed help with the housework. A former student of his named Lynda O'Regan agreed to clean the house and do some cooking on a three-days-a-week basis. Lynda had been one of the few who'd never believed the ugly stories circulating about the professor. Her own parents had struggled to put her and her younger brother through college, so the opportunity to earn money by helping out with the professor's household chores, while still being immersed in music, came as a godsend. During this period Oonagh's visit to the house became less frequent. She'd met Lynda and been impressed by the young woman's attitude and her hero-like deference to the professor. When Oonagh did see her father, he was either occupied with a student or drunk, hung over, or simply noncommunicative.

Almost a year to the day after Trevor Kavanagh had lost his job he was involved in a fatal road accident. His Ford Sierra was crushed beneath an articulated lorry; his body battered beyond recognition. The crash investigators were satisfied that he had been to blame, a factor backed up by the discovery of excess alcohol in his bloodstream. The funeral had been a harrowing experience for Oonagh and her brothers. They contacted their mother's sister in London, asking if she would contact their mother. The sister rang back a few hours later, saying that Stella had no wish to attend the funeral.

It would be eighteen years before Oonagh discovered that her father's death might not be as black and white as had been assumed. The facts, when they finally emerged, forced a re-evaluation of everything she thought she knew about the family history. The current murder investigations into the death of Mansfield would provide another significant insight to her family's unfinished saga and, in particular, the tragic tale of her father's life.

7

Ciarán Bailey was dying. No need of a doctor's diagnosis to confirm the fact; Emma had only to look at the wasted face and the eyes that no longer pulsed with life. Sadness welled up inside her.

How can nature be so cruel?

As a patient in the Oaklawn Lodge complex, within the grounds of St Luke's, Ciarán had been subjected to ongoing radiotherapy and specialist oncology treatment for several months. On two of Emma's previous visits to the hospital she'd encountered her ex, Vinny. Since the split, he'd refused to bow out gracefully. The situation had become especially difficult since it transpired that his father, Ciarán, was dying. Emma had formed a firm bond of friendship with Ciarán and had taken time out of her busy schedule to visit him, but Vinny had used her calls to the hospital as an excuse to be around her and generally make a nuisance of himself.

He had been the one to inform her that the prognosis for his father's condition held out no hope of recovery. Even though she'd been married to Vinny for ten years — and separated for eighteen months — confronting him in the presence of his father had been awkward. Vinny's doom-laden prediction aside, it had been difficult to gauge what exactly he hoped to achieve by his pretence in front of his father that they were still sharing a life, still united, still the happy couple.

Ciarán was not fooled. Death's door might beckon but his brain still functioned; he understood better than Vinny, it seemed to her, that his son's marriage had run its course, moved to a plane beyond salvage. For many years, Ciarán's life had been concerned with operating Bailey's Fine Art and Antiques Studio in Bray, twelve miles south of Dublin City. He had a reputation as the country's finest restoration artist, specializing in the reconstruction of damaged canvases. Vinny, who shared the business with his father, had made his mark in the art world by buying and selling original paintings and establishing himself as a dealer in antiques and rare books.

For ten years Emma had become, in a roundabout sort of way, part and parcel of both the Baileys' lives. Even before she'd married Vinny, he had taken her to the studio to meet his father. She loved the place and had grown to like Ciarán and his somewhat eccentric ways. He was close to death now but Emma would always carry an indelible image of Ciarán, absorbed in his work, wearing his customary multidaubed smock, immersed in an odour-filled world of brushes, palettes, linseed oil, turpentine, varnish and tubes of paint. Even back then, when Ciarán showed initial signs of the onset of angina, his stamina and enthusiasm for life had greatly impressed her.

It was hard to reconcile that vibrant image with the man now staring up at her from his hospital bed. Drained of colour, the face that normally bespoke a merciless pragmatism and intelligence now looked gaunt, his cheekbones protruding, his mouth drooped at the corners, the visage emphasizing his frailty. It was as though some pitiless sculptor had hewn his features from a block of carbolic soap with a blunt chisel.

'So good of you to come,' he said, holding Emma's hand with more strength than she would have thought possible. 'You've just missed Vinny, but I suppose . . . ' He stopped mid sentence, a barely noticeable twinkle in eyes that no longer held the mischievous beam they once harboured. The twinkle, Emma suspected, meant he'd twigged that her visit had been calculated not to coincide with his son's timing. His mental faculties, it appeared, still operated to a degree that belied his physical condition.

'Good to see you, Ciarán,' she said with genuine warmth, trying to ignore the metacarpal bones of his near-skeletal hand that pressed into the flesh of her own. 'How are they treating you here?'

'Couldn't be better, doing all they can for me, you know how it is . . . even had me out on the putting green they have here. Made me regret I'd never taken up golf. D'you know, I might've been a dab hand at it.'

'Oh, a regular Padraig Harrington, I'd say.'

'Ah, no, Emma, far too late for anything like that but, damn it, when all's said and done, I've no real complaints. I've had a good innings, yes indeed, a good innings. But you, Emma, just seeing you bucks me up better than any tonic. I've gone through so many damn clinical trials here; chemotherapy, radiation therapy, biological therapy, hormonal therapy and the devil knows what, but seeing you beats them all, hands down.'

'Well, it's good to see you haven't lost your old silver-tongued blarney. You can still charm the birds out of the bushes, whether they want to come out or not.'

'Go way outta that, I mean every word. You're a sight for sore eyes, Emma, and no mistake. D'you know what I'd like to do right now . . . ?'

'Let me guess: a pint of Guinness?'

'Wouldn't say no to a pint, right enough, but what I'd really like to do, if I had the strength, is paint your portrait . . . capture the expression on your face, the beauty in those bright, sparkling eyes. Do you still have the canvas I did of yourself and Vinny?'

'Yes, yes of course, my most treasured possession.' Emma was not lying. Ciarán had presented her and Vinny with a special painting as a wedding present: a full-scale copy of Renoir's masterpiece, *Luncheon of the Boating Party*, but it was more than just a reproduction of a group of young friends sitting by the banks of the Seine. Ciarán had superimposed portraits of Vinny and her into the composition with a subtlety that did not debase the beauty of Renoir's original. At the time, he had explained how the young woman in the picture, the one playing with the dog, resembled Emma, having similar golden brown whorls of hair, the same bright happy eyes, full lips, slight upturned nose and an identical strong profile. Ciarán admitted he'd had to do rather more extensive alterations to merge Vinny's likeness seamlessly into the space that originally contained a study of a French man straddling a chair.

The painting was one of the few possessions that caused dissension between Vinny and her when it came to dividing the spoils of their defunct marriage. After protracted argument, Vinny allowed her to retain the painting, wrongly assuming she wanted it as a reminder of their happier times together. In reality, she wanted it because it represented Ciarán; every brush stroke had been painted by his hand, the same hand that clasped hers now.

'More's the pity that life can't be like a painting,' Ciarán said sadly, his eyes fixed on Emma. 'Oh, I'm not just talking about you and Vinny breaking up, though I wish that hadn't happened, but I suppose I mean life in general. We have our time and then in the blink of an eye it's gone. 'Tis as I say — nature's a cruel mistress. It allows us to glimpse beauty, then just when we've learned to appreciate it properly, takes it away. The important thing is to make the most of it. There's little else we can do. I'm sorry, Emma, didn't want to subject you to the ramblings of an old man. How are you keeping? Still chasing the bad guys and reporting their wrongdoings?'

'Yeah, something like that . . . though I have been taking it a bit easier lately.'

'Hmmm, that doesn't sound very like the

Emma we all know and love. Everything's OK, yeah? Can't help noticing that you've lost a bit of weight. Not having trouble with that big-shot detective you're living with, I hope?'

'No, no, not at all: everything's fine as far as Connolly is concerned.'

'Do you intend to marry him?'

The question surprised Emma. It wasn't like Ciarán to probe into her personal life, certainly not in such a direct, unsubtle manner. Maybe his mental faculties had, after all, dimmed a little, or could it be that knowing his time was short, he decided to dispense with niceties, get straight to the point. 'No,' Emma answered, uneasily, 'we haven't decided to formalize our relationship. For the moment we're happy — '

'I ask for a good reason,' Ciarán interrupted, 'and I hope you'll forgive my impertinence, but I'm concerned about . . . how do I put this . . . I'm concerned about Vinny. The lad is still in denial as far as you're concerned. I want him to let go, get on with his life, move on, pick up the pieces, get married again, have the family he so desperately wants.'

'That's what I've begged him to do,' Emma said, feeling the surge of guilt that always assailed her whenever the subject of her failed marriage came up. 'I've tried to make it clear to him that — '

Ciarán interrupted again. 'There *is* a way to resolve the matter, a way to get through to Vinny, a way to give him back a meaningful life.'

Mist formed in Ciarán's eyes. Emma could feel the bones in his fingers strain as they attempted to hold hers more tightly. She dreaded to think what he was going to say to her but knew she had to ask. 'If there's any way I can help,' she offered, 'just tell me, I'll do whatever — '

'You could marry your detective friend.'

'What? I don't understand, I mean I don't — '

'Let me explain.'

8

The hospital façade faded as she drove away but not the devastating image of Ciarán Bailey's emasculated body. Jostling into the traffic crush on Highfield Road, she found it hard to grasp how a once vibrant artist like Ciarán could be reduced to a mere shell. On her way now to interview Scott Mansfield's widow, Emma needed to get a piece into the *Post*. In the absence of any startling new developments in what the media labelled 'the vampire slaying', Crosby wanted to keep the story running, and that meant chasing all the peripheral angles. In Emma's case it entailed talking to people who'd been close to the victim when he was alive. Doing little more than going through the motions, she still felt peeved at not having been given the lead.

To keep her juices flowing, she needed to be close to the centre of action, allowed to follow her instincts, have the freedom to create her own agenda, sniff out her prey like she'd done in the past. Limiting her role to that of a mere observer was like cutting off her oxygen supply.

Exiting Rathgar, Emma's thoughts remained tethered to the cancer wards of St Luke's, still feeling the imprint of Ciarán's emaciated fingers, hearing his strangulated voice enunciate his master plan for bringing an end to Vinny's reluctance to let go of their relationship. Couldn't be simpler, he'd insisted, all she had to do was marry Connolly. Emma had listened politely, feeling disquieted. Ciarán's rationale was not nearly as simple as he believed. 'Blame Vinny's Catholic upbringing,' he'd said. 'Vinny retains an unrealistic, old-fashioned respect for the sanctity of marriage. Even though the two of you are legally separated, he still thinks of you as his wife . . . in the sight of God. To rid him of this outmoded ideology, you must marry Connolly; that will act as a dose of reality and force him into accepting that the marriage is history.'

As it happened, Connolly had, on a number of occasions, suggested that very course of action to Emma, though not for the same reasons put forward by Ciarán. Connolly was all for tripping down the aisle but only if that was what she wanted. The problem, if you could call it a problem, was inside her head. She'd done the marriage bit once already and it had been no bed of roses. Baggage remained. Mostly guilt. The loss of her baby. Her fault. The barely concealed censure in Vinny's eyes. The weight crushing her spirits. Vinny's desire to start again, raise a family, destroyed every vestige of the love and trust they'd once shared. She wasn't ready to go there again. What she now enjoyed with Connolly was liberation. *Why risk that?* They stayed together because they loved each other, not because of some formal marriage certificate or spoken vows. Even so, Ciarán had got her thinking. If marriage to Connolly was the price she had to pay for setting Vinny free, then perhaps, just perhaps, it was a price worth paying . . . but not yet, not today.

Her musings were interrupted by her mobile.

It was Crosby.

'Emma, can you get to St James's graveyard ASAP?'

'Why, what's happening?'

'Spot of bother. Machines have moved in on the site and the protesters are up in arms. Better see what it's all about.'

'Yeah, OK. I was on my way to see Mansfield's widow but I suppose that can wait.' Emma's response had the kind of enthusiasm she normally displayed prior to a visit with her dentist for deep root canal treatment.

'Mansfield's widow can wait; see what this agitation is about first.'

'Right boss, whatever you say boss,' Emma replied, adding *three bags full boss*, under her breath.

Five minutes later, Emma pulled her Hyundai Coupé to the side of the road near St James's churchyard. Crosby was right. A crowd of placard-waving protesters pushed and shoved against a chain of uniformed gardai, observed by a group of onlookers, huddled by the old churchyard wall. A television team, complete with van and communications dish, had got to the scene before her. A female reporter attempted to coax sound bites from the protesters while being pushed back by two uniforms.

'How's it goin' there, Miss Boylan,' a voice called out from among the protesters. 'Hope you're getting all this for your paper.'

Emma recognized Hugh Foley and gave him a half-hearted nod of recognition, unwilling to get involved. Last time they'd met, he'd taken advantage of the situation, falsely admitting to the murder of Mansfield. *Once bitten, twice shy.* Besides, Hugh Foley had spotted something more advantageous to his cause; he had managed to position himself in front of the television camera and was attempting to talk into the microphone being held by the female reporter.

The sound of barking drew Emma's attention to the onlookers. She recognized Dick Burke and his dog. He didn't appear to notice her as she moved to his side, his attention concentrated on the protesters. 'Hello, Mr Burke,' she said, gently tapping him on the arm. 'We spoke the other day. I'm with the *Post*; my name is — '

'Oh, hello there, yes, yes, I remember you. Your name is — don't tell me, don't tell me — your name is Emma, Emma something-or-other. Must be a slow news day if you've got nothing better to do than come here to report on this farce.'

'Well, I suppose the people protesting don't think it's — '

'That's exactly it,' Burke interrupted, 'they don't *think*, period. They've got the wrong end of the stick as usual. You see the machinery in the graveyard? Well, those protesters — gobshites, the lot of them — think that work has begun on the proposed development.'

'Isn't that what's happening?'

'Not at all, the machinery is just drilling holes for the workmen to erect a fence and secure the site. Since the murder, the place has been overrun by sightseers, trampling the ground, no respect for living or dead.'

As Burke spoke, the television camera crew moved to include the onlookers. A woman, weaving a microphone, moved along the line of people, soliciting reaction. Emma realized she knew this reporter; she'd worked with her a decade earlier as rookie journalists for a magazine called *Business World*. Emma's stint with the magazine had been short lived. She'd written a damning indictment of a wealthy beef baron, outlining his alleged involvement in a scam to defraud the EU bureaucrats out of millions of pounds in intervention payments. Unfortunately, she'd omitted to include the word 'alleged' in her article. When the publication hit the shops, the beef baron obtained a court injunction compelling the publishers to withdraw the magazine from the shelves. Almost bank-rupted the publishers. Could have put paid to her career, but being young, stubborn, idealistic, and convinced of her own right-eousness, she'd refused to let the incident stall her chosen pursuit of employment. One of the few people sympathetic to her point of view at the time had been the reporter now approaching her. Her name was Evelyn Morgan and she'd obviously gone on to greater things since her days with *Business World*.

'Emma Boylan,' she said, a pleasant

surprise in her voice, before remembering to remain professional, neutral. Turning to camera, she said, 'I'm speaking to the *Post* investigative reporter, Emma Boylan. Tell me Emma, what's your reading on this protest? Do you have any inside information to share with us?'

'Afraid not,' Emma answered, knowing that this was a non-story, but anxious not to appear uncooperative. 'I'm talking to this man beside me,' she said, indicating Dick Burke. 'He's the one who discovered Scott Mansfield's body; I think he's the best person to fill you in on what this is about.'

Evelyn smiled, accepting Emma's helpful deflection. Burke needed little encouragement to launch into his, by now familiar, opinion of the protesters. His dog, as though aware that his master was being interviewed, barked more loudly than before, leaping up at the camera, anxious to feature on the TV footage. The dog wasn't the only one trying to make it on to the evening news; several of the crowd, attracted by the lure of the camera, poked their faces into frame, determined to be seen on the news later that night. One woman appeared anxious to make her way to where Emma stood, as though needing to speak to her, but as soon as Emma caught her eye she changed direction and veered away. What the woman's intention had been, Emma could only guess at.

Does she want to speak with me?

Has she backed off because of the television camera?

Emma was in no mood to find out. Another time, she would have pursued the woman. Not today.

9

'I was an air hostess when I first met Scott,'
Connie Mansfield said. Sitting in her late
husband's den with Emma, she seemed
almost glad to discuss the life she'd once had,
as though talking could obliterate the ugly
truth, restore things to the way they had
been. 'He used to fly Aer Lingus, Dublin-
Heathrow on a regular basis. Always a
gentleman, always pleasant, you know, a
ready smile, a joke or two. He took me to
a musical in the West End on our first date;
we enjoyed a meal afterwards in a posh
restaurant — can't remember the name —
cost him a packet; he wasn't nearly as well off
then. I was impressed. I was plain Connie
Smith back then, and because of the airline I
worked for he gave me the nickname
'Connielingus'. I was pretty naïve, didn't get
the joke. I used to tell my friends about the
name he'd given me and they'd crack up; I
couldn't understand it. Then one day a friend
explained the joke, the wordplay, the
meaning, and I . . . '
    Connie stopped talking, tears rolling down
her face. Emma moved to comfort her,

patting her back gently, feeling Connie's body heave with sobs. Emma had been impressed by Connie as soon as she'd been invited into the Mansfield house. Wearing a silver-coloured suit with black and white beads, Connie maintained a façade, holding things together as best she could. Even allowing for the dark circles beneath her eyes it was possible to get a glimpse of the passion that had so recently been dowsed. Small but vibrant, she had the high etched cheekbones of a model, arched eyebrows, a strong forehead and her hair, cut in a boyish fashion, showed all the signs of a high-maintenance regimen.

They were sitting in what Connie called Scott's den, though it didn't look like any den Emma had ever been in before. In the first place, there was the size to countenance: an enormous room that took up the entire ground floor. On Emma's arrival at the restored, three-storey Georgian mansion she'd climbed a set of granite steps and entered through an elevated front porch. One of the more upmarket districts on the city's north side, the area rivalled anything on the more prestigious south side. The tree-lined avenue that led to the house left Emma in no doubt as to Mansfields' financial status and standing in the community.

Inside the house, a dozen, maybe more, elegantly dressed people spread throughout a large reception area in small groups, talked quietly, the pall of grief unmistakable. The period-style drawing room and anteroom had the requisite high ceilings and spectacular plasterwork, chandeliers, mirrors, and pristine white marble fireplaces. Scott Mansfield had to have been at the top of his game as a property developer to afford such a pile. It was equally evident that he had style and good taste to complement his wealth. That good taste, Emma concluded, included his choice of wife. As soon as Connie had realized that Emma was not one of her late husband's relatives or a family or business acquaintance, she'd ushered her downstairs to the den.

Connie Mansfield talking endlessly, cathartically, with pent-up energy, appeared to be glad of the excuse to get away from the mourners. The den was, in reality, a music room. A row of guitars stood on their stands: two acoustic Spanish models and three electric ones. Stacks of CDs and DVDs were lined up beside a large book cabinet that had been packed with best sellers and literary classics. A grand piano and two keyboards stood next to an array of microphones, music stands and recording equipment. Shelves loaded down with office files, a row of steel cabinets, a desk, and soft furnishings accounted for another section of the room. This area, Emma assumed, was where Scott Mansfield kept track of his business interests.

Connie allowed herself a smile as she watched Emma observe the musical instruments. 'He came down here to unwind, to get away from business associates, to indulge his passion for music,' she explained, gesturing to the instruments. 'Half of what he played was, according to him, for the salvation of his soul; the other half, he used to jokingly concede, was the devil's music.' Connie wiped a tear from her eye and walked over to a modern keyboard. 'He played this for the church choir and he liked to play classical guitar but his guilty secret was that he would have loved to be part of a rock 'n' roll band. A split personality, of sorts. One half dark, rebellious, the other half righteous and pure. He could perform Beethoven's piano sonatas with the best of them but down here in his den . . . '

She stopped briefly, moved to one of the guitars, and continued with a sudden infusion of ebullience. 'With just me and the boys as the audience, he'd pick up this Gibson Les Paul and play the solo from *Sweet Child of Mine*. You'd swear you were listening to the Guns 'N' Roses recording. He'd liked nothing better than to sit here for hours on end, looking out at the front lawn through that big window there while playing the guitar. Music allowed him escape to another world. Of course, he also ran the business from down here but I think he'd always regretted not following music as a career.'

Emma moved to a sideboard festooned with photographs. 'Your husband?' she asked, pointing to a smiling young man in a study of four men posing with various musical instruments.

'Yes, it was taken some years before I knew him. They looked so happy then, don't you think?'

'Yes, they did. Was Scott playing professionally then?'

'I don't think so. He formed some sort of chamber ensemble with his friends but I gather it didn't last very long. He never talked much about that period but I know he'd been serious about music at one point, took lessons, and from what I've been told, had enough talent to go all the way. But for some reason — a reason he refused to discuss with me — he gave up, opted to go into his father's property business instead.'

'What about the other people in the photograph?' Emma asked. 'Did any of them go on to become full time musicians?'

'To be honest, I couldn't say. Whenever I asked Scott about them he became uneasy, downcast, almost as though there was something malevolent contained in the picture. I was intrigued but I never pushed him on it.'

Emma took a closer look at the photograph, studying each face in turn, all of them smiling for the camera, their mouths forming the silent word *cheese*. A young Scott Mansfield posed by a grand piano while the other musicians, all male, proudly held their instruments like badges of honour: a violin, a double bass, and a clarinet. An older man, probably the tutor, Emma supposed, and two young women stood to one side, beaming radiant smiles.

'This is us on our wedding day,' Connie said, handing a framed picture to Emma. 'A wonderful day . . . happiest moment of my life.'

'I recognize Slane Castle,' Emma said, studying the photograph. 'Looks like you had beautiful weather.'

'Sunniest day of the year. The reception was like something out of a fairy tale.' Connie gave Emma a chronicled account of all the photographs on display, her narrative, it seemed to Emma, an attempt to blot out the awfulness of the killing by concentrating on the better times: christening shots of the two boys, school groups, Christmas parties and holiday snaps. One photograph showed Scott wearing a builder's hard hat and holding a spade at a 'turning the sod' ceremony on one of his property developments.

'This is all I'm left with,' Connie said, her voice breaking with emotion. 'How could anyone . . . how could anyone do what was done to Scott?'

'Did he have any enemies that you know of?'

'Enemies? Well, until this happened I would have said no. Certainly there were people he had differences with . . . bankers, suppliers . . . architects . . . planners. He was in a difficult business, a tough business, but he tried to be fair with those he dealt with.' In an instant, her grief turned to rage. 'He certainly never did anything to warrant the brutal butchery that — '

'Yes, it was dreadful,' Emma agreed, leading Connie back to a chair. 'I know the detective who's in charge of this investigation; he's a good man. Nothing can undo what's happened but at least you'll get justice when they find whoever is responsible.'

'Yes, the big man, he was the one who broke the news to me. Can't recall his name, it was something like — '

'His name's Connolly, Detective Inspector Jim Connolly; he won't rest until he tracks down the person responsible for what's happened.'

'What's the world coming to when ordinary decent people like Scott, going about their business, are killed . . . and for what? All this mindless violence, it's so wrong, so unfair, so, so . . . I just don't know . . . '

Emma listened as Connie talked about her two children and how she would now have to take sole responsibility for their upbringing. There was no doubt that the woman was broken-hearted but there was also an underlying reserve of strength and resourcefulness. After Emma explained the kind of background article she planned to write, Connie agreed to cooperate fully. 'If what you write can focus attention on the wanton savagery of what's happened, if it helps the investigation, I'll do whatever I can.'

'Would you mind if I borrowed a few of your photos,' Emma asked.

'What good will they do?'

'I'm not sure,' Emma answered honestly, 'but I'd like to get a better handle, a more rounded impression of your husband's life. I'd like to let my readers know the kind of man he was.'

Connie looked unsure, perhaps a little unwilling to part with such personal belongings, but after a moment's hesitation, nodded in compliance. 'Well, yes, I suppose anything that gets the nauseating and insulting vampire nonsense off the front pages has to be a good thing. I'd like them back as soon as possible, though, if that's OK with you?'

'No problem, I'll scan them as soon as I get back to the office and — '

'Tell you what, you can come back here to the house after the funeral tomorrow, bring the pictures with you. We'll have a little spread laid on here for Scott's friends who've travelled a long distance to pay their respects. I'd be pleased if you could join us?'

Emma had not planned to attend the Mansfield funeral but made a quick decision. 'That's very kind of you,' she said. 'Yes. I'll be here and I'll bring them with me.'

10

Emma toe-heeled her shoes off, hoisted her feet on to the sofa and allowed her head to sink gently into a pile of cushions she'd arranged against the armrest. Time to chill out. It had been a long day and she felt more strung out than usual. She wasn't feeling hungry but she'd taken the time to put some ingredients together for Connolly's supper. She'd been tempted to pop the cork on a bottle of wine but resisted, preferring to wait for Connolly, share the bottle with him. She'd quit cigarettes because of evidence that claimed tobacco affected the kidneys and caused renal failure, blood pressure, anaemia and liver damage. By comparison, wine was a safer bet; apart from the minuscule risk of breast cancer, it actually lowered cholesterol levels.

Connolly had phoned earlier. 'Going to be late,' he said. 'The suits are restless and our beloved Minister for Justice has been on the blower to the Chief Super, all hot and bothered because the murder is monopolizing press, radio and TV and has, surprise, surprise, produced nervousness among his fellow cabinet ministers and backbenchers. And, of course, the flog'em-and-lock'em-up brigade are extremely exercised, demanding instant results so that decent law-abiding citizens can sleep easy in their beds at night.'

'No pressure then,' Emma said with mock cheerfulness.

That had been an hour ago and she hoped he wouldn't be much longer. No matter which way she lounged on the sofa, she remained uncomfortable, ill at ease. She'd sometimes felt like that in bed when she'd been overtired, on the point of exhaustion, her brain in overdrive, refusing to shut down. Her current unease, she knew, was not due to work overload or having to juggle too many chores simultaneously. Quite the reverse, in fact. Not having enough meaningful activity or responsibility for the case now assigned to her was doing her head in. For the past three days she'd just been tinkering around on the periphery, spinning wheels, getting nowhere.

Crosby's fault . . . and that scheming little shit, Willie Thompson.

Getting up from the sofa, she moved ponderously to the picture window that overlooked the Liffey. Darkness had descended. Street lamps reflected their orange illumination on the surface of the river's fast-flowing current. Traffic had eased considerably since the mad, congested teatime city exodus but a steady flow of cars continued to push along both quaysides, criss-crossing the bridges, spewing their fumes into the night air with little consideration for global warming.

To Emma's way of thinking, November represented the most depressing month of the year. Long, dark evenings, cold nights, frigid mornings. To shut out the city's gloom, she pulled the curtains, returned to the sofa, rearranged the pillows, and picked up the remote. She flicked through the channels, rejecting each within seconds, before settling for the home channel news. The top report concerned itself with the murder of Mansfield. Connolly might not have made it home but he was here, if only by proxy, answering questions at a packed press conference. The screen suddenly filled with a close-up shot of *Post* reporter Willie Thompson, his eyes alight with indignation, his lips flapping like a braying jackass, as he fired questions at Connolly.

This, for Emma, was akin to having an inflamed sore probed with a red-hot poker, the irritation slightly mitigated by the fact that his questions were studiously ignored. She was about to channel-hop again when footage of the protest outside the St James's graveyard filled the screen. Emma watched as

Evelyn Morgan, microphone in hand, approached the group where she had stood. Emma's own exchange with the reporter flashed on to the screen but she paid little attention, being more concerned with the activity taking place in the background. At the time, she'd felt reasonably sure that a woman in the crowd had moved towards her, but now, seeing it re-enacted on screen, it was obvious that she'd been right. The woman had definitely approached her, then suddenly veered away. Emma would like to have had more time to study the woman's face but the picture dissolved as a fresh news item rolled on to the screen.

Emma closed her eyes, concentrated. She attempted to recreate the woman's face in her mind's eye. Her age: difficult to tell, mid-thirties perhaps, maybe more. Hair: mouse-brown and longish. Eyes: large, probably hazel. She was tallish, well-dressed, wearing little or no make-up, could be called pretty if she'd made an effort.

Who is she? What does she want with me?

Emma was still thinking about the woman when Connolly finally made it home. He slumped down beside her, kissed her and apologized for being late.

'Just seen you on the news,' she told him.

Connolly dismissed this with a shrug, proceeded to give her a potted version of his day. Emma would ask for more detail later and discuss her own experiences, but first she wanted to place the food in the oven: seafood and fresh vegetable lasagne.

'You dining?' he asked, eyeing the bottle of wine.

'Eaten already,' she lied. Even though this was one of the dishes that formed part of her newly acquired dietary regimen — rich in omega-3, containing polyunsaturated fat to protect against coronaries and strokes — she didn't feel like eating this evening. In the half-hour that it took to cook, Connolly had a shower and changed into comfortable clothes.

She sat at the table, refusing all his entreaties to join him in the meal, but happy to share the bottle of Italian Pinot Grigio. Under normal circumstances, Connolly was reluctant to discuss his work in the evenings but Emma hoped, now that she was consigned to second-fiddle reporter status, he'd be more willing to share the ins and outs of his caseload.

In this assumption she was wrong. After giving him several openings to unburden himself on the finer details of the murder, he took hold of her hand and said, 'I'm all talked out; why don't we open another bottle of wine and do what we do best, what you say?'

'I'll drink to that,' Emma replied, leaning over to kiss his cheek. She wanted to give herself fully to him, no reservations, but she couldn't help thinking that something dark and foreboding lay ahead. What that something might be, she had no idea, but the fear that her idyllic life with Connolly was headed for choppy waters seemed inescapable.

11

Funerals. Emma hated them. Something to do with the rituals. She'd never felt comfortable expressing condolences, having to listen to the inane banalities of mourners who, like her, struggled to express appropriate sentiments while conveying all the expected gestures. Apart from the sadness and anguish of bidding final goodbyes, the subliminal thought that the grim ceremony would one day be enacted on her behalf was a reality she'd rather not acknowledge. Today's obsequies would, she hoped, be a little less stressful. She had never met, or known, Scott Mansfield. It was enough that she'd met his wife.

Since her visit to the Mansfield house, she'd scanned and downloaded the photographs she'd borrowed. One of the better prints would come in handy to bolster the slight piece she'd put together for the next edition of the *Post*, a contribution that was supposed to complement Willie Thompson's lead story. The image depicted Scott Mansfield alongside his wife and children. A happy picture. She would have preferred to have used the black-and-white study of Mansfield with the group of musicians because it was far more illustrative and complementary to her text but she held it back on account of the lack of information available for a caption. Apart from Scott Mansfield, seated at the piano, she couldn't put names to the others. Might have helped if she had some idea of where and when the photograph had been taken. All she had to go on was a partially faded stamp on the reverse side of the print that identified the name and address of the studio that had shot and processed the photograph.

She'd brought the original prints to the funeral so that she could return them to Connie Mansfield. She deliberately arrived late for the service, hoping to merge quietly with the mourners as they made their way from Sword's picturesque Protestant church to the adjacent graveside. In Emma's experience, it usually rained cats and dogs during funerals but thankfully on this occasion the church, with its distinctive round belfry, was bathed in midday wintry sunshine. The manicured graveyard with its uniformly well-maintained headstones was surrounded by mature oaks and elms and an old-fashioned ivy-clad stone wall.

Easing herself into the crowd, she watched the coffin being lowered into the earth amid prayer, sobs and muffled words. Mourners watched uneasily, their feet moving involuntarily on the gravel, an audible manifestation of the heightened emotions present: sadness, compassion, pity. Connie Mansfield, attired in black suit and lace-trimmed hat, flanked by her two boys, stared at the space where her husband's remains had disappeared as though not fully believing her own eyes. She remained in this limbo state of consciousness as two grey-clad undertakers masked the grave with a covering of artificial grass. Emma decided not to join the mourners who'd lined up to shake hands with the family and offer sympathy, waiting instead until the people had begun to leave the cemetery, before approaching Connie Mansfield.

She was about to reach out to Connie when, from behind her, a woman said, 'May I speak with you, Ms Boylan?'

Emma pivoted to see who had spoken, instantly recognizing the woman. 'I know you,' Emma said, slightly flustered, her mind running in two directions simultaneously: needing to know what the woman had in mind, aware too that Connie Mansfield's car was about to pull away. 'I saw you yesterday at the protest,' she said, opting to concentrate on the woman. 'I got the impression you wanted to talk to me, but then you disappeared. Am I right?'

'Yes, you are right . . . didn't think you'd

noticed. I wanted, needed to talk to you . . . talk to somebody, but I chickened out. Saw you here today and . . . please, can I . . . can we talk. I have to . . . '

Before Emma could reply she saw Connie Mansfield's car drive away. She hid her annoyance at missing the opportunity to return the photographs and turned her attention to the woman responsible. 'How can I help you?'

'I'm not sure, Ms Boylan,' the woman said, a slight quiver in her voice, 'but I don't know who else to turn to.'

'You know my name . . . I'm afraid I don't know yours?'

'Sorry, should have told you who I am, sorry.' She spoke in a deep, almost masculine, voice but her words were soft and hesitant. She might have been attractive but the lines around her mouth made her appear fretful and anxious; her hazel eyes, slightly sunken, studied Emma with piercing intensity. She held out a shapely hand with a broad gold bracelet around the wrist. 'My name is Oonagh Kavanagh . . . I know it means nothing to you, but, well, I wanted to tell you something that could be important . . . something relevant, I mean, something to do with the murder.'

12

The house was small, poorly maintained. A terraced dormer bungalow on Leeson Street Upper, close to the Grand Canal Bridge and separated from Mespil Road by Grand Parade. Emma had followed Oonagh's black Micra from the graveyard in Swords, through the city centre, and into a private parking space off Sussex Road. From there, she'd accompanied Oonagh on the short walk that took them to the back entrance of Oonagh Kavanagh's house.

Oonagh motioned Emma to a leather couch in a small television room, apologized for its untidy state and offered to brew coffee. Emma nodded her agreement, wondering what information, if any, would be gleaned from this sad-eyed woman. If the bookshelves were an indication of the owner's state of mind then prospects were far from encouraging. Shoe boxes, hat boxes and various-sized file folders were packed haphazardly on the shelves, wads of newspaper cuttings and what might have been correspondence, stuck out from bulging files held together with elastic bands and twine. Emma frequently encountered people who believed they possessed earth-shattering revelations to impart. Trouble was, once revealed, they usually turned out to be either unreliable or downright fabrications. There was, however, something in this woman's eyes, a gleam of repressed desperation that held out the prospect of yielding something positive, something worthwhile.

Oonagh placed a tray containing coffee and chocolate biscuits on a small occasional table, smoothed her skirt across her thighs and sat down. 'Sorry to drag you here,' she said, 'but I didn't know who else to turn to. I've got your articles on the murder filed right here,' she said, indicating the overflowing book shelves. 'From what you've written, I feel you might be the kind of person willing to listen to what I have to say with a sympathetic ear.'

Oh, Christ! A fruitcake.

Emma hid her scepticism, anxious to move things along. 'You've got information about the murder of Scott Mansfield, yes?'

'I do, yes. I most definitely do.'

'Well then, my first question is simple: why haven't you gone to the authorities? Shouldn't you be talking to them, not me?'

'When you hear what I have to tell you, you'll understand. I'm involved in the murder

. . . my family's involved . . . I knew Scott Mansfield.'

'How did you know him?'

'Knew him through my father's work.'

'Your father? And your father is . . . ?'

'My father *was* a music professor; he tutored Mansfield back when he was a student. Because of him, he lost his life. It's a complicated story . . . one I'd like to talk to you about . . . if . . . if you've got the time.'

'I've got time,' Emma said, impatient to know where this was going.

Oonagh took a deep breath, sighed. 'My father, Trevor Kavanagh, was fired from the Metropolitan School of Music after a seventeen-year-old student named Norma Somers claimed he'd made her pregnant. She said he'd demanded sex as payment. The scandal — at least that's what it was considered back then — made the newspapers and the news bulletins on radio and television. Our family was shamed. People whispered when we walked down the street. It was terrible . . . especially for Dad. Two months before giving birth, Norma Somers withdrew the accusation and announced her engagement to the young man she now claimed to be the real father. The exoneration came too late for Father. The School of Music refused to reinstate him, claiming that he'd compromised his professional standing and brought the school's name into disrepute.

'Without a job, he was forced to give lessons in our family home. My brothers, Fintan and Owen, were working by then and had moved from home but father's loss of steady income meant I had to drop out of university. Mother never fully accepted Dad's innocence and moved into a separate room. Father began to drink heavily, the atmosphere in the house deteriorated to an intolerable level. I couldn't stand the constant fighting and bickering and decided to move out. Six months later, Mother left for London where she had an older sister.

'Dad managed to get an ex-student of his to do part-time cleaning in the house; I got a job in the civil service but I looked in on him as often as I could. Even though he'd taken to the booze he never lost his talent as a tutor and was never short of students. Almost a year to the day after he'd lost his job he was involved in a fatal road incident. The crash investigators blamed him; said there was excess alcohol in his bloodstream.'

Oonagh stood and exhaled loudly. 'Until three months ago, I had no reason to doubt the verdict. I assumed alcohol had fogged Dad's brain and contributed to what happened. And then, three months ago, I found out it might not have happened in the way I thought it had.'

Emma didn't know where Oonagh Kavanagh was going with her story and couldn't quite see how it tied in with the current murder. She was, nevertheless, riveted by the unfolding tale and moved by the quiet catch of grief in Oonagh's voice and the total earnestness of each word.

'If it wasn't an accident,' Emma asked, 'what was it?'

Oonagh looked past Emma, as though striving to solidify some intangible thought. Colour drained from her face. She remained lost and silent for several seconds, her jaws and lips striving for words before finally emitting in a low throaty rasp, 'Scott Mansfield pushed my father to his grave.'

13

'What?' Emma said, stunned by Oonagh's assertion. 'Mansfield . . . *pushed* your father. I don't follow, I mean, didn't you say he was killed in a car crash? How could — ?'

Oonagh's etiolated face remained immobile. Eyes unfathomable. Only the bloodless lips moved. 'He was responsible . . . Mansfield, the others . . . hounded him, pushed him — '

'Pushed him? The others? Who . . . I mean how — '

'Suicide! My poor demented father took his own life . . . wanted out, couldn't take any more.'

'And you think — '

'Think? No, I don't just *think*. I *know*.'

'You have proof?'

'Proof! Yes, I have proof.' Oonagh went to a bookshelf, removed a small cardboard box. 'I've got a letter here that explains everything.' She returned to her seat, removed the lid. 'This,' she said, extracting an envelope, 'was written by Dad eighteen years ago on the morning of his death. He addressed it to Mother but it was meant for my brothers and me; she was supposed to call us together and read it but for reasons best known to her she ignored his wishes. Couldn't be bothered, I suppose. It was only after her death that we discovered the letter. The thing that surprises me is that she didn't burn it. Aunt Kathleen, Mother's sister, that is, found it among mother's bits and bobs after the funeral. She had no idea what it contained but she decided we should have it.'

Oonagh removed three typewritten sheets from the envelope, offered them to Emma and said, 'Read this, it'll explain how the murders tie in with my family.'

Emma took the letter, read:

Dear Stella
It is not my intention to place a further burden on your shoulders but I feel that certain facts ought to be put on record for Fintan, Owen and Oonagh. I'm painfully aware of the huge disappointment I have been for all of you but I feel obliged to put a true and accurate account of what actually happened, actions that got lost in the ballyhoo surrounding my ignominious fall from grace.

I was exonerated on the charge of having unlawful carnal knowledge with my student, Norma Somers. The stigma and shame remains, however. I could hardly expect my employers in the School of Music to stand by me when you, my wife, refused to believe me. I like to think that Oonagh believed me but the doubts evident in my boys' eyes are all too easily read. I should have been stronger, should have weathered the storm with fortitude, but a man can only take so much battering before fault lines appear. Alcohol became my crutch, my refuge. But even with this self-inflicted debilitation, I could have survived were it not for the evil scheme hatched up by four of the students I tutored in my house.

The students I refer to are:

Alan Gibney,
Dom Sutton,
John-Joe Moody and
Scott Mansfield.

Talented young men undoubtedly. Arrogant assuredly, but not quite as gifted as they'd like to think they are. Because of the various instruments they played, I encouraged them to form a quartet. They had connections in the world of show business and managed to wangle a televized spot on RTE. The exposure should have provided a worthwhile springboard but the disruptive element within the group proved counterproductive.

I wished to confine myself exclusively to their musical abilities but when their pernicious behaviour impinged on my character, the situation became intolerable. They were aware of my troubled history, vis-a-vis my association with Norma Somers and because of it, they saw an opportunity to concoct a scenario that placed me at the centre of another sex scandal.

After Oonagh left home, I employed an ex-student of mine as part-time help to keep a semblance of normality in the house. Her name is Lynda O'Regan and, unfortunately, she became an unwitting participant in the scheme the musicians devised to destroy me.

After one particular practice session, during which time I'd consumed too much whiskey, I invited them to join me for drinks, my intention to talk about their musical talents. They jumped at the chance but what should have been an exploration of musical pursuits turned into a marathon bender. I remember Lynda O'Regan being quite annoyed as she attempted to get the lads to leave the house, but being inebriated myself I told her to relax and join us for a drink. Whether she did or not, I can't say because I blanked out and don't remember anything else from the session.

The following day Lynda telephoned me to say she'd been sexually abused during the drinking session. I was dumbfounded and drove to her house straight away. When I got there, her brother John refused to let me speak with Lynda. He accused me of raping his sister, claiming that the four musicians were willing to swear to my culpability. He physically threw me out of the house when I denied the accusation.

I do not wish to face another case of false accusation, nor do I wish to subject you and the children to further humiliation. With that in mind, I've opted to take myself away from the situation in order to spike their conspiracy. I've no idea why these students should condemn me to such a fate but should they persist with their malicious lies, I feel it important that Fintan, Owen and Oonagh know the truth.

Your troubled husband — Trevor

Oonagh remained silent while Emma read the letter, the fretful expression on her face appearing to deepen as she stared into the middle distance, trance-like, her bottom lip quivering.

'That's quite something,' Emma said, handing back the pages. 'Have your brothers seen it?'

'Yes. I met them in London when Aunt Kathleen gave me the letter.'

'How did they take it?'

'Bit like myself; furious that Dad got such a raw deal, furious for not having been more supportive, furious with the students who'd orchestrated the situation in the first place.'

'Did they intend to do anything about it?'

'You mean, did they want to track down the musicians?'

'Did they?'

'Like me, they were mad as hell, and yes, we wanted to get back at them but our greatest condemnation was directed inwards. We met in London's Tara Hotel. Wanted to see if there was something we could do.' Oonagh stopped talking and took a handkerchief from her pocket and wiped her eyes. 'Fintan, my oldest brother was incandescent, wanted to go after each of them.'

'Go *after*; what did he mean by that?'

'Well, he was so angry . . . if he'd got hold of them he would've killed them, no question about it. Owen and I had to calm him down, explain that were we to take such action we'd be no better than them.'

'So, what action did you take?'

'We agreed to do nothing until we came up with something the three of us could agree upon. It's over six weeks since we last met face to face and that particular meeting was something of a shambles. We ended up screaming at each other, disagreeing on what we ought to do. All we succeeded in doing was to create animosity and mistrust among ourselves. We're due to meet again in two weeks time. If that happens, it will be the first time we'll have a chance to talk about the murder.'

'So, who killed Mansfield?'

'I don't know, I really don't know. That's why I'm talking to you, not the law. The thought that Fintan might have taken things into his own hands is just too mind-blowing to contemplate . . . simply not credible. He would never do such a crazy thing but I'm so afraid, I'm afraid of what he might have started. I've tried to contact him over the past few days but he's not responding to my calls. I don't know what to do. I hate those men for what they did to Father but God in Heaven, I'd never dream of doing, or condoning what's happened . . . that's barbaric.'

'What do you think *I* can do?' Emma asked.

'I think you can do something that the law can't.'

'Like what?'

'You can prove that my brother is not involved without setting up a manhunt. You can prove it without branding him a prime suspect. I would hate to be the one to ruin his career, hate to see history repeat itself. What happened to Father can't be allowed to happen to Fintan.'

'But what if he *is* guilty?'

'He's *not* guilty; I believe that . . . I do, but I'm cursed with this all consuming, nagging doubt that he just might be involved . . . in which case I wipe my hands of him, let the law take its course. I've decided to place my trust in you. If you're willing to work with me to establish the truth . . . without recourse to the law, I will fill you in on all the relevant information you'll need to get to the bottom of this.'

'I'll need to hear a lot more before I can take such a leap of faith. If what I hear satisfies me then maybe, just maybe, we might be able to work something out.'

'That's fine by me. Where do you want me to start?'

14

Guidelines had been ironed out, conditions and rules of engagement agreed upon. The most awkward moment came when Emma had to forcefully reiterate her role in the exercise, spell out her *raison d'être*. 'I'm an investigative journalist,' she'd repeated, 'you contacted me, not the other way round. What I discover ends up in the public domain.'

Oonagh had teased this dilemma every which way before finding an acceptable modus operandi. She'd wanted sight of each article and the power of veto on disclosures, something Emma resolutely opposed, insisting she retain freedom to publish what she deemed germane to the subject. As a concession, Emma agreed to appraise Oonagh on the outline content of articles that had the potential to embarrass or adversely reflect on her or her family.

'If Fintan's got nothing to do with this madness,' Oonagh said, 'which is what I truly believe, then we won't have dragged his name into the mire and damaged his reputation; if, on the other hand, he's guilty, it won't matter a jot what you print.'

With this uneasy understanding, they got down to business. Oonagh extracted a photo album from one of the countless cardboard boxes that seemed to form part of the very fabric of the house. 'This,' she said, handing it to Emma, 'contains photographs of the students who received tuition from my Father. Friedrich Schiller, the photographer, was a good friend of Dad's; he used to operate a studio with his son Walter in Dame Street. They were frequent visitors to our house.'

The mention of a photographic studio made Emma think of the picture she'd borrowed from Connie Mansfield but she decided to say nothing about it for the moment, preferring to hear more first.

'Schiller was older than Dad,' Oonagh said, 'but the two men hit it off, spent hours discussing music, sipping schnapps and beer, listening to their collection of vinyl LPs. Wonderful music by composers like Wagner, Berg, Mahler, Richard Strauss . . . all the greats.' A rare smile appeared on Oonagh's face, her eyes appearing to visualize a time long passed. 'I can still hear them playing the operas . . . speakers going full blast, drove the neighbours nuts . . . didn't bother the old boys in the least, worse than teenagers, they were. I sat there sometimes, enjoying the look of bliss on their faces.

'Other times Walter Schiller, the son, sat with me; he usually came to the house when Friedrich wanted to take pictures. Walter's job was to lug the camera and photographic equipment about and help set up the shots. Sometimes, especially on days when the students were giving special performances or rehearsing for important exams or concerts, my father would invite both the Schillers. Photographs were always taken at times like that.'

As Oonagh spoke, Emma leafed through the contents of the album. Each photograph was dated and contained the names of those in the shot. Several pictures showed a bespectacled Trevor Kavanagh posing beside his students. A family grouping included a young Oonagh Kavanagh standing next to her two brothers. The siblings appeared somewhat stilted in the company of their parents, a handsome couple who looked into the camera's lens with an air of confidence and, to Emma's eye, maybe a touch of arrogance.

'Excuse me,' Oonagh said, stretching slender fingers across the album and flicking several pages over, 'but this is what I want you to see.'

When Emma saw what Oonagh showed

her, she took an audible intake of breath. 'You're not going to believe this,' Emma said, 'but I've already seen this photograph. As a matter of fact, I happen to have it on me now.'

Oonagh seemed mystified, said, 'You're not serious?'

'Dead serious,' Emma replied, opening the envelope she'd intended to return to Connie Mansfield and extracting the photograph. Smaller than the image in Oonagh's album, the print had been taken from the same negative. Emma placed the two photographs side by side and would have said *snap* if it weren't for the look of utter bafflement on Oonagh's face.

'Where? I mean, how? I don't understand . . . I didn't know anyone else had this . . . how did you . . . ?'

Emma, anxious to quell Oonagh's growing anxiety, explained about the visit she'd made to the Mansfield house and how she'd come upon the duplicate image. 'When you approached me at the cemetery, I was about to return it to Connie Mansfield.'

Oonagh pursed her lips and frowned. 'Didn't think the students had copies,' she said, looking past Emma as though trying to remember something.

'I see Scott Mansfield's name,' Emma said,

'but I wouldn't have linked his youthful looks with the current pictures in the newspapers; he looked so different as a young man.'

'Like his pals, he was an arrogant tearaway back then,' Oonagh cut in. 'They were into amphetamines, grass, morphine and, of course, alcohol; they were responsible for my father's death; they thought they'd got away with it but somebody out there wants them to pay for what they've done.'

'And you think your brother Fintan is the one who — '

'No, no, I do not. That's the whole point, I don't. But — and this is the crazy part — simple logic tells me he'll be seen as prime suspect. I know it has to be someone else but for the life of me I can't think who it might be.'

'You have a second brother; isn't it possible that he — '

'You mean Owen? No, no, never in a million years, not Owen. He's a pacifist, wouldn't hurt a fly. When he read the letter he went dumb — a sort of *see no evil, hear no evil, speak no evil* attitude, if you follow me. He refused to listen to Fintan when he suggested that Dad's tormentors should pay for what they'd done.'

'Who are the others?'

'That's me standing next to father,'

Oonagh said pointing to a smiling young woman wearing a chic, flower-print dress, chunky necklace and matching wrist bangles.

'Wouldn't have recognized you,' Emma said.

'Hey, even I don't recognize me,' Oonagh said with an unsmiling smile. 'I looked pretty good back then but that was before . . . well, doesn't matter. Lynda O'Regan, the girl mentioned in Father's letter, is standing next to me.'

'The one the students accused him of raping?'

'Yes. I think Dad might possibly have been a bit smitten by her but she was at least thirty years his junior. The very idea that they were *having it off*, as the saying goes, is simply ridiculous. I knew my Father, knew Lynda too, it didn't happen . . . couldn't happen.'

'Is Lynda O'Regan still around?'

'No, the poor woman's dead. I attended her funeral, thought some of the men in the photograph might be there.'

'And were they?'

'No. A few of Dad's other students turned up but none of those named in the letter. I saw Walter Schiller and Lynda's brother John in the church but I hadn't the heart to go up to them. I really wanted to talk to John but I couldn't pluck up the courage, knowing he blamed Dad for his sister's misfortune. I used to meet him back in the days when Lynda worked for Father. He was studying architecture at the time and used to drop Lynda off at the house and pick her up in his clapped-out Mini. Their family was strapped for cash, found it difficult to put John and Lynda through college. That's why Lynda worked part-time . . . helped to pay the fees for her and John. I tried to make contact with Lynda about six months after the scandal but her family made it clear they wanted nothing to do with me. I desperately wanted to find out what exactly happened on the night she was raped.'

'What about the others in the group; any idea what's become of them?'

'Haven't a clue. Until Father's letter, I'd never given them a second thought.'

'Three of the people in the photograph are no longer with us if we include your Father and Lynda O'Regan,' Emma said, trying to get her own fix on the situation. 'That's a pretty high rate of attrition. And you say you haven't been in touch with or spoken to any of the others since getting your Father's letter?'

'That's what I said.'

'What about your brothers? You told me you met face to face six weeks ago. But have you talked to either of them since Mansfield's death?'

'That's another thing,' Oonagh said, her throaty voice taking on a note of agitated alarm. 'I've been ringing and leaving messages at the numbers where they usually hang out but I can't make contact.'

'Can you give me a little more background on the musicians?'

'You might be better off talking to Walter Schiller. From what you've told me, it appears he might have given each of them a copy of the group photograph. He was a great one for keeping records, so it's possible he can point you in the right direction.'

'You have an address?'

'Yes, I can let you have it. After his father died he moved out of the old premises in Dame Street and opened up a studio in the Essex Gate district of Temple Bar.'

'That's great, thanks. Do you have any addresses or numbers to help me make contact with your brothers?'

'Well, like I say, both of them are incommunicado at the moment but I can let you have a rummage through my files. How much time do you have?'

'As much as it takes.'

Oonagh came close to giving Emma a genuine smile as she gestured to the shelving.

'There's eighteen years of my life tied up in what you see here. I'll guide you through the sections that are relevant.'

Emma smiled back. 'Lead the way,' she said.

15

Emma listened to Connolly's deep breathing, watched his chest rise and fall, the whisper of post-coital bliss still discernible on his handsome face. He was assuredly the best lover on the planet as far as she was concerned, no question about it; he knew instinctively how to please, tease, tingle and excite every erotic nerve ending in her body. Pure ecstasy. She'd responded to every caress and thrust with wanton abandonment, unafraid to let loose her cries and moans of fulfilment. Times like this made life worthwhile; the rest of the world shut out, removed, nonexistent.

She'd come home late. Connolly had waited on her, his intention to enjoy dinner together. He'd pulled out all the stops, conjured up mouth-watering delights, but she just nibbled and pushed the ingredients around the plate while downing a glass and a half of wine. Afterwards, in front of the telly, sound muted and fresh glasses, they'd swapped stories about their day's workload.

Before this mutual exposure to each other's trials and tribulations, Emma had been concerned about what she'd learned from Oonagh Kavanagh and, in particular, how much she could divulge without breaking a confidence. The significance of the files she'd looked at in Oonagh's living room could be vitally important. Kavanagh's letter could have a bearing on the investigation.

Do I pass it on? Yes? No? Damn it!

'Saw a pal of yours today,' Connolly said, interrupting her thoughts.

'A *pal* of mine?'

'Well, not a pal exactly; more a rival, really, a colleague who — '

'You don't mean — '

'I do! Willie Thompson, the very man. Saw him in the television studio.'

'Interesting! What the hell was he doing there?'

'Search me! The guy appears to be stalking me, everywhere I go, he turns up. He was in the television canteen today; giving it large with the gob; licking up to a few of the back room boys, big time.'

'Biggest lick in the business, that's our Willie. He'd lick his own granny if he thought he'd get a story there.'

'Yikes! That sounds vaguely obscene.'

Emma smiled. 'Just your bad mind,' she said. 'So, tell me, what were you doing out in RTE?'

'You remember me telling you about finding fragments of a musical score down Mansfield's throat, yeah? Well, since then we've been looking for a connection that might link the murder in some way to music. I went to the parish where he played the organ and talked to his vicar. He told me that Mansfield once played music in some sort of classical outfit and had performed on RTE's *The Late Late Show* back when Gay Byrne hosted the show. Turns out our victim was a member of a quartet named *Con Spirito*. So I went to the studios in RTE to see if I could dig up anything that might shed light on that appearance. The production people were most helpful; they unearthed the footage from the show and let us have a print. We're going to make stills and have the newspapers run with them over the next day or so; in that way, we hope to put names to the other musicians.'

Emma felt the need to say something. 'I can give you the names of the other musicians.'

Connolly looked at her askance. 'No, I don't think so; we've only got our hands on the footage late this evening. Nobody, apart from me and my team have seen it.'

'I don't need to see the footage. I have a photograph of the musicians.'

'But you couldn't have; I told you we only got — '

'I got it yesterday from Connie Mansfield.'

'What? You've known since yesterday and didn't bother to open your mouth. Dammit, Emma, this isn't like you; we're in the middle of a serious investigation and you've taken it upon yourself to withhold evidence?'

'Whoa! Hold it just a sec. Yes, I've had the photograph since yesterday *but* I didn't have the names until today. Didn't recognize the younger Mansfield until someone pointed him out.'

'Who pointed him out?'

'I'd prefer not to say, at least not yet, OK? But, I can give you the names of the other musicians . . . if you want.'

'Damn right *I want*. I want everything you've come up with.'

'You can have the names, no problem but I need to check out a few leads before giving you anything else.'

'Dammit, Emma, come on, I don't have time for this. I shouldn't need to tell you about obstructing the law, withholding evidence, and — '

Connolly stopped in mid sentence and allowed a thick silence to fill the space between them. Emma put her glass down, took hold of his hand. 'Jim, you remember our deal?'

'Our deal?'

'Yeah, the one we decided on back when we moved in together?'

Connolly nodded. ''Course I remember: I wouldn't use you to gather information for my police work and — '

'And I wouldn't rely on you to pass on tip-offs for my journalistic endeavours. Well, I think we've reached a situation where we need to honour those commitments.'

Connolly had been ready to argue the toss but after a long brooding silence, a broad smile slowly surfaced. 'Yeah, you're right . . . 'course you're right. Let's hit the sack and work things out the best way we know how.'

'Yes, let's,' she'd replied, dragging him from the chair.

16

Connolly emerged from Chief Superintendent Smith's office, the recipient of a right bollocking. Four days had elapsed since Mansfield's body had turned up in St James's churchyard and the Chief Super was not a happy bunny. 'I want results, Jim, not tomorrow, not next bloody week, I need them now,' the Super had boomed, before trotting out what had become something of a mantra for him, 'the politicians are crawling up my arse'.

Connolly was left in no doubts, if he couldn't provide positive results in double-quick time, a new team of investigators would take over from him.

Bearing this in mind, Connolly faced his team in the hastily created Incident Centre, two rooms converted into one by the removal of a foldaway partition, known unofficially as The Branigan Suite. Named after Jim 'Lugs' Branigan, Dublin's most famous cop who, back in the 40s–60s period, earned the *Lugs* tag on account of the size of his ears. The big-framed Branigan had learned to box in his youth, a skill he'd put to devastating effect when dispensing one-on-one justice to the 'gougers' on his Dublin beat. They were given three choices: *you take your chances in court, a punch in the gob, or a swift kick up d'arse.* He only used as much force as he deemed necessary, measured justice, Lugs style. His unorthodox, yet efficient method gained infamy, notoriety and respect in equal measure and, over time, attained mythical status. On the wall of the Incident Room, a framed triptych of photographs showed highlights of Lugs's illustrious career: Lugs holding a gloved hand aloft after winning the Leinster heavyweight boxing championship in 1937; Lugs in the company of film stars Elizabeth Taylor and Richard Burton as their personal bodyguard when they came to Dublin to film *The Spy Who Came in From the Cold.* The third photograph showed him in retirement, working as head of security at the Zhivago Nite Club in Baggott Street. The great man died in 1986 but his exploits as the city's favourite policeman were enough to bestow his name on the Incident Room.

Connolly moved to the large whiteboard erected at one end of the room. Desks and computer flat-screens had been assembled back to back along the central axis of the room, extra clerical staff brought in to assimilate data and deal with the huge public response, mostly tip-offs from cranks and crackpots. Some of them, though, appeared to offer genuine information, warranting further investigation.

A doom-laden unease oppressed the gathering as detectives glanced anxiously at one another, avoiding direct eye contact with Connolly. They'd overheard the carpeting in the Chief Super's office, heard their own efforts on crime detection being ridiculed. Lack of results hurt them all. The remarkably uncluttered Incident Board told its own story. Apart from sealed plastic bags containing items of the victim's clothing and a selection of mortuary photographs showing grotesque depictions of torture, humiliation and per-verted savagery, images that created emotional upset among those present, there was little else of consequence on display.

Connolly ran through some of the informa-tion he'd gleaned from the forensic lab report. The toxicology results showed that Mansfield had evidence of poison in his systems. DNA samples, taken from the cadaver and clothing, to be of any use, would necessitate the taking of samples from friends and acquaintances. That work was being carried out and results were due within days. The forensic scientists were still examining the fragments from the musical score, attempting to match up five-line bars, clefs, staves, crotchets, quavers and such. As yet, they'd failed to establish the identity of the score except to say it was classical in structure and might possibly have been composed for a chamber orchestra.

DS Bridie McFadden, minus her chewing gum for once, spoke next. She outlined the actions she'd overseen in the past twenty-four hours. Ever cheerful, the rosy-cheeked officer had nothing of any real consequence to offer. She'd been diligent, hard working as always, assimilating clues to Mansfield's lifestyle. She'd checked his address book and mobile phone records, found names of associates, friends and escorts, all of which were being followed up. She'd been unsuccessful in digging up a single witness who might have seen him on the evening before his body was discovered. There had been no CCTV available and nothing she'd done so far had got them any closer to getting a result.

DS Dorsett, his thick Donegal dialect sometimes indiscernible, took longer than McFadden to brief the team and list the actions he'd taken, actions that, like McFadden's, had been exhaustive. Found nothing out of the ordinary. After a few further inputs from other detectives, Connolly decided it was time to view the footage from *The Late Late Show*.

The picture flashed up on a large flat monitor positioned at the end of the central bank of desks, giving all those present an unimpaired view. Perfect quality. Full volume. Everyone in the room watched and listened as the show's host, Gay Byrne, introduced a group called *Con Spirito*, presenting them as a treat for middle-brow music lovers. Polite studio applause and individual spotlights marked the four young musicians' appearance. The music had a familiar ring to it, prompting someone to say, 'Hey, isn't that from the movie, *Shine* . . . the one with Geoffrey Rush, remember?' Another voice, determined to show superior knowledge of the classics offered, 'It's the *Flight of the Bumble Bee* by Rimsky-Korsakov.'

'We're not concerned with what they're playing,' Connolly cut in. 'Study the faces, OK? The guy on the piano is Scott Mansfield, a very young Scott Mansfield. Remember, this show was transmitted more than eighteen years ago. Think about the fragments found in his gullet; anything that ties in with that aspect is worth following up. We have to assume that the score has significance for our killer.' Connolly froze the image on the monitor and pointed to each of the other three musicians in turn, naming them as, Alan Gibney, Dom Sutton and John-Joe Moody. He was still rattled that Emma, who'd provided the names, and matched them to the appropriate faces, had not taken him fully into her confidence.

'We need to track these three men down,' he said, forcing his thoughts back to the task in hand. 'We'll presume they're still alive. I'm hoping we unearth some helpful leads by confronting them. Right now, we've got frig all to go on so let's dig into their backgrounds, find out who their friends are, what they were up to at the time Mansfield was murdered. I'd like to know how close they were to each other back when the TV show was aired; if there were any great rivalries, jealousies, grudges . . . over lovers . . . male, female, whatever? Do any of them hold resentments? Have they kept in touch?'

After a general discussion, Connolly gave the task of chasing down Alan Gibney to DS McFadden and her team; he gave Dom Sutton to DS Dorsett. As for himself, he would try to make contact with John-Joe Moody. He arranged for the full investigative team to meet again at seven o'clock that evening. 'It's important we make contact with the three men by then,' he told them. 'Better still, I'd like to have all three of them sitting in our interview rooms so that we can establish whether or not we're pissing against the wind.'

17

The sulk was over.

Emma felt energized. First time since being sidelined she was anxious to do what she was being paid to do. Still bothered that Crosby had given Willie Thompson lead reporter status but she let that slide. She didn't rate Thompson at all; he believed in style over substance, peppering his prose with buzz words and phrases he'd lifted from CSI, writing smart-ass pieces, always chasing street-cred. Emma's take on journalism was different; she wasn't afraid to go out on a limb, undertake painstaking research to back up a hunch, go down the road less travelled. Instinct. Imagination. Thinking outside the box. Yeah, sure she got it wrong occasionally, but when she got it right, *boy*, the pay-off was simply euphoric. Right now, she felt born again, a woman on a mission, determined to show Crosby, prove to herself that she was bloody good at her job.

Talking to Oonagh Kavanagh had gotten her juices flowing, her adrenaline pumping. Action stations. She'd already checked on the details Oonagh had provided. The saga of

Trevor Kavanagh's ignominious fall from grace was pretty much as she'd been told. Revisiting newspaper reports came as second nature to Emma. The case against Trevor Kavanagh had been reported on a daily basis.

Norma Somers, the student responsible for Kavanagh's plight had indeed retracted her allegation and married Tomás Lee, the father of her child. Emma had traced Somers and Lee's whereabouts to Ann Arbour in Michigan, USA. After several false starts she'd managed to get their telephone number. A house-sitter, who gave her name as Cindy Castillo, answered the phone. She sounded like a cheerful soul who might, Emma suspected, have helped herself to a bottle or two of house wine. She informed Emma that the Lees had left for Ireland a month earlier and she couldn't say when they'd return to the States. Norma and Tomás wished to spend Christmas in their native land and planned to move in and around the Dublin area. Cindy was unwilling to provide a contact number or address where the Lees might be reached. Emma left her mobile number with Cindy and asked her to pass it on to the Lees. The phone conversation had established that the Lees had stayed in the Dublin area during the time of the killing. Didn't prove anything, but it was something Emma would keep in mind.

Taking heed of Oonagh Kavanagh's advice, Emma decided to contact Walter Schiller. The photographer tried to fob her off when she'd phoned but as soon as she mentioned Oonagh's name, he agreed to see her. His studio, a large ground-floor room beneath a solicitor's practice in Essex Gate, was set up for a Christmas season fashion shoot. Walter Schiller, with light meter in hand, was busy firing orders at his assistants, telling them where to place lamps and deflector sheets, directing them to position props precisely where he needed them. An old-time shop-front set had been erected on the studio floor to mimic a scene reminiscent of the images one associates with traditional Christmas cards. A realistic footpath, complete with kerb stones and street lanterns, was being manoeuvred into place while a snow machine waited in readiness to add atmosphere to the Yuletide setting.

Barely glancing at Emma, Schiller called out, 'Be with you in a minute. Take a pew in my office; it's through the door next to the one with the props sign on it.'

Emma entered a tidy, shelf and glass case-lined room not much bigger than the average bathroom. A circular glass-top table and three tubular stainless steel chairs took up the middle of the floor. A large highly polished timber-encased camera with shiny brass fittings and bellows sat on the table. The absence of a desk or computers suggested to Emma that this space was more a reception-cum-waiting room than a working area. A brass nameplate with the engraved legend FRIEDRICH SCHILLER — PHOTOGRA-PHER was given its own display case, a note beneath proclaiming it to have come from Friedrich Schiller's original premises in Dame Street. Other glass encased units displayed cameras, flanked by cards showing dates and brand names, some going back almost a century, names like Leica I — 1925, Argus C3 — 1939, and Asahiflex — 1954. Beautiful objects.

Absorbed in her inspection of the equipment, Emma hadn't noticed Walter Schiller enter the room. 'Father's collection,' he said, with a sweeping hand gesture. 'I like to keep his spirit alive.'

'It's absolutely fantastic,' she said, impressed. 'How on earth did you manage to hold on to so much stuff . . . it's all so well preserved?'

'Take a seat and I'll tell you,' he said pulling back one of the steel chairs for her. With light meter suspended around his neck, much as a doctor might wear his stethoscope, he subjected Emma to full appraisal, eyes unashamedly travelling the length of her body before coming to rest on her face. Emma's inspection of him was enacted with a deal more subtlety. Walter Schiller, who remained standing, was attractive, mid thirties, strong forehead, steely blue eyes and brushed-back luxurious locks of sandy hair that evoked Germanic ancestry. At six feet plus, and wearing black leather jacket, T-shirt, jeans and trainers, his physique made him look like someone from the world of athletics. He'd been born in Ireland but Emma detected a slight 'v' inflection in his 'w' sounds, something he'd probably picked up from his German-born father, she presumed.

'Father died eight years ago,' he said. 'Until then, he looked after these items in the old Dame Street studio. He was an obsessive hoarder, held on to everything that related to the two great passions in his life — music and photography. Look at these,' Walter said, pointing to a series of photographs on the wall depicting Wagner's operas. 'Father loved Wagner, especially the operas, travelled the length and breadth of Europe to see his works staged; photographed all the heroic tenors and divas. Used the camera to fund his love of music. After he died, my wife looked after the collection, made sure his belongings remained in pristine condition.'

'Your wife? She works with you?'

'She used to, yes, she was the one who helped build up the business into what it is today but unfortunately she's no longer with us.'

'I'm sorry to hear that, it must — '

'Life goes on,' he said, dismissively. 'So, tell me, how can I help?'

'I'm hoping you can fill in some background for an article I'm putting together. Oonagh Kavanagh told me that you and your father used to visit their house when Trevor Kavanagh gave music lessons . . . this would be eighteen years ago or more; I'm wondering if you remember?'

'Remember? God, yes, I remember. My father and Trevor were kindred spirits. When Dad visited the Kavanagh household I got dragged along. As I recall, father never charged for our labours; the exercise was just an excuse to listen to the musicians and teach me the art of photography. Truth is, I enjoyed listening to the old guys discussing the great composers and, in spite of myself, I began to take an interest in the pupils' performances. I learned to appreciate the power of composition, structure, admire the beauty of a late Beethoven quartet or be moved by a Schubert sonata. I became aware of the more contemporary innovators too, people like

Harrison Birtwistle and Elliott Carter.'

Emma nodded knowingly, though in truth, Birtwistle and Carter might as well have been premier league footballers for all she knew.

'For me,' Walter continued, 'the Kavanagh household was my university, my private concert hall, a place that opened my eyes, my ears, my senses to the wondrous world of music. My father was greatly upset when Trevor got into trouble at the School of Music. After that, after he began to tutor in the house and hit the bottle, my father tried his best to help but you can't help a person who doesn't want it. It was heartbreaking to watch the professor self-destruct.'

Walter Schiller shook his head slowly and sighed. 'I'll never forget the day Trevor met his end. Such a waste of talent; such a waste of life.' He paused, shook his head again, and finally sat down. 'So, tell me, was there something in particular you wanted to talk about?'

Emma produced a print of the photograph she'd borrowed from Connie Mansfield. (She'd returned the original to Connie with a note apologizing for not having gone to her house after the funeral.) 'I was hoping you could tell me something about the four musicians in this photograph.'

Walter raised his eyebrows as he looked at

the print. 'Interesting,' he said. 'I assume you want to know what I know about the man who's been murdered, right?'

'Right!'

'I was shocked when I heard about it. The fact that I'd set up this very shot for my father sent a cold shiver down my spine.'

'It *is* shocking,' Emma agreed. 'I was wondering if you might have any details about him . . . and the others in your files. Oonagh Kavanagh tells me you're a great one for keeping records.'

'She's right about that, it's something I inherited from my father. I do have records, names, addresses, basic information, but it'll take me some time to go through old files. I'll be happy to let you have what I've got. What do you hope to do with them?'

'I want to track down the other band members, find out if they can shed some light on the fact that one of them has been murdered.'

'You think there might be some sort of connection?'

'I don't know, at least not for sure, but I have to start somewhere.' Emma could not tell him about the fragments of musical score found wedged in Mansfield's throat. Connolly had sworn her to secrecy on that account; it represented vital data held back

131

from the public by the investigation team. It was one of the factors in the case that Willie Thompson knew nothing about and that, Emma hoped, might give her an edge, allow her to explore leads that her rival wouldn't be au fait with.

'It was a long time since they had played together,' Walter said with a little twist of his lips. 'From what I remember of them, they had talent, at least I thought so. A bit full of themselves, though, you know, too smart for their own good.'

'You didn't like them?'

'No, not a whole lot. Like I said, as musicians they had natural ability but as people . . . well, forget it. They were what I might call well-heeled shits, cretins, always taking the piss out of those around them.'

'Did that include Trevor Kavanagh and your father?'

'No, they appreciated Trevor. They could see he was a top-class tutor and respected his judgement. They were OK with my father too. Mind you, he wouldn't have taken any crap from them if they'd tried it on.'

'How did they treat you?'

'Me? I don't believe I even registered on their radar. I was just Dad's assistant — invisible as far as they were concerned. Didn't bother me.'

'Did you get to know Fintan and Owen Kavanagh?'

'The two boys? Yes, I got to know them quite well. They were likeable young men, good manners, studious, interested in the performing arts . . . had their father's ear for music. I knew Oonagh somewhat better. You've met her so I don't have to tell you what a nice person she is; her ambition was to become a musician like her brothers but Trevor, who didn't believe in deluding people, let her know she didn't have what it takes. Hurt her deeply, as I recall. Could have made her bitter, probably did to some extent but, well, she got over it. When he took to the booze she could have walked away, nobody would have blamed her, but that wasn't her style. She tried really hard to help him but, well, in the end no one could help the poor man. My heart went out to Oonagh; always thought the boys should have offered more support at the time . . . but they pissed off, left it all in her lap.'

Emma wanted to ask more questions but conversation was interrupted when one of the assistant photographers poked his head through the door to tell Walter that the models were in situ for the shoot.

'Got to go,' Walter said, 'I'll dig up what I have on the four men and give you a bell.'

Emma handed him her business card and allowed Walter to guide her out of the office. The backdrop in the studio could well have been a scene from Dickens's *A Christmas Carol*. The snow machine created the finishing touches by sprinkling the set with what looked like a realistic fall of snow. To one side of the set, four female models, all dressed in winter fashion of contemporary design, awaited the signal to parade through the make-believe world. Schiller moved to where his camera was set up and issued a string of orders to his assistants before giving the signal for the models to strut their stuff.

Emma slipped out of the studio, pleased to have spoken with Schiller, but none the wiser as to why Mansfield had been murdered or whether his one-time fellow musicians had any hand, act, or part in the killing.

18

Connolly rocked the phone back in its cradle, a tingle of excitement coursing his body from head to toe. The phone conversation he'd just concluded with Sergeant Tony Lynch promised imminent developments. Wishful thinking? Perhaps. In the five days since the investigation began he'd had precious few leads to follow up, no arrests, no prime suspects, not a single encouraging prospect to pacify Chief Superintendent Smith. Blanks all the way. Since discovering that Mansfield once played with *Con Spirito*, the investigation had got a much needed straw to clutch. Enquiries established that John-Joe Moody, one of the other musicians, had moved to Skryne in County Meath six years previously and had set himself up as a sheep farmer.

Tony Lynch, sergeant in charge in Skryne, (assisted by two back-up officers) told Connolly that John-Joe Moody lived on his own in the old miller's house and farmed sixty acres of good grazing land. According to the sergeant, Moody had called at the barracks on a few occasions, requiring the signature of a member of *An Garda Síochána* for various documents. Lynch had formed the opinion that Moody was a decent, if distant, sort of bloke. Moody was known to enjoy a drink, sit in on the odd card game with the locals in Pearson's, and play the double bass with a group of jazz musicians in the pub's Saturday night sessions. *The musical connection again*, Connolly thought, but hearing that John-Joe Moody hadn't been seen in the locality for three to four weeks set his antenna buzzing. According to Lynch, one of Moody's drinking buddies had driven to Moody's house to enlist him in a charity whist-drive and found the place deserted, a coal delivery in the open yard, not put away. This hadn't caused any undue alarm because Moody wasn't known for keeping his place all that tidy.

'Didn't anybody wonder whether or not anything might have happened to him?' Connolly asked.

'Why would we?' Lynch had replied, unconcerned. 'Moody's place is always something of a tip-head . . . a bit like himself; dresses like a tramp, has a problem with personal hygiene. Besides, wasn't as if anyone had reported him missing or anything like that. I mean, people go away all the time; no law says they have to tell anybody.'

The sergeant had a point, Connolly

conceded, but a gut instinct told him that Moody's vanishing act might be significant, something that necessitated further investigation. He hoped he wasn't being paranoid but, given what had happened to Mansfield, he couldn't afford to let it go without further probing. He decided to drive to Skryne, meet with Sergeant Tony Lynch and together, visit John-Joe Moody's sheep farm.

★ ★ ★

On her way back from Walter Schiller's photographic studio, Emma pulled to the side of the road in response to a bleep from her mobile. It was a text message, the sender, Oonagh Kavanagh — *Got word from brother, call me.* This was unexpected. Emma needed to find a safer place to park in order to get back to Oonagh. Half a mile along the road she pulled into a service station forecourt and punched the numbers Oonagh Kavanagh had given her. The connection was bad. White noise, crackle and static. Emma tried a second time, still lots of crackle but the signal got through. She recognized Oonagh's voice.

'Had a text from Fintan,' Oonagh said, her voice sounding nervous above the interference. 'He'd heard about the murder and says he's not sorry but he swears he had nothing to do with it.'

'That all he had to say?' Emma asked.

'Well, yes, isn't it enough? If Fintan says he had nothing to do with it, that's good enough for me, end of story. I've never known him to lie. He just wouldn't, I know he wouldn't.'

Emma sensed that Oonagh was confused, unsure, on edge, as though trying to convince herself. 'Where is he now?' she asked.

'He's staying in The Grosvenor House on Park Lane. He usually books in there when he's working in London.'

'Do you think it's possible I could talk to him?'

'Oh, gosh, no, no, I don't know about that,' Oonagh said hesitantly. 'He'd be mad at me if I put you — the press — on to him. I swear to you we can accept his word on this.'

'But when you contacted me, you thought he might — '

'I know. I feel a fool for having considered him in the first place.'

'I still think it would be a good idea for me to talk to him, put the whole thing beyond question, ask him — '

'No, that'd just add insult to injury. Please forgive me for wasting your time on such a hare-brained notion, I'm truly sorry.'

Emma wanted more but the connection

crackled loudly and died. *Damn*. For several seconds she stared at the phone, frowning, mentally rerunning the conversation. Oonagh had been the one to bring up the possibility of her brother being seen as suspect. And now, she'd had a text from her brother and sounded frightened, fearful that Emma would proceed with enquiries.

What else did her brother put in that text?

The course of action Emma needed to take was becoming ever clearer. She would fly to London, meet Fintan Kavanagh. The only problem she was likely to encounter lay in telling her boss Crosby and her partner Connolly. Crosby, depending on his mood, would probably give her the go-ahead once she assured him she was on the trail of a scoop. He knew from past experiences that her instincts were usually on the money. She would have to be more economical with the truth when it came to Connolly. It wasn't that he minded her doing her own thing — he knew her job entailed travel from time to time — but he would be miffed if he thought she was holding back or interfering with his investigations.

19

His mind in a spin, Connolly motored towards Skryne, an hour's journey north of Dublin. Before leaving, DS Bridie McFadden had reported success in tracing Alan Gibney and had set up a meeting with him for the following morning.

DS Dorsett hadn't been quite so fortunate. Locating Dom Sutton, the fourth member of *Con Spirito*, was proving more difficult. Sutton, it transpired, had a criminal record and had spent a few stretches behind bars. His most recent release had taken place less than two months previously. Since then, he'd gone to ground. DS Dorsett had spoken to several of Sutton's acquaintances and felt it would just be a matter of time before the felon was tracked down. Dorsett was excited, feeling confident that this development signalled the breakthrough so badly needed. Experience had taught Connolly to be more cautious. Because a person had form didn't automatically mean that that person should be regarded as the prime suspect. Even so, he gave serious consideration to the prospect, knowing that both his sergeants would cover all bases in that respect. Hopefully, by talking to the one-time musicians, they might get a line on why Mansfield had met with such a bizarre death.

Overlapping all aspects of the case, gnawing at his consciousness, the domestic awkwardness that had developed between Emma and him refused to be stilled. His first marriage had disintegrated after some of the most miserable years imaginable. Moving in with Emma had rescued him from a virtual hell on earth. He'd discovered a state of happiness, bliss, all the whistles and bells. In recent days he felt that ground begin to shift. He refused to contemplate the thought of losing what they'd found together and would move heaven and earth to ensure history didn't repeat itself. But, for reasons he couldn't fathom, this case was exerting hitherto unknown stress on their relationship. Only this morning Emma had informed him that she wouldn't be home this evening. When he asked her why, she told him she was staying overnight in London.

'Something to do with the murder?' he'd queried.

'Might and it mightn't,' she'd replied. 'Can't say more than that. I'll call you in the morning, let you know where I'm at.'

He'd pleaded with her to tell him more but

Emma was not for turning. After that, he'd done something dumb, something that went against his better judgement: he rang her boss, Bob Crosby. The two men had attended the same college in their youth and had remained close friends, using each other as sounding boards, trusting each other's judgement, fiercely loyal, always discreet. There was, however, one area they invariably sidestepped: their domestic life. That being the case, it should not have come as any great surprise to him that Crosby was less than forthcoming when asked about Emma's trip to London. 'I'm just her boss, damned if I know what she's up to,' Crosby said, attempting a joke but failing miserably.

Annoyed with himself for having put Crosby on the spot, he beat himself up trying to figure why Emma was behaving so secretively. Wasn't like her. In the past, when her journalistic interest clashed with his, they talked about it, respected each other's positions and usually agreed on how little, or how much, they could compromise or encroach on each other's territory. Invariably, it worked out.

What's so different this time?

The unease still gnawed as he drove northwards along the M2, heading for the barracks in Skryne. As he bypassed Ashbourne, a great bank of dark clouds loomed ahead, hovering above the rich pasturelands of Meath, mirroring the dour, intangible thoughts circling his brain. He hoped the rain would hold back until after his meeting with Sergeant Lynch. He spotted the road sign for Skryne at the last second and just managed to make the sharp left with the aid of heavy breaking and the accompanying squeal of tyres. *Shit, nearly lost it there*. Five minutes later, driving at the recommended speed limit, he pulled into a space in front of Skryne's barracks.

Sergeant Tony Lynch, wearing uniform and stripes, stood beside a Garda squad car and watched Connolly pull in. He approached as soon as the car stopped and leaned down to the driver's window before Connolly opened the door. 'If you follow me and Garda Reilly, I'll lead you to Moody's farm. That OK with you?' he said, indicating the Garda car. A young uniformed officer sat in the passenger's seat, buckled up, engine running, ready to go.

'Sure, no problem, lead on,' Connolly replied, amused by the sergeant's brusque, businesslike attitude. No small talk. No hand-shake. Connolly, who'd never met Lynch, had, on the strength of their earlier phone conversation, pictured him as a stout man with hangdog looks, short of stature, mid fifties, untidy, reeking of nicotine, and perhaps a mite lazy.

Wrong on all points.

Lynch was tall, of slender build and in his early forties; his face was impassive with eyes that held an air of calculation. He moved like someone who used the gym on a regular basis, capable of handling himself in a scrap, and ne'er a cigarette in sight. Lynch and his driver, it appeared, also knew how to handle a car on the narrow hedge-lined, pot-holed roads that snaked through the countryside on the way to Moody's farm. Connolly followed the white Garda car, with its distinctive blue and yellow strip as it skirted the slopes of Skryne Hill. He stayed on its tail as it turned into an open gateway with the legend MILLER'S LODGE carved on one of the four granite pillars at the entrance. The squad car sped along a gravelled driveway that terminated in front of a period stone-faced, two-storey residence. Lynch and his sidekick were out of their car by the time Connolly brought his Passat to a halt. Smells of farm manure and sounds of bleating sheep assailed his senses as he stepped out of his car. He wrinkled his nose in distaste. Times like this he was glad he lived in the city. By the time Connolly joined the two cops, they'd already pressed the doorbell.

'Doesn't look like John-Joe's at home,'

Lynch said. 'Door's locked.' He levered the flap from the letterbox slot and peeped through it. 'Pile of post scattered in the hallway,' he said. 'Several weeks delivery, I'd say. No one's been here for weeks.'

The young cop, the one called Reilly, studiously ignoring Connolly, spoke to his sergeant, 'Why don't we poke around the back, check out the yard and the barns.'

Lynch and Reilly were, it seemed to Connolly, determined to let him know this was their patch. They were in charge, running the show. No 'suit' from the city was going to dictate what, or how, they conducted their business.

'Is there a back door,' Connolly asked, in no mood to play silly buggers or bother about jurisdictional boundaries.

'Usually is,' Lynch answered, striding quickly in that direction, the young cop in tow like a faithful lapdog. Connolly followed and watched as Reilly wriggled the handle and pressed his weight against the solid, back porch timber door. The young cop, with short-cropped dark hair and skin smooth as a baby's backside, had Connolly wondering if Reilly had yet begun shaving.

'Bolts are not secured on the inside,' Baby-face offered, his deadpan baritone voice and pronounced Meath accent belying his

145

age. 'Only thing holding this door a simple Yale.'

'We could push it in,' Lynch suggested.

'If I might make a suggestion,' Connolly cut in. 'Let's not break in for the moment. Let's do as Garda Reilly first suggested; let's scout around the barns, see what's what.'

The two uniforms stared at him as though seeing him for the first time. What was it he saw in their expressions: a measure of acceptance? He could visualize the wheels turning inside their heads, hear the message percolating through: *hey, this bloke's probably OK*.

'Why not?' Lynch said, this time including Connolly in a hand gesture as he strode towards the outbuildings. The first building contained a Peugeot 4007 SUV. 'Nice wheels,' Baby-face said, 'but I bet it guzzles fuel. I've seen John-Joe in this a few times.'

'Why is it here?' Lynch asked. 'He can't have gone far.'

Next to the barn with the SUV, an old building, with an antique mill wheel attached to its gable end, looked as though it had recently undergone some restoration work. Connolly presumed there must have been a stream to drive the wheel at some point in the past but he could see no sign of any flowing water. The word GRANARY was carved into a timber beam above the door. Inside, sacks of animal foodstuff, plastic containers of disinfectant agent, remedies for everything from the control of blowfly strike to lice, scab, keds and ticks, lay scattered around. Agricultural implements were housed towards the back of the barn, everything strewn about with no discernible order or logic. A mud-splattered quad bike, with mini-trailer attached, stood in the centre.

'Hey, I like it,' Baby-face said, strolling around the bike and trailer as though he was in a dealer showroom. 'Wonder what he uses this for?'

Lynch pointed to a sprinkler unit affixed to the rear of the trailer. 'John-Joe fills this with food pellets and spreads them on to the land for the sheep to eat.'

'What happens if he's not here to feed them?' Connolly asked.

Lynch frowned. 'I know a little bit about farming,' he said. 'Enough to know that the sheep shouldn't be making such an almighty racket. This time of the year the ewes are in lamb and need feed to supplement the poor grass available to them. It's my guess that John-Joe's sheep are not being looked after. I'm pretty sure that if he'd gone away, he would've got a neighbour to take on the task.'

'You think — ' Connolly began to say.

'Something's wrong.' Lynch said, turning to stare at Connolly. 'I think you'd better tell me what's prompted your visit. The sooner I know what this is about, the sooner we can figure out what kind of situation we've got.'

20

No longer interested in sparring, Sergeant Tony Lynch cocked his head to one side, listening intently as Connolly outlined the perceived connections that tied John-Joe Moody to the murder of Mansfield. The link, Connolly conceded, if it existed at all, was tenuous but he feared it might become an issue if the whereabouts of Moody wasn't quickly established. Even before he'd voiced his fears, the cursory inspection of the outbuildings had triggered the need for a more thorough search. Images of Mansfield's dead body forced Connolly to contemplate the consequences should a similar fate befall John-Joe Moody.

Unable to dispel a sense of foreboding, he allowed Lynch give Reilly the go-ahead to force the back door. It was immediately apparent that all was not as it should be. The place reeked of dampness, putrid air and an overwhelming premonition of dread. An eat-in kitchen with small counter, not much bigger than an ironing board, jutted out from a row of dark timber cabinets, complete with 1970s-style Formica top. On a small central table they found the remains of an unfinished meal. A partially eaten egg, a portion of a sausage and a half-eaten slice of blue-mould bread remained fixed like some frozen still-life study in a fossilized bed of grease on a plate.

'Looks like Moody's breakfast was suddenly interrupted,' Connolly said, examining the plate more carefully. 'Look at this piece of bread, there's teeth marks on it.'

'The smell is getting to me,' Lynch said, his nostrils twitching, 'I'd say whatever happened took place three, maybe four, weeks ago.'

A quarter-full jug of milk had congealed and turned into a soggy white substance, giving off a sour, fermented odour. Two chairs remained overturned amid broken cups and saucers on the kitchen's stone-flagged floor.

Off the kitchen, in a slightly larger room, they found a double bass lying in the centre of the floor. CDs, DVDs, vinyl albums, sheet music and magazines lay strewn haphazardly around. Connolly squatted next to the instrument. All four strings and the bridge of the double bass had been broken. Dark splatters of blackened, dried blood stained the polished timber surface on the uppermost belly of the instrument. In another part of the room, they found an upturned hi-fi set and speakers alongside a broken television set.

Connolly warned Lynch and Reilly to avoid touching anything before enlisting their help in carrying out a systematic search of the house. The place was dank and badly lit, its small multiple-paned windows and lace curtains, allowing little of the outside winter gloom to penetrate. The walls, built long before damp proofing was an option, were covered in 1950s-style wallpaper, the design featuring symmetrical flowers wound into elaborate shapes that nature never intended. The nauseating impact was somewhat ameliorated by a series of framed watercolour prints on the wall, depicting old-world equestrian scenes. Odours of rancid cabbage and boiled bacon impregnated the whole interior, each room giving off a decidedly fetid atmosphere as Connolly, Lynch and Reilly intruded on the privacy of another man's domain. Evocations of loneliness and regrets poked out at them from every shadowy cubbyhole. In the scullery, Connolly inspected a poorly stocked fridge and noted that the 'best before' stamp on a plastic milk container had lapsed three weeks earlier. A thorough search of every room, cupboard, nook and cranny made it obvious that the owner wasn't hiding or secreted in the house.

Sergeant Lynch needed no prompting from Connolly to arrange the acquisition of extra gardaí to search the farmlands. Within half an hour, uniformed officers from the nearby towns of Ashbourne, Trim, Navan and Kells were organized into a search party. A degree of urgency was required if they were to complete the sweep with the benefit of daylight. A steady downpour added its misery as six men and two women, clutching long sally rods, began a systematic trudge of the farmlands, their efforts accompanied by the persistent bleating of sheep.

Barely visible in the haze, a fourteenth-century church and round tower, ruined in Elizabethan times, created a ghostly back-drop to the search. This was, after all, a historic part of the country, in sight of the Hill of Tara, home to the High Kings of Ireland in ancient times. Connolly, who'd always taken a keen interest in Celtic history, suspected that the searchers now plodding the mucky fields, soaking up the rain, didn't give a tinker's curse one way or another about the significance of the land they trod. That was fine as far as he was concerned; he needed them to focus on the task in hand: to find John-Joe Moody. Of course, he couldn't be sure whether or not Moody was, in fact, hidden on his own farm, but the probability existed and that was reason enough to proceed. On the good-news front, their task was eased considerably due to the fact that, it being November, the grass was short and, because of John-Joe's husbandry, the hedges and ditches were properly maintained. On the bad-news front, the rain was now bucketing down with a vengeance, and the last of the evening's light fading fast.

Twenty minutes into the search, a shout went up from one of the uniforms. 'Over here, over here,' the officer yelled, excitedly waving his sally rod. Connolly's reaction was immediate; he dashed to where the call had come from. The other searchers stopped in their tracks. The garda causing the commotion, a tall, gangly man in his mid twenties, pointed to four planks, the size of railway sleepers, covering a rectangular pit. One of the planks protruded above the others, forced from beneath by an odd-shaped, leather-covered container with smooth, contoured sides. Sergeant Lynch, who'd rushed to join Connolly, hunkered down and reached out to touch the disturbed plank.

'What *is* that?' Connolly asked.

'It's a sheep dip,' Lynch said. 'They fill the trough with water and chemicals, then plunge the animals into it . . . disease prevention, I think . . . something like that.'

'No, I mean, what's the object beneath the plank?'

'You got me there,' Lynch said, attempting to push the disturbed plank aside. 'Haven't the foggiest notion. Moody was an untidy devil but I doubt if he'd leave his sheep dip in this state. Give us a hand to shift it.'

Reilly, with the help of another garda, joined forces with Connolly and Lynch, the combined efforts enabling them to lever the plank away from the pit's opening. The object remained jammed by the other planks, submerged in muddy liquid.

'I think I know what this is,' Lynch said as rain pelted his face, his breathing heavily laboured after the exertion. 'I'm pretty sure we're looking at the holding case of John-Joe's double bass.'

'That's exactly what it is,' Connolly agreed, recognized the contours of the case's narrow extremity, the part that housed the instruments neck, scroll and pegs. The belly of the case remained sunken, its bulky size wedged against the side walls of the sheep trough. By now, the field searchers had abandoned their positions and had come to watch. Lynch gave them instructions on how best to remove the remaining three planks. After some awkward manoeuvres, made more difficult by the slippery conditions, the men succeeded in prizing the planks clear. Three-quarters of the instrument's container remained immersed below the surface of the liquid.

'Going to be a bitch to get this out of there,' Lynch offered, circling the pit, sizing it up from all angles.

'We need to tread carefully,' Connolly warned. 'This is most likely a crime scene so we don't want to go destroying any crucial forensic evidence.'

'Yeah, right,' Lynch said, sarcastically, 'with this rain pissing down there's going to be sweet fuck all forensic evidence for anyone to examine. So, I suggest we take it out, open it up, see what the fuck we've got before calling in the antiseptic crew, yeah?'

Connolly nodded, knowing what Lynch said made sense. 'Go ahead then, let's see if we can open the damn thing.'

Using his handkerchief to loop around the clasp that held the case closed, Lynch eased the lid up. As soon as he saw what was inside he gasped. 'Ah, Jesus no!' he said, averting his gaze momentarily. Connolly pushed up beside him and looked into the case. Two hands, severed at the wrists, lay half-submerged in blood-tinged water.

'Moody's hands, I presume?' Lynch said, an expression of bewilderment on his face.

'Most likely,' Connolly agreed, shaking his head.

'Look!' Reilly cried out. 'There's something here.' He'd moved to one end of the sheep dip and had got down on his hands and knees. 'See, here,' he said, using his sally rod to probe a liquid-filled space between the inward curve of the case's belly and the wall of the trough. Two fist stumps were visible beneath the murky liquid. Even in the dying light it was evident that the blood had drained from the baby-faced officer. 'There's a . . . oh shit, the body's down here,' he said, his voice just audible above the pounding rain. Groans came from the others who now stood and watched, some with their mouths open, some holding their hands in front of their mouths.

'OK, everyone, move back,' Connolly ordered. 'Try not to touch anything. We need to secure as much evidence as possible . . . anything that's not washed away. We need to get some floodlights, plastic sheeting and the biggest tarpaulins we can lay our hands on. I'll have to call in the technical bureau people and the state pathologist. Looks like we've just found John-Joe Moody.'

21

Watching a recording of his appearance on *The Russell Parker Chat Show*, Cecil Charles nodded approvingly at the replies he'd given to the host. The BBC had gone the extra mile in an effort to dig up clips from two of his earlier West End successes. The first clip, showing his production of *The Beggar's Opera*, had been a thumping great triumph, providing a significant boost for his career and marking him out as an impresario to watch. He'd taken a chance by reviving the old John Gay comic farce/ballad opera and it had paid off handsomely. For a follow-up, he'd played safe, plumping for the obvious choice: *The Threepenny Opera*.

The second excerpt showed just how accomplished and sophisticated his productions had become. He'd renamed the show, *Mack the Knife*, it being the best-known song from the show. By doing so, he'd upset those purists who felt he had taken a liberty with Bertold Brecht and Kurt Weill's original work. He'd hit back by pointing out that Brecht and Weill had themselves taken liberties by adapting the plot from John Gay's original plot for *The Beggar's Opera* in the first place. The controversy that followed, mostly carried out by passionate, and sometimes irate, music lovers in the letter pages of the *Guardian* and *The Times*, created free publicity and guaranteed full houses for the show's entire run.

After applause from the live studio audience, (encouraged by a 'prompt' board) the host asked about his current plans. Cecil became entranced with his performance, almost as though watching someone else talk to Parker.

'Tell me, Cecil,' the host asked in his well modulated actor's voice. 'Is it true that for your next production you're planning to adapt Tarantino's *Pulp Fiction* into a stage musical?'

'Well, yes, it's been an ambition of mine for some time.'

'This is something of a departure for you, is it not? What attracted you to the Tarantino classic?'

'Saw it at the Cannes Film Festival back in 1994 and was blown away. Never seen anything like it before, a crime drama with a nonlinear storyline, rich eclectic dialogue and an ironic mix of humour and violence. I had what you might call an epiphany there and then, knew it would work on stage. It's been in the back of my mind ever since.'

'Aren't you taking a huge risk?' Parker asked, stroking his chin in thoughtful pose.

'A risk? In what way do you mean?'

'I mean, are you not afraid of generating a backlash against your interpretation of such a highly stylized — one might say *iconic* — depiction of graphic violence?'

'No, I don't have a problem with — '

'Really?' Parker said, with undisguised scepticism. 'I'm thinking in particular of the explicit depiction of buggery as portrayed in the film . . . and the scene in the car where Travolta's character — what's his name?'

'Vincent, the character's name is Vincent.'

'Ah yes, Vincent. When he blows the head off the passenger in the back seat? Surely, these scenes are . . . well, let me put it bluntly: unpresentable to a live *theatre* audience?'

'I disagree. You underestimate the intelligence of an audience at your peril. Harnessing their imagination to an appropriate presentation of mood music, dialogue, lighting, pace and illusion will ensure acceptance of any idea, no matter how outrageous.'

'I don't know . . . I think that — '

'Take the scene you mentioned, the one in the car where Vincent's .45 goes off accidentally and hits Marvin in the throat.

159

It's a horrific scene but we don't actually see the half-severed head, do we? No, we don't. What we see is a gush of blood — which, of course, isn't really blood — as it splatters around the interior of the car, right? All smoke and mirrors. Nothing that can't be simulated convincingly on stage provided the direction and imagination are up to scratch.'

Parker nodded; he'd had enough of that argument. 'What of the great man himself? What if Tarantino sees your production as an attempt to turn his movie into an all-singing, all-dancing, camp-take on the neo-noir genre?'

'If it were an all-singing, all-dancing romp, as you put it, then I'm sure he wouldn't be too happy but, fact is, it's not going to be like that. I'll handle it with deference to the original intent.'

Cecil took the remote in his hand and stopped the DVD. He felt content with how he'd acquitted himself. Taking on *Pulp Fiction* represented his biggest challenge to date. In the current financial climate, it would require all his negotiating skills to entice the big-money backers. He'd reached a crucial juncture in his career; he could remain in the second division, producing safe, successful shows for the rest of his life *or* he could go for it, make a grab for the big time and create a blockbuster to rival the likes of *Les Miserables, Miss Saigon*, or even *Phantom of the Opera*.

Bringing the project to fruition would see him recognized as a player on a par with the likes of Mackintosh and Lloyd Webber. An introspective half-smile creased his face. How strange, he thought, to be sitting here, in a luxury suite in London's Grosvenor House, contemplating such a thing. What a fascinating journey he'd undertaken to arrive at this point. His life had changed out of all recognition since jettisoning his previous existence as the son of a disgraced music teacher in Dublin.

For eighteen years he had worked like someone possessed to make a success of his life. He'd been ruthless in the pursuit of a dream, a dream that set achievement, acceptance and the approval of his peers as a central objective. In this single-minded quest, he had reinvented himself, cleansing his mind of the unpleasantness he associated with his youth, banishing the feelings of embarrassment and shame he felt to be synonymous with his family. His first act of cleansing had been to change his name by deed poll from Fintan Kavanagh to Cecil Charles, a moniker he felt would sit comfortably in the world of musical theatre and show business.

22

Crosby sanctioned the London excursion, grudgingly, insisting on knowing the game plan and how the 'expenses paid' trip would provide the *Post* with an exclusive scoop. Emma convinced him, without giving specifics, to trust her instincts on this one. Her assurances hadn't totally swayed the editor but her track record for ferreting out stories won the argument. She'd been given forty-eight hours to uncover whatever it was she wished to uncover in London; after that, Crosby warned, she'd better provide some shit-hot headline grabbing news or there would be, to use his term, *wigs on the green*. His oft-used expression might not make a whole lot of sense but those around Crosby knew it spelled trouble.

Emma took the early morning flight from Dublin to London, not at all sure how the next forty-eight hours would pan out. Coming into Heathrow, she'd never been more aware of just how much her mission hung, literally, on a wing and a prayer. The airport seemed to double in size every time she passed through but it never failed to send a tingle of excitement through her; the prospect of spending time in London never lost its allure for her.

Waiting to collect her baggage, she got a call from Connolly. After exchanging stilted pleasantries he told her there had been another murder. 'Would've told you last night but it was 2 a.m. when I got in. You were asleep. And this morning, you'd left before I'd a chance to tell you.'

'Didn't want to wake you,' Emma said, immediately regretting that she'd missed out on the latest development. 'Linked to the Mansfield's killing, yeah?'

'Looks that way. We found John-Joe Moody's body on his farm; been dead for three weeks. He was one of the musicians — '

'Yeah, I know. Was he mutilated?'

'Severed limbs. The body, submerged in a sheep dip. Not pretty.'

'Any other similarities with the Mansfield murder?'

'You're referring to that information we're holding back on the first case, yes?'

'Yes, exactly.'

'Again Emma, let me warn you to keep this strictly to yourself, but yes, similar matter has been found inside the victim.'

'Jees-zus,' Emma said, swallowing her breath, 'This gets crazier by the minute. What the hell's going on? Better get in touch with the other two musicians, let them know their lives could be in danger.'

'Already in hand,' Connolly said, the edge in his voice growing sharper, not taking kindly to being told what to do by Emma. 'Look,' he said, after a short pause, 'you said it yourself: there's a maniac out there; we're faced with one of the biggest murder hunts ever undertaken here. If you know something — something we don't know, something that might help our investigation — it's imperative that you level with me. Can you tell me why you're in — '

'Jim, please,' Emma said, taking a deep breath, her equivalent to counting to ten. 'We've been down this road already. I don't have anything concrete to give you or anybody else; I'm skating on thin ice as it is, could be on a wild goose chase. Hell, I couldn't even tell Crosby what I hoped to achieve, that's how flimsy a hunch I'm riding on. Soon as I find out anything that connects or throws light on the murders, you'll be the first one to know.'

'Yeah, of course I will,' Connolly said, with undisguised sarcasm. 'Have a nice time in London.'

Before she could reply, he'd cut the circuit. *Damn*, she thought, *that didn't go the way it should have*. Making her way through the hustle and bustle that was Heathrow, it troubled her; she wanted to be scrupulously open and honest with Connolly but disclosure of her plans at this point would entail long explanations and exposing Oonagh to police investigation. The rationalization didn't help. It was one thing to play cute with Bob Crosby, that never bothered her, but it was another thing altogether to hold out on Connolly, the man she loved. She shook her head in an effort to dismiss the quandary, knowing she would have to resolve the problem as a matter of some urgency.

Reunited with her travelling case, she sat in the back of a London taxi as it ate up the M4E on its way to the city centre. If this had been an ordinary trip she would've indulged in a shopping spree on Oxford Street, taken in Harrods in Knightsbridge, but the way things stacked up right now, the prospect of doing anything of that nature didn't look too promising. Everything depended on making contact with Oonagh Kavanagh's brothers.

She hadn't a lot to go on; just what Oonagh had given her when she'd visited the house in Leeson Street Upper. She'd learned about Fintan's name-change and had been shown newspaper clippings tracking his career from that of small-time theatrical agent to successful impresario. The articles always referred to him as Cecil Charles, never Fintan; no reference or hint of his Irish upbringing. In the photographs that accompanied the text, he looked trim, a striking appearance, eyes alive and burning with intensity.

Oonagh had filled her in on the career path of her other brother, Owen. He hadn't changed his name but, unlike Fintan, Owen maintained a low profile, almost to the point of being a recluse. The brothers collaborated on all of their musical enterprises; Fintan — now Cecil — wore many hats: front man, ideas man, salesman, fund-raiser, business coordinator and production manager. Owen, on the other hand, was more of a one-trick pony; he limited his tasks to that of musical director, content to remain in the background. According to Oonagh, Owen was the more sensitive of the brothers, the one who'd inherited their father's gifts for interpreting and respecting the music of the great composers. He'd brought that gift to bear on his interpretation of contemporary music and had, in the process, attracted critical acclaim for his musical scores.

Walking from the taxi to the entrance of The Bonnington Hotel, her long olive coat flapping in the breeze, revealing tan knee-length skirt and boots, Emma felt apprehensive, unsure of how best to proceed with the half-baked plan she'd envisaged before setting out on the trip. The four-star luxury provided by The Bonnington — everything from bathrobes and slippers to high-speed internet connection — was appreciated but this was a working trip and she was under pressure to deliver, and to do that she needed to make contact with Cecil Charles. According to Oonagh, her brother was staying in The Grosvenor House. That was all she had to go on.

Emma looked around her sumptuous surroundings, wishing Connolly was there with her but glad in another way that he wasn't. She had work to do and wanted to get on with it without distractions of the amorous kind getting in the way. It was mid morning already and she was on a tight schedule. The Bonnington, situated between the City district and the West End, was separated from Park Lane and the Grosvenor House by Oxford Street. In the past, she'd spent many pleasurable hours walking the full length of the street, shopping in Selfridges, John Lewis, Chloe, and the other department stores that lined the famed high street, but not this time. This occasion, she would avail of the London transport system and use the underground as a means of negotiating the route.

Cecil Charles had just finished crucial telephone calls to Drury Lane and Covent Garden and, stimulated by two positive responses, scored some snow ahead of schedule. He did not consider himself what health professionals liked to call *a problem cocaine user* or what tabloids generally refer to as *an addict*. He thought of himself more as an experimental or recreational user who mixed with mainstream society where like-minded friends sniffed the occasional line of coke. Feeling high, an unnatural smile fixed on his face, he reflected on the pitch he'd given both theatres in regard to the *Pulp Fiction* project. They'd been enthusiastic, eager to meet him, happy to discuss it in more detail. It was like pushing at an open door, attestation to the old maxim *nothing succeeds like success*. His spirits were floating on air.

This feeling of euphoria was in marked contrast to the mood upheavals that had bedevilled his life of late. His recent trips to Dublin had proved to be something of a downer. This was the city he'd tried to obliterate from his past but it refused to let go, always there, attaching itself to him like some invisible umbilical cord. He'd talked to the powers that be in the Gaiety and The Helix Theatre and their responses had been lukewarm. He could understand how James Joyce must have felt at being rejected by his native city and been sorely tempted to tell them to get stuffed, let them know he didn't need them, assure them he'd be doing them a favour by offering to bring his show to Dublin, but he'd desisted. He had yet to talk to the people who operated the Cork and Belfast opera houses, get their reaction. This would mean further trips to his homeland, something he had already made soundings about. Some need in him, like that of the salmon's need to return to its spawning ground, obsessed him. It was a need he didn't fully understand, a need that yearned for approval, acceptance, acclaim, from his own kind.

This pull, this need, he felt had never impinged on his consciousness until he'd read the letter his father had left behind. Since then, his mind had become preoccupied by the terrible injustice suffered by his father. Never, until now, had he experienced such a sense of shame, loathing and guilt. He'd been found wanting when his support was needed most. Since revisiting the events that had pushed his father over the edge, he'd found it hard to concentrate on the business of producing his forthcoming show. Sometimes, while in discussion with potential investors, his mind wandered, reconstructing events as outlined in the letter.

Luckily, his brother Owen appeared less affected by the revelations. He'd locked himself away in his loft in Chelsea, swamped himself in the works of Quentin Tarantino, and had come up with some of the best music he'd ever composed. Collaborating with the acclaimed lyricist Anthony West, Owen had created a credible, rhapsodic interpretation of *Pulp Fiction* with all the required ambiguities of graphic violence and gallows humour. In similar vein, West had penned the words of what sounded to Cecil's ears like a show-stopper — *Killing and Thrilling*. If he could get someone like, say, Michael Bublé or Harry Connick Junior to record it, it would generate massive interest and guarantee exposure on the television chat show circuit.

Cecil put aside the empty snifter of brandy he'd been sipping from and proceeded to snort a second line. He didn't usually mix cocaine with alcohol, fearing the mixture might create the cocaethylene toxin he'd read about recently, but today he decided to treat himself to a double hit. His mind afloat, he visualized the stage set for *Pulp Fiction*, imagining the lighting plot, hearing the music and lyrics as clearly as though he were there in the auditorium with every aspect of the production already a reality. Eyes closed, head tilted upward, he experienced a moment of sheer ecstasy, sure in his heart that he was on the cusp of the kind of career break he'd always longed for. The drug had taken hold of his consciousness when the phone rang. Thinking it might be a reply from one of the theatre people he'd spoken to earlier, he picked up immediately. 'Yes, Cecil Charles here, who is this?' he asked expectantly.

'Sorry to bother you, Mr Charles,' a sonorous male voice intoned. 'Front desk here; we've got a lady in reception wishing to see you, a Miss Boylan; says she's come from Dublin and that she's a friend of your sister Oonagh.'

Cecil froze for a fraction of a moment. He was glad no one could see the shocked expression on his face. He took a deep breath before speaking. 'Tell this woman she's got the wrong person. I don't have a sister Oonagh, or any other sister for that matter, and even if I had, I've no wish to see this woman.'

23

Two hours she'd waited. Mid-afternoon. Feeling foolish. In the vast lobby of the Grosvenor House hotel, doubts concerning the wisdom of her trip to London playing large on her mind. Three helpings of coffee to pass the time. Silver service, plate of biscuits, the whole nine yards. The predictable effect on her bladder. *To pee or not to pee.* Not funny. She refused to vacate her vantage point less her quarry, Cecil Charles, slipped out of the hotel while she surrendered to nature's demand. She ignored the barely audible sounds of the city on the outside: buses, a bobby's whistle, laughter. Watched as the non-ending stream of people passed through the enormous foyer. People checked in. People checked out. Porters, in stylish livery, weaved luggage trolleys to and from lifts. Business executives conversed earnestly. Couples on city breaks consulted maps, deciding on which tourist spots to visit. Emma observed all, but her mind remained focused on one objective: Cecil Charles.

Her call to his room, via the desk clerk, had got her nowhere, but her stubborn streak, something she'd inherited from her father, kicked in; she would remain in the lobby for as long as it took, the need to 'go' notwithstanding. At some point her quarry was bound to come down from his room. She just hadn't counted on it taking so long. Checking her watch for the umpteenth time, she caught sight of him emerging from a lift.

At last.

She wanted to jump up, confront him, but remained immobilized, staring wide-eyed as Charles moved towards reception and spoke to a young desk clerk. Emma had no trouble recognizing Charles from the photograph Oonagh Kavanagh had provided. Oonagh had told her that her brother was forty but he looked slightly older. The ravages of time, it seems, had not been kind to him. Wearing a stylish grey suit, he moved with an assured stride, retained a full head of hair and carried about the average weight for a man his age. Emma watched him turn away from reception and head in her direction.

He'd got within touching distance before she shot to her feet and offered her hand. 'Mr Charles,' she said. 'I'm here because of your sister Oonagh; I'm hoping you can spare a moment to talk to me.'

Flustered, he stopped mid stride, ignoring the outstretched hand. He stared at Emma with undisguised irritation, before glancing around the lobby sheepishly to see who, if anyone, was watching. 'I'm sorry lady, but you're mistaken; you've got the wrong person. I don't know you and I don't have a sister.'

'No, I'm not mistaken, *Fintan*,' she said, emphasizing the name he'd been born with. 'I've talked to Oonagh. I've read the letter your father wrote. I know what happened to him and I have a photograph of the four students he accused of destroying him. Please, can we talk, can we — '

'Shsss,' he said, putting a finger to his lips, a mixture of shock and indecision on his face. Frowning deeply, he took her by the elbow in a forceful grip, guided her towards a three-seater at the far end of the lobby, sat her down, plonked himself next to her. He said nothing for several seconds, appearing to consider how best to handle the situation.

Seeing Charles up close, Emma thought she detected dilation in the pupils of his wide-set eyes. Drugs, she thought. Slight bags were evident beneath the eyes, a degree of puffiness in the cheeks and an overall unhealthy pallor, signs perhaps that he'd been spending too much time indoors, spending too many late nights poring over manuscripts. While Emma studied Cecil Charles, he

174

looked her up and down, his face twitching. 'Right,' he said with an obvious effort to control his annoyance, 'Just who the blazes are you and what exactly is this about?'

'Your sister contacted me, she wanted me to — '

'Whoa! Hold it there; why did she contact you . . . I mean, why *you* in particular?'

'Name's Emma Boylan. I work for the *Post.*'

'The Post Office?'

'No, a newspaper. Oonagh read some pieces I'd written on the subject of the recent murder and she — '

Charles looked dumbstruck. 'What? You're a *journalist?* You saying my sister contacted a journalist to discuss my family history? That what you're saying?'

'Yes, I know it sounds odd but you're jumping to the wrong conclusions. Your sister means well; she's horrified by what's happened; she needed someone to confide in, claims you and your brother have shut her out. As a last resort she turned to me . . . there was no one else, no one she could trust. And she's right, I *can* be trusted.'

'Trust you? A journalist, a muck raker, Christ in Heaven! I'd sooner trust Stevie Wonder to drive my car. I don't believe this. Oonagh's really gone and done it this time.

You're the last person she should be seen with . . . unless . . . unless she's playing tricks, messing with my mind.' Charles paused for a second, shook his head as though seeking divine intervention, then stared intently at Emma. 'OK, OK, all right,' he said, his voice now calm, 'let's knock this on the head. Just tell me what you want? Ask your questions . . . be done with it. If they're relevant, I'll answer; if you're bullshitting me, well . . . '

This was the opportunity Emma wanted. She produced the photograph of the four musicians. 'The people in this photograph, you know them, yes?'

'Yes, I do . . . what about them?'

'What about them?' Emma repeated, thrown by the attitude. 'Well, for a start, two of them have been murdered. You aware of that?'

'Yes, I am. And I repeat, what about it?'

'Well, your sister is concerned and, on the basis of your father's letter, she's worried that the investigation might conclude you have a powerful motive to go after these people. She's concerned that you might be linked to their deaths. She told me — '

'Jesus, I don't believe I'm hearing this. You've come here to see me because my sister told you she thinks *I* might have killed — '

'Look, I know how difficult this is for you

176

and I can understand your hostility towards the men in the photograph.'

'I doubt that very much,' he said with an ugly sneer. 'Look, Ms Boylan — that's your name, isn't it? — can you get to the point? I'm a busy man and I need to be somewhere right now. So what exactly do you want from me?'

'Oonagh knows it's only a matter of time before the investigation team begin nosing around you and your brother. She knows they'll get to her too, ask a load of questions; she's looking for assurance that there's no need to worry.'

Charles pursed his lips. The lines around his eyes and mouth deepened and his eyes seemed to become vacant. 'She mentioned my brother?' he asked, as though unsettled by what she'd said.

'Yes, she did. She told me how she'd brought you and Owen together to discuss your father's letter. According to her, you expressed the opinion that the men who'd persecuted your father ought to pay the ultimate price.'

'Look, look, this is ridiculous, it's bonkers, couldn't be more out of line. Yes, goddamnit, my first reaction was to go after the bastards, get them all — it's how any normal human being would react. I'd always felt guilty for not being there for Father when he needed me but when I read what really happened, I damn well blew a fuse. Who wouldn't? I wanted to strike out; I don't deny it but I'm a rational man, always have been. When I thought about it, when I analysed the situation, I knew I could no more kill another human being — no matter what the crime — than fly to the moon. What surprises me about this is that Oonagh should have told you about it. I mean, she took it pretty bad herself, she was the one who . . . well, I'm not going to go there.'

'Would you say your brother Owen feels the same way?'

'My brother Owen? What's he got to do with anything? You leave him out of this, OK?'

'Well, he read the letter . . . he must have felt — '

'Owen is in denial. He's not strong enough, mentally speaking, to revisit the past. He suffers from depression and is in no condition to contemplate the horror visited on Father. Right now, he has shut himself away in his loft. I want it to stay that way. No one, and that includes you Ms Boylan, is to bother or disturb him from his work, you hear me?'

'I hear what you're saying but I think your sister would feel better if I had a quiet word with Owen. I promise I won't disturb his work or interfere with what he's — '

'Good God, woman, are you deaf? Didn't you hear what I just said? I don't want you anywhere next to or near Owen under any circumstances.'

'But your sister — '

'Enough! As for Oonagh, I'll deal with her, OK? I'm flying to Dublin tomorrow and I'll make it my business to talk to her. In the meanwhile, I'd appreciate it if you would kindly butt out of our lives. You got that?'

'Yes, Mr Charles, but I think Oonagh is right about one thing: it's only a matter of time before the investigation throws up the connection that exists between the victims and your father. When that happens, they'll come down on Oonagh and you . . . and your brother. It might be worth your while to talk to me about the relationship that existed between your father and the four musicians. Someone out there is killing his ex-students and it's possible that with your help I can identify who that someone is.'

Charles replied, 'That's not going to happen, Ms Boylan. To be honest, I'm not too bothered about the scumbags in the photograph. I can't pretend I'm sorry that two of them have got their just desserts. If the cops come after me, then so be it. Come to think of it, the publicity might work in my favour considering the genre of the current musical Owen and I are working on. So, Ms Boylan, not to put too fine a point on it, I don't give a monkey's. But just to make matters crystal clear, let me assure you that my brother Owen and I are not the ones putting an end to anybody's miserable lives. Now, Ms Boylan, you can quote me on that when you're dishing the dirt in the rag you work for, go and print the bloody thing. You got that? Goodbye!'

24

Ensconced in Interview Room No. 2, DS Bridie McFadden sat across from Alan Gibney. Diligent research had provided her with a profile on Gibney's business activities. He ran a successful recording studio, sometimes taking on the role of recording engineer/session musician for the many top-flight artists who used the studio. Why then, McFadden wondered, did he need to garb himself in such a bizarre get-up. Sporting an untidy ponytail, he wore a fawn coloured suede leather jacket with stringy cowboy fringe and Cuban-heeled boots that made him walk with a slightly awkward gait. McFadden wouldn't swear to it, but she was fairly certain he employed a corset to hold back the expanding thirty-nine-year old gut that, in turn, stretched his loud T-shirt to breaking point. Ripped blue jeans, Bono-style Ray Bans and studded ear completed the look, giving the impression of a man clinging to youth with all the desperation of a drowning man clutching a lifebuoy.

Earlier in the day, when DS McFadden called to the recording studio in Rathmines,

181

he'd been obstinate and rude. After some gentle persuasion and fluttering of eyelids she'd persuaded Gibney to comply with her wishes. She disliked resorting to girly ploys but, in truth, it helped achieve compliance. She'd let him think she was impressed by the scale and lavishness of his two-storey, purpose-built studio. With spliff between his fingers, he gave her the grand tour after she'd positively gushed with enthusiasm about the calibre of singers and bands who'd recorded in his establishment.

The entrance lobby and the walls leading to the soundproofed studios were crowded with framed, top-selling CDs, discs and glossy portraits of recording artists. Through a slotted window, McFadden saw a group of young singers and musicians in the process of recording, the soundproofing denying her the benefit of hearing what kind of music they made. An enormous clock dominated the space behind the reception desk, the hours denoted by numerals superimposed on gold discs. Across the face of the clock, large letters spelled out the name of the business:

HIT-TIME STUDIOS

Pointing to the portraits of the entertainers, Gibney trotted out anecdotes, saying things like: I'm in demand to do session work for most of the artists who record here . . . played lead guitar on that track . . . played keyboard on that one . . . that group — only thing they play with is their dicks — got me to play piano on their last album . . . went platinum. When McFadden had finally got down to talking about the purpose of her visit, he'd gone quiet for a change. He told her he'd read about the murders of Mansfield and Moody, and that he'd been shocked to see his own name linked to the old *Late Late* clip. He'd told her that he'd known it would be only a matter of time before someone like her called on him.

Facing DS McFadden and Connolly in the Garda station, he removed the shades. Deep-set eyes peered back at the two detectives, the lack of shades accentuating his aquiline nose and the spasmodic behaviour of a rodent face. Connolly was happy to allow McFadden lead, content to listen, observe, as she asked Gibney about the time he'd spent with Trevor Kavanagh. 'We had a blast,' he told her, 'we were young bucks then, none too sure about what we wanted to do with our lives. Nearly made the big time, but like the man says: *nearly* never bulled the cow. We achieved success and could have gone all the way . . . if we'd a mind to.'

As he spoke, he rested his right ankle on his

left knee, and gave the detectives a world-weary smile. 'Con *Spirito* were hot, man, even if I do say so myself. Music for middle-brows was our bag . . . we performed the well-known classics, arranged our take on the better contemporary works . . . tunes like Lennon and McCartney's 'Eleanor Rigby', Queen's 'Bohemian Rhapsody' . . . even did Presley's 'In the Ghetto', made them sound like they'd been composed by Mendelssohn or Vivaldi or whoever. The pseuds of the corporate world, bankers for the most part, couldn't get enough of us, they ate up that kind of crap, booked us for quite a few gigs . . . dammit, it was cool . . . helped pull chicks. I suppose it was inevitable, given our disparate personalities, we'd go our separate ways . . . and that's exactly what happened.'

'Can you think of anyone who might feel aggrieved enough to take out members of your group?'

'We weren't a group,' Gibney insisted, rotating his shoulder sockets like Rocky on his comeback trail. 'We were a *band*.'

'There's a difference?'

'Yes, there's a difference. Chalk and cheese. We were the real thing, real musicians, read music, we had talent, none of that saccharine drivel you hear today. How in God's name do they get away with it?'

184

'I was asking if you knew of anyone who might have a reason for — '

'Yeah, yeah, heard you the first time. Nope! Can't think why anyone would want to knock us off. It's crazy, I mean, we were just four high-spirited lads having a blast. I'll grant you the music we played didn't float everyone's boat — down side: we pissed off the *real* classic heads, pissed off the rock brigade even more — but, hey, we didn't upset anyone enough to bump us off.'

'And you can't think of anyone who might have held a grudge against a particular member of the band?'

'Nope! Hey, you mind if I light up?' he asked, sounding uneasy for the first time since he'd sat down.

'Yes, I do mind, smoking's not allowed. I was asking you — '

'What? You think myself or Dom Sutton, being the only dudes still breathing, might be on some kind of vendetta kick, knocking the other heads off?'

'No, I hadn't been thinking that,' McFadden replied, realizing that such thoughts hadn't entered her head, at least not until now. Her reasons for getting him down to the station had been twofold: firstly, she'd considered the possibility that he could be a potential victim and, secondly, she'd hoped

185

he'd be able to shed light on the period when he played with *Con Spirito*. She glanced at Connolly to see if the thought had crossed his mind that either Gibney or Sutton might be suspects. His face was blank. He looked bored, his mind elsewhere . . . or nowhere. McFadden felt disconcerted as she continued to question Gibney. 'How did you get on with Trevor Kavanagh?'

'The old maestro! Our fifth Beatle. A class act, without a doubt. Lived for the music, knew how to get its beauty across to the rest of us. Had his faults, liked the hooch a little too much.' Gibney mimed a drinking gesture with one hand and made a glug, glug, glug sound in his throat. His other hand went to his crotch. 'Liked the chicks even more as I recall, randy old goat.'

McFadden refused to return his smile. 'You're referring to the incident where he was accused of an improper relationship with a female student?'

'*Improper relationship with a female?* Jesus, where'd you learn to talk like that? What you mean is: was he banging the arse of some slapper. Well, yes, I knew about that of course, but — '

'And did you also know that he was exonerated?'

'*Exonerated*? There you go again! Yeah, I

knew he'd got away with that caper, but I was talking about the shapely babe who cleaned for him.'

'Are you saying he had a thing going with — '

'Lynda! Her name was Lynda O'Regan, a fine little filly, believe me, the kind I'd let squeeze my lemons any day of the week,' this said with a dirty grin. 'The old professor was not backward in coming forward as far as she was concerned. I was jealous, but hey, I couldn't begrudge him a share of the honey pot. You know what they say; the older the fiddle . . . '

This revelation was news to McFadden but her expression remained in neutral mode. 'And how about Kavanagh's daughter and two sons; were they aware of what their father might or might not have been up to?'

'Now that, I couldn't say. The daughter carried a chip on her shoulder, if you ask me; she could've known something, I suppose, but the boys weren't around all that much; they disowned their old man after the scandal. His wife legged it to England, didn't hold with the gospel according to Tammy Wynette, didn't stand by her man like Tammy or Hillary Clinton, couldn't stomach the disgrace, I suppose.'

'Tell me, Mr Gibney, have you kept in

touch with Mansfield or Moody?'

'No reason I should. Truth be told, we didn't have all that much in common, if you discount the music, oh yeah, and our partiality for some hot totty. We were young dudes, sap rising, easily aroused, know what I'm saying. Way things are going now, though, we'll soon be able to organize a comeback tour in Heaven, playing electric harps . . . unless, of course, the bells of Hell call us downstairs. Hey, now, there's an idea, we could — '

McFadden cut across him. 'Have you spoken to Dom Sutton recently?'

'Nope! Last I heard he was in the clink. Doesn't surprise me. Dom was a prize stud, used to say of every tart he pulled: *give it to her big, send her home early, someone will rear it*. Horny whore, fancied himself as a dancer, had all the moves, and a temper too . . . a love machine with attitude.'

'Could he have had anything to do with Lynda O'Regan?'

'Now that, my friend, I don't know. He could have, I suppose, he was always primed, hot to trot, the kind that'd get up on the crack of dawn . . . if *Dawn* would let him.' He snorted at his own feeble joke while McFadden and Connolly remained impassive. 'Sorry about that,' he said pulling a sad clown's face, 'Forgot they gave all recruits a humour bypass in Garda boot camp. As to whether Dom Sutton did the dirty thing with the lovely Lynda or not, well, you'll just have to ask Dom, or better still, ask the little princess herself.'

'Might have a problem with that,' McFadden said. 'Seems like Dom Sutton has gone to ground since being released from jail and as for Lynda O'Regan, she's dead. You didn't know?'

'Nope! First I heard of it. Didn't know Sutton was out of the clink . . . didn't know Lynda was dead either.' For a fleeting second, a reaction that might have been remorse flashed across his sunken eyes, the first expression he'd displayed that carried a hint of conviction. 'As for Sutton,' he said, quickly recovering, 'I couldn't give a toss, but Lynda, ah jeez, she had a body to die for . . . sorry to hear she's dead.'

Connolly, who'd been observing McFadden's interview, had switched off. He'd taken a dislike to Gibney as soon as the musician presented himself in the station. He disliked the man's sham, loquacious joviality, his limp humour and the leer on his face as his feral eyes ogled McFadden, mentally undressing her. But it mattered little what he thought of Gibney; his main concern was to decide whether the man could be considered a potential victim, a suspect, or unconnected to the case. Gut instinct told him Alan Gibney was not involved in the murders but it was less easy to dismiss the possibility that Gibney's life might be at risk. With two members of *Con Spirito* already dead, it would be foolish in the extreme to discount such an outcome.

He stopped short of offering Gibney round-the-clock protection. With the recent spate of cutbacks, expenditure of that nature would not be approved by his paymasters. The best he could do was to keep a close watch on Gibney, look out for anything that might be seen as remotely suspicious. He left the rest of the interview to McFadden and made his way to the Incident Room.

25

The Branigan Room should have been abuzz with the ongoing investigations. It wasn't. Instead it exuded about as much excitement as a backstreet funeral parlour on a wet Wednesday. A double workload to contend with, inadequate resources and no prime suspect in sight, the team was in a state of abject dejection. The meagre contents of both whiteboards told their own story. Connolly pulled them together to give an appearance of progress. The reality, though, amounted to a great big zero. Apart from location diagrams, photos of the dead, victims' names, addresses, next of kin, and details of their grizzly demises, no data of any great significance, no prospects of a breakthrough, nothing that would lead to an arrest, had been attached to the boards.

Giving the two murders top priority didn't mean the city's other villains could be ignored. Connolly was all too aware that everyday crime never let up, the likes of bank robberies, armed hold-ups and breaches of the peace. The past year had seen 78 murders, 66 attempted murders, more than 1,000 sex attacks. Not pretty. Old ladies were still being mugged and households burgled as junkies sought the wherewithal to obtain their daily fix. But it was the two murders in particular that had caught the public's imagination. Natives were restless. Citizens were in full cry, needing to vent their rage, wanting authoritative heads to roll, demanding results, egged on by the press, fury stirred up to unprecedented heights.

Connolly, who'd never known such pressure, felt decidedly out of sorts. The past few days had been as rough as he could ever remember. Confronted by microphones and cameras at every turn, he'd been sorely tempted to tell them all to bugger off, but he hated crass language and so desisted. Instead, he offered stock platitudes, terse answers, deftly sidestepping the more awkward queries, citing the requirements of the case for withholding certain information.

In the twenty-four hours since Moody's body had been dredged from its watery grave, a measure of progress had been achieved. The state pathologist established the victim's identity, confirmed that he'd been dead for three weeks, and established that the sheet music fragments found in his gullet were from the same musical score that found its way into Mansfield's body. The crime scene had been sealed off but, because torrential rain had swamped the area during initial discovery, forensics are unlikely to discover any worthwhile evidence.

A worrying and unexpected development added a wrinkle to the investigation that Connolly could have done without. The *Post* had run a front-page story about the footage from *The Late Late Show*, the one featuring *Con Spirito*. As well as identifying the dead musicians, the report named the two remaining members. Connolly assumed Emma was responsible for the article. *I screwed up. Never should have told her about the footage.* It was only after he'd read the report a second time that he noted the by-line. Willie Thompson had written the piece.

He remembered seeing Thompson in the television studio on the day he'd gone to view the footage. Obviously, Thompson had seen him too, and that had been enough to make the reporter curious. He'd probably put feelers out to discover what the police were doing there. And bingo, one of his inside contacts at the station had come up trumps for him.

Connolly had been carpeted again by Superintendent Smith who'd demanded to know how he'd allowed such a cock-up to happen. It was obvious from Smith's demeanour that he blamed Connolly's friendship with Emma for what had happened. Wasn't a lot Connolly could do about that. He admitted his mistake, took the bollocking without protest and got on with the investigation. His mistake meant that the media felt they had carte blanche to pursue their own investigation. Unhindered by the rules of engagement that governed the official investigation, individuals like Willie Thompson were not inclined to let simple matters like natural justice or lack of evidence get in the way of a good story. All Connolly could hope for was to get to the truth before the case was knocked out of shape by irresponsible journalism.

He freely acknowledged that there were a number of trustworthy reporters, ones with integrity, ones willing to check facts thoroughly before going to press, but, in his experience, these were the exception rather than the rule. He could trust Emma, of course, but for reasons he couldn't comprehend, she'd been acting peculiarly since this case kicked off. The previous evening, after he returned home from writing up his report on the discovery of John-Joe Moody's body, her absence had got to him.

It was hard to shake the notion that something bad, something lacking definition, something corrosive, was eating into their relationship. The not-knowing was getting to him. Yes, the case was difficult, but they'd worked through such difficulties before. Understanding each other's professions had until now enabled them to withstand the pressure. So, why was this case turning out to be such a stinker? Why, for instance, did Emma act as though she was in competition with him? What had he done or said to bring about that? The realization that, maybe, he didn't know Emma as well as he thought he did, hit home.

Do I know her at all?

Nothing new there; he'd never really known his first wife either, even after ten years of marriage. *Christ!*

He had been, to use the hackneyed phrase, economical with the truth when briefing the press. He wondered if one of the things he hadn't shared with them could be connected to Emma's sudden flight to London. The discovery of the 'Late Late' footage had steered the investigation back to the music professor. Trawling through records, Connolly discovered that Trevor Kavanagh had a daughter and two sons. So far, he'd only managed to chase down the address of the daughter whose name was Una, though she spelled it Oonagh. One of his team called at her house but she wasn't at home. She

195

worked for the Department of Social Welfare but she wasn't there either. An officious sounding department head stated that Miss Kavanagh had been on sick leave for the past three weeks . . . and, no, she couldn't say when Miss Kavanagh would be back at work. The sons, Fintan and Owen, were proving even more elusive but one snippet of information he'd gleaned suggested that both men were in the music business and used London as their base.

London! Emma's in London.

Connolly's mind raced, conjuring up a whole series of scenarios. *Should never have told Emma about the music score fragments. Has she stolen a march on me? Has she already managed to meet Oonagh Kavanagh? Is that how she got the names of the musicians? Is she now meeting the Kavanagh brothers in London? Could she be in danger? Is that what's happening?* His mind in a spin, he didn't know what to think. *Why is she deliberately keeping me out of the loop?*

Another thought struck him. *Is it possible that Emma is far more upset about being sidelined than she'd admitted to me? Maybe I'm just part of the collateral fallout, a proxy punch bag to absorb the hostility that she should, by right, be directing towards Crosby and Thompson?*

Connolly put thoughts of Emma on hold. The other detectives were filing into the Incident Room, ready to compare notes, move the investigation along. He had no idea what connection, if any, Trevor Kavanagh's daughter and two sons had with the murders, nor was he sure if the student who'd accused Kavanagh of sexual impropriety was connected to the case. Equally, he couldn't tell if the two remaining musicians from the ill-fated *Con Spirito* should be treated as potential victims, suspects or unconnected. With few solid facts to go on, it was difficult to know how best to proceed. Even as he prepared to address his team, the image of Emma, working on her own in London, continued to bother him.

26

Buddy Holly's death was, it seems, in part down to his laundry. The 1950s pop star had taken the ill-fated plane to get to his next performance in Fargo, North Dakota, early, in order to have his laundry cleaned in time for the show. This was the kind of trivia you got by tuning into morning television. It was something Emma rarely indulged in, but, settled in her comfortable bedroom in London's Bonnington, she'd gone and activated the flat screen. Felt almost compulsory to do so. Earlier, she'd declined the room-service's offer of full English breakfast, the very notion of all that fried food on a plate was enough to make her stomach heave. Settled instead for cereal, fruit juice, toast and coffee. With no one to talk to, and Connolly never more than a wish away, she helped herself to a second coffee as Bill Wyman looked out from the screen, recounting his days as a member of the Rolling Stones.

She supposed that there were plenty of people who found this kind of inane morning television fare interesting, conscious of the irony that she too was now caught up in the ex-Stone's tale of the difficulties he'd encountered finding same-day laundry services when touring with the Stones, performing continuous one-night stands. Wyman, looking seriously old, was relating the Buddy Holly anecdote when the telephone purred.

Twenty minutes earlier she'd put a call through to Oonagh Kavanagh's mobile and left a message asking her to call back. This, she hoped, was the expected call.

It was.

'Had to move from my house because of you,' Oonagh said crossly.

'Because of *me*?' Emma echoed, a puzzling grimace flitting across her face. 'How'd you make that out? What have *I* done?'

'Cops came to my house, that's what you've done. And they've been in touch with my workplace. You gave me your word — we agreed — you would not talk to anybody about me . . . or about what I told you. You promised.'

'And I've kept my word,' Emma cut in. 'I never mentioned your name.'

'So how come they're on to me?'

'Could be any number of reasons,' Emma replied, trying to figure out how the investigation had picked up on Oonagh, anxious to reassure the woman that it wasn't down to her. 'I know the investigative team got hold of some footage from an old television show that featured the murder victims back when they were members of *Con Spirito*. Wouldn't take a genius to track down your father's involvement. And then, as soon as his name pops up on their records, hey presto, they see he once faced an accusation of rape. Dig a little deeper and they find out how he died. Most natural thing in the world would be to chase down his children. I'd say that's what happened. I assure you I had nothing to do with it.'

Silence ensued for a moment before Oonagh spoke. 'Yeah, could be something like that, I suppose; sorry for jumping on you, it's just that I'm so bloody furious. But I'm not going to make myself available for questioning, at least not until I find out what you've come up with in London. Have you talked to Fintan yet?'

'Yes, I've met him, had to use your name before he would see me and, well, I'm afraid he's pretty annoyed with you for contacting me. He's adamant that he had no hand, act, or part in what's happening. He's on his way over to Ireland as we talk, so I thought I'd better let you know.'

'Ah, that doesn't bother me. Fintan's a bit inclined to fly off the handle but he's all right.

So, having heard it from the horse's mouth, so to speak, do you accept that he's innocent?'

'You've got to appreciate my position, Oonagh. I'm an investigative journalist, got to keep an open mind until every '*i*' is dotted and every '*t*' crossed. In fairness, your brother sounds pretty convincing. His main concern is that I keep away from Owen.'

'Well, he's right on that score. Owen is a sensitive soul. Lives for his music, in his own little world, wouldn't hurt a fly. No need to bother him, you'll only upset him, and to what benefit?'

'You could be right, Oonagh, but from my point of view, he represents a loose end. I want to meet him; I give you my word that I will be the soul of discretion. Can you let me have his London address?'

'Gosh, I don't think he's lived in London for years. Far as I know he's in Amsterdam . . . lives there with a . . . with a friend.'

'Hmmm, I got the distinct impression that Owen has a place here in London. I heard Fintan refer to Owen's loft. That mean anything to you?'

'The loft? Oh, yeah . . . *The Loft*! That's the place he bought years ago. It's in Chelsea. I thought he'd got rid of it but it's possible he's held on to it.'

'Do you have the address?'

'Hold on a sec, Emma. As it happens, I have my contacts book with me; that old address should be in it, if I'm not mistaken.'

27

The taxi dropped Emma off near the Cheyne Walk/Oakley St junction on Chelsea's riverfront. She would have preferred to walk from her hotel, look at the shop windows on King's Road, but there was a nip in the air sharp enough to skin a whippet. Didn't help that she'd forgotten to pack her warmest winter coat. Her legs ached and her feet pinched by the time she made it through an arch that opened on to a tree-lined courtyard on the periphery of Cheyne Gardens.

Oh God, how much further do I have to walk?

Oonagh had given Emma a telephone number for Owen Kavanagh but it was out of date, missing two recently added digits. Consequently, she'd no way of setting up an appointment beforehand, which she hoped might work out just as well; fore-warning would probably increase the odds that he'd find an excuse not to meet her. So, cold-call it had to be. Five minutes laboured walking brought her to a well-maintained eighteenth-century red-brick building, similar to most of the neighbouring houses, all of them giving the area something of an old village atmosphere.

A young, black doorman admitted her in to a small reception to one side of a spacious hallway. 'Which apartment, Madam?' he enquired in a clipped, English accent.

'I'm here to see Owen Kavanagh,' she said, with false assurance.

The doorman, or concierge, or whatever he called himself, gave Emma a knowing smile, said, 'Oh, The Loft . . . you want The Loft?'

Emma nodded and watched as he put a call through, heard him say, 'I've got a young lady here wishing to see Mr Kavanagh.' After a moment's silence. he looked at Emma enquiringly, said, 'Your name is . . . ?'

'Emma Boylan, I'm a friend of Mr Kavanagh's sister. She told me — '

'You're expected,' he said, cutting her off. 'Take the lift to the top floor and someone will meet you there.'

On her way up, Emma wondered why she should have been expected. Had Oonagh managed to get word to her brother, told him to expect her? As she stepped out of the lift, squinting her eyes to adjust to the change of light, a gangly, middle-aged man with several day's stubble, bleary dark eyes and unruly hair held out his hand to greet her. The name JUDY was branded across his

T-shirt; his trousers, yellowish-brown cords, barely reached the ankles, revealing stocking-less feet and shoes that struck Emma as having attitude, a hybrid of Moccasin/Hush Puppies and Desert all rolled into one.

'Emma Boylan, I presume,' he said theatrically. 'Welcome to The Loft.'

'Owen Kavanagh?' Emma said, accepting his handshake.

'No, no, no, no, God no! I'm not Owen, goodness me, no. I'm Anthony, Anthony West. I'm the other half of the music collaboration that pays the rent on this establishment. I write the words that make the whole world sing,' he explained, opening his hands upwards to mime singing. 'Owen is the genius who makes it worth singing in the first place. So, my pretty Irish colleen, come in and let me tell you what's what, OK?'

Emma followed West into a large brightly lit lounge, lavishly decorated in a style reminiscent of the 1950s, understated wealth, taste and refinement. A large picture window offered a panoramic view of the River Thames, the Embankment, the Albert Bridge and the Cadogan Pier. 'Wow!' she said, genuinely impressed. 'This has got to be one of the best views in all of London.'

'Yes, I rather think it might be,' he said. 'Watching the seasons change from this

205

vantage point is such a thrill, I never tire of it. But you didn't come here to discuss the sights, I presume, yes? You came to converse with Owen, I do believe.'

'Yes, that's right, I wanted to — '

'Let me stop you there,' he said with a theatrical flourish of the wrist. 'Owen and I are currently working on a special project with Cecil Charles. It's behind schedule and we're both under considerable pressure. For that very good reason we've declared The Loft a no-go area to visitors.'

'Oh, I'm really sorry, I didn't mean to — '

'It's OK! Cecil called us from Heathrow yesterday and mentioned, among other things, that you'd most likely show up on our doorstep. Insisted, in the strongest possible manner, we turn you away, but his very insistence intrigued us, made us curious. It's why you've been allowed up here. That, plus the fact that we're both suffering cabin fever bunged up here 24/7 without sufficient interaction with the outside world. It's driving us nuts.

'Your timing, however, is less than perfect. Right now, as we speak, Owen is having a bad hair day, experiencing a spot of bother working on a tricky musical passage and doesn't want a break in concentration. But, a little distraction could be just the job to free up his creative juices. So, Ms Emma, here's the deal. I'm going to allow you into the inner sanctum. He's due his once-a-day nicotine fix any minute now and while that little ritual is being enacted he might, I say *might*, talk to you. No promises. He'll probably bite my head off, throw a hissy fit and refuse to play ball but I'm hoping you might be the one to get his mojo firing again.'

Owen Kavanagh looked similar to, yet quite different from, his brother Fintan/Cecil. No puffiness in the cheeks, no bags under the eyes, and no suspicious dilation of the pupils, but his features definitely sprang from the same gene pool. Like his brother, he had a bountiful mane and no sign of the bad hair day alluded to by West. Owen, it appeared, believed in careful grooming, his appearance complimenting the 50s decor of the studio, almost as though he'd contrived to coordinate the two, an ample handkerchief flowering from his breast pocket. He sat in front of a grand piano, playing notes every few seconds, not bothering to acknowledge Emma. His profile, for that's what Emma was looking at, reminded her of old Hollywood glamour and sophistication — more Rock Hudson/Tab Hunter than Humphrey Bogart/Spencer Tracy.

Feeling uneasy, Emma was about to

introduce herself when West pressed a finger to his lips and made an inaudible shissing sound. Apart from the unconnected series of notes coming from the piano there was a sense of tranquillity about the place. West sat beside a small occasional table and took up a brandy snifter. He signalled to Emma with the glass, enquiring if she wanted a drink. Emma declined with a shake of her head and a tight smile, at which point West shrugged his shoulders, put the glass to his mouth and drank deeply.

Waiting for what seemed like an interminable amount of time gave Emma the opportunity to examine every aspect of the music room. She resisted a devilish impulse to heel off her shoes and free her aching feet. There was lots of space, lots of house plants, lots of ornaments, lots of everything. A rectangular block of wood sat atop a free-standing, truncated ionic column that held the model of an elaborate stage set, every miniature detail in perfect proportion, including figurines in costume. Framed posters, advertising successful musicals, took pride of place on one wall. Emma assumed that Owen and West had been involved with these shows but, as she wasn't a big fan of that particular arm of entertainment, she couldn't be sure.

At odds with everything else in the room, a large screen, positioned across from the piano, displayed a projected shimmering movie still that showed actors John Travolta and Uma Thurman in dancing mode. Emma recognized it as a scene from *Pulp Fiction*. Back in the mid-90s, Vinny had persuaded her to see it with him in their local cinema. As it turned out, she'd thoroughly enjoyed the film, and came away with a lasting impression of the sequence in which Travolta and Thurman did a fantastic dancing display in order to win a prize in a twist competition. Back then, she'd been smitten by Travolta as he danced in his socks to the old Chuck Berry hit, 'C'est La Vie — You Never Can Tell', balancing his body on the balls of his feet, pulling hand movements and splayed fingers rhythmically before his eyes. Why this image should be projected on to a screen in front of Owen Kavanagh and Anthony West, she'd no idea.

Looked as though she was about to find out. The tinkling on the piano keyboard stopped. Owen stood up, but didn't move away from the instrument. He looked tall, thin, angular, and slightly effeminate. Flexing his fingers, he took a cigarette from a pack of Gauloises that, along with a slim gold lighter, had been placed on the piano. Ceremoniously, he brought cigarette tip and flame together before inhaling deeply, savouring the nicotine hit. He looked at Emma for the first time but made no attempt to speak. Emma watched as he allowed his head tilt back to slowly exhale a plume of smoke towards the ceiling. As the plume dissipated he gave a sardonic little chuckle. 'Fags gonna kill me,' he said, temporarily setting the cigarette down on the rim of a glass ashtray, 'but what a glorious way to go.' This remark he aimed at Anthony, accompanying it with a lecherous wink.

Emma stood to introduce herself but he waved her back to her seat. 'Do you know how difficult it is to kill someone and make it look entertaining?' he asked, as though they'd been having an ongoing conversation. 'Consider this: Stephen Sondheim brought his gore-fest musical, *Sweeney Todd: The Demon Barber of Fleet Street* to Broadway back in 1979.' Owen no longer looked at Emma, no longer talked to her, or to West, who continued to drink; he was now talking to himself, or some invisible presence that only he could see. 'The audience lapped it up,' he said, replacing the cigarette between his lips, his eyes partially closed against the rising smoke. 'They couldn't get enough throat slashing, blood, guts and grisly death. Won eight Tonys. And then in 2008, Tim

Burton, with a little help from buddies Johnny Depp and Bonham Carter, made a screen version. Well, it's one thing to take a smash hit musical and film it . . . that's easy! But Anthony and I are doing it arse-about-face; we're taking a hit movie and attempting to turn it into a stage musical. Blood, gore and guts, live on stage, all set to music and song.'

Owen stopped talking, stubbed out the cigarette butt and sat down next to Emma, looking at her with an impish grin. 'My brother, the great impresario who must be obeyed, warns me to have no truck with you, Ms Boylan, so gratify my curiosity and allow me a modicum of pleasure; tell me why I should ignore him.'

'I've talked to your sister Oonagh. She's concerned about — '

'I know, I know. Little sis is concerned about the fate of the men she blames for father's death.'

'Yes. Two of the men named in your father's letter have been murdered. She's terrified in case you or your brother becomes embroiled in the whole nasty business, concerned that the police will jump to the wrong conclusions. My purpose in talking to you is to put her mind at ease, confirm the fact that you . . . and your brother . . . have no involvement in what's happened. Mr West tells me you haven't been outside these walls for weeks on end. Is that right? If that's the case, then I can — '

'Anthony's wrong! I've made several trips back to the auld sod. I've killed those bastards, looked into their miserable eyes before snuffing their lights out. I've listened to their confessions, smelt their fear, saw the evil in their eyes and heard their last breaths.' As Owen spoke, he appeared to become detached from reality, his expressions flitting through a series of emotions: weariness, scepticism, exasperation, and others that eluded Emma.

'Inspiration,' he said, the impish glint back on his face. 'If the theatre-going public are to be subjected to brutal slaying on stage, then by all that's sacred, I'll give them a musical score fit to sustain and reinforce their suspension of disbelief. Killing those bastards gives me the impetus, the fire in my belly to live the moments . . . to infuse those hellish, murderous impulses into every note I set down. Sometimes, sometimes, I feel a divine intervention flow through my body as I lay waste the bastards. I wash my hands to remove the blood, I smell the stench from their rotting bodies. I make it my solemn duty to ensure they get no curtain call.'

Emma wanted to speak but stopped when West signalled that she should keep her mouth closed. Owen turned away from her and moved towards his piano, wafting a dismissive hand in her direction as he did so. West rested his brandy snifter, crossed to Emma's side and gently took her by the elbow.

'Exit stage left,' he whispered, 'that's all we're going to get for now.'

28

Forty-eight hours in London. Little to show for it. Crosby would not be pleased. Strapped into her seat above the clouds, the drone of the Airbus's engines failing to lull her into a sense of tranquillity, her mind insisting on regurgitating the events that had buffeted her life during those two days. It would be wrong, she decided, to write the trip off as a total failure; it might pay dividends eventually, but the hope that it would yield front page headlines like KILLER TRACKED DOWN IN LONDON, well, that wasn't going to happen.

Fintan Kavanagh, known to the theatre fraternity as Cecil Charles, looked like a 'possible' for the killings. He had motive — revenge for his father's death — and opportunity: on his own admission he'd been over and back to Ireland. He, of course, denied involvement. *Well he would, wouldn't he*! Emma needed to establish his arrival and departure times to see if they tied in with the dates of the murders. She'd seen them do that on all the top TV crime shows. Worked for them. There was, however, one little problem in casting Charles as the villain, what one might call a fly in the ointment: Emma believed he was innocent. Having talked to him, looked him in the eye, she'd been inclined to believe his denial. Was he just a very good liar? Had her usually reliable bullshit detector failed? One way or another he would remain on her list of possible suspects, an area for concern, a loose end needing further scrutiny.

Soon, Aer Lingus flight E157 from Heathrow to Dublin would touch down but Emma's mind continued to wrestle with the strange — no, make that *weird* — encounter she'd had with Owen Kavanagh. After West escorted her from The Loft, he'd assured her that in spite of what she'd heard, Owen hadn't killed anybody, at least not in the physical sense. Owen's outpourings were, he assured her, pure flights of fancy. 'His imagination conjures up things he couldn't possibly have done. These fantasies empower his music. It works. His music sometimes sounds like God Himself descended from on high and etched every crotchet and semiquaver, the notes materializing in perfect order from some other dimension. There's a downside of course: the images swamp his brain, cause confusion and a sense of dislocation. In the end, he's no longer sure what's real and what's imagined.'

An announcement to fasten safety belts and bring seats into an upright position brought an end to her musings. The plane banked for final approach, the familiar thumping sound of landing gear being lowered enlivening all those on board. She would soon be back on terra firma, forced to face Crosby, compelled to level with Connolly. She'd missed Connolly. Two days away from home had made her realize just how much the big man meant to her. Discussing the case, however, would be a different story entirely. How much to tell him? She possessed information that might, or might not, be pertinent to the investigation. She had promised to keep Oonagh appraised of her enquires but that undertaking might not be all that easy to honour. Having spoken to Oonagh's brothers, she got the distinct impression that they were as suspicious of her as she was of them. Oonagh, a suspect? What a turn-up for the books that'd be. It was possible. Anything was possible. Oonagh had the same motive as her brothers — revenge. But, if she was involved, why would she have contacted Emma in the first place? *Why indeed?* Emma had reached one of those make-your-mind-up moments: how much to divulge, how much to hold back. She had very little time in which to decide on how best to handle the situation.

After collecting her belongings from the carousel she headed for the car park, feeling the Arctic chill cut like a blade. *Where did I leave the bloody car?* Parking facilities at the Dublin Airport were, Emma decided, designed by someone who hated cars, the objective to cause maximum chaos and frustration, but on this occasion she spotted her silver Hyundai without undue bother. She was about to get in when her mobile sounded. The incoming number belonged to Crosby. Moment of truth. Crunch time.

Damn, what do I tell him?

'Hello Bob,' she said, trying not to betray her unease.

'Where are you?' he asked, speaking softly, not at all his usual gruff self.

'Just landed and it's bloody well freezing . . . hold on a sec, I'm getting into my car. Right, Bob, now I'm with you, is something wrong?'

'No, well, I don't know. I've had Vinny on to me, he — '

'Damn! He rang you? I'm really sorry, Bob; he has no right — '

'No, no, it's OK, Emma. He couldn't get you or Connolly so he contacted me; he wanted you to know, well, I'm afraid there's been some bad news. It's his father, I'm sorry to say, Ciarán Bailey passed away yesterday.

Sorry to be the one to tell you; I know how fond of him you were.'

'Ah no! Poor Ciarán, Lord have mercy on him. I knew he was . . . but I didn't think . . .' The words caught in Emma's throat. 'Thanks for telling me, Bob. I'd better contact Vinny, try to talk to him, find out about the arrangements. I'll get back to you as soon as I can, tell you about London, tell you — '

'Hey, don't worry, Emma. You do what you have to; we'll talk as soon as you sort this out, OK?'

Emma cut contact with Crosby and wiped a tear from her eye. Ciarán Bailey was dead. A million thoughts flashed through her head, fond images of the old artist standing in front of his easel, brush and palette in hand, a look of concentration on his face; images of his smiling face and the mischievous twinkle in his eyes as he told some joke or anecdote. She would miss that. He was Vinny's dad, sure, but he'd been the one to understand and appreciate her point of view throughout the sometimes fraught marriage she shared with his son. He'd been more understanding, more sympathetic, than her own parents when the break-up finally came.

And now she must call Vinny, express her sympathy and offer to be there for him during this sad time for him . . . for both of them.

29

Connolly had jockeyed his day's commitments hither 'n' thither in an attempt to squeeze in lunch with Emma, his curiosity at boiling point, impatient to know about her London sojourn. It wasn't just the not knowing that had got to him; something else had taken hold of his senses. He'd missed her, missed her more than he would ever have believed. Stuck in the middle of a double murder, all hell breaking loose around him, superiors demanding results, the press snapping at his arse, and all he could think about was how much he was missing Emma. Ciarán Bailey's death had knocked the lunch reservation on the head, obligating Emma to go directly from airport to funeral home. Given the circumstances, he couldn't very well argue.

The investigation was bogged down, getting nowhere fast. All the usual avenues had been exhausted: interviewing relations, friends, neighbours, acquaintances, anyone and everyone who'd come in contact with the two victims. His team had followed up on flimsy leads, appealing to the public on radio, television and press. They'd gone the extra mile, and then some. The Branigan Suite finally looked like an Incident Room, piled high with stacks of paperwork, DNA records, dossiers of forensic photographs and autopsy reports. So much slog, so little gain. Connolly's feeling that the key to the mystery lay rooted in the past had solidified. The link between the two murdered men went back eighteen years to a period when they were members of a band named *Con Spirito*. He'd looked up the name, thinking it sounded a bit like the word *conspiracy*, only to discover it was a musical term, an Italian instruction to play *in a lively manner*. Not much help there.

He considered the basic facts. All members of *Con Spirito* had been tutored by music professor Trevor Kavanagh. The professor had been involved in a minor scandal, concerning a female pupil, and had died in a traffic accident. The pupil in question had moved to America but inquiries established that she was currently in Ireland with her husband, her exact whereabouts unknown. He needed to find her, ask her some questions.

Forensic experts had finally established that the music sheet particles had been torn from a classical opus; they hoped to be in a position soon to put a title to the work and name the composer. It would be helpful to talk to Kavanagh's two sons and daughter about this discovery but so far efforts to track them down hadn't got very far. He had no idea if, when found, they would shed light on the music aspect of the case but it would at least enable him to check their DNA against the samples lifted from the crime scenes.

Right now, though, he was intent on focusing on Dom Sutton, the fourth band member. His profile was interesting in that he stood out as being quite different from the others. All four musicians had fared reasonably well in the material possessions stakes, but Sutton, unique among them, had chosen the criminal route to amass his wealth. He'd first come in contact with the law at the age of twenty-one. This, Connolly discovered, was shortly after *Con Spirito* had disbanded. Convicted at Dun Laoghaire District Court on a housebreaking charge, he was fined IR£500 and bound over to keep the peace. A year later, records showed he'd been sent down for the first time; eighteen months for robbing a warehouse and receiving stolen goods. On the inside, Sutton mixed with a number of like-minded criminals and formed what would become the nucleus of a gang.

After his release, he moved in with his

girlfriend, well-known model, Patricia Dean, and appeared to go straight for a while, settling down and becoming the father of a baby girl. But old habits die hard; before the baby's second birthday he came to the attention of the authorities again, this time for his involvement in a VAT swindle that involved smuggling luxury cars from the Continent into Britain and Ireland. In a sting operation, Customs and Excise managed to expose the scam. Sutton, estimated to have made millions out of the racket, was arrested and sentenced to seven years.

In the two months since his release from Mountjoy Jail, having served five years of that sentence, he simply disappeared. Instead of going back to the house where his partner and daughter lived, he dropped below the radar. Even the usual snitches claimed not to know the ex-con's hideout. This struck Connolly as odd. After all, Sutton had served his time and had no reason to hide from the law. So, where was he? Who was he hiding from? More to the point, what did he know about the deaths of the two men who once played music with him?

Connolly pulled the unmarked squad car to a halt outside the gated entrance to Dom Sutton's palatial home. Situated in the leafy suburbs of Foxrock, one of Dublin's more affluent districts, home to corporate executives, barristers, bankers, consultant doctors, and a handful of shady characters who'd taken more dubious routes to get there. DS Bridie McFadden sat in the passenger's seat chewing gum, her arms folded across her chest, her shoulders huddled to conserve body warmth. On what was probably the coldest day of the year, the car's heater had packed in. 'I'm freezing me tits off,' she said to Connolly who seemed not to have noticed that the previous night's frost continued to hang about. 'Nice piece of real estate, don't you think?' he said, indicating the big house.

'How can Dom Sutton afford such a pile?' Bridie asked, the chewing gum visible on her tongue as she looked at the wrought-iron gate guarding the mock-Georgian three-storey residence.

'It would appear that crime has proven more lucrative for Dom than the pursuit of a musical career. The Criminal Assets Bureau have been trying to confiscate the property for the past few years, claiming it to be the proceeds of criminal activity.'

'So, what's stopping them?'

'Sutton's put the property in the wife's name but the CAB will eventually get it. Meanwhile it's private property and we've no right to barge in.'

'What the hell are we sitting here for, then?'

'Well, I thought it might be an idea if you were to go over to the speaker on the pier and ask nicely if we could speak to Ms Dean.'

'And if she tells me to bugger off, what then?'

'Oh, I'm sure you'll find a way, a resourceful lady like you.'

McFadden made a moue of distaste, shook her head and gave Connolly her best men-are-such-shits expression before getting out of the car. Connolly smiled as he watched her approach the intercom, thinking, this won't work but, hey, it's worth a try. Ten seconds later, to his amazement, McFadden turned and waved at him, a radiant smile on her face.

The gates had already begun to open.

30

They approached the granite entrance portico, glancing at each other with raised eyebrows. McFadden had expected to get an earful when she'd spoken to Sutton's partner on the gate's intercom but, as soon as she'd identified herself as a Garda detective, she'd been invited in. Like his sergeant, Connolly fully expected the bum's rush and was striving to second guess why they'd been allowed in. A shiny new Range Rover stood in the brick-paved driveway, its tyre tracks visible in the frost-covered surface, an indication that the powerful 4WD had recently been in use. Walking past it, McFadden removed the gum she'd been chewing and, unseen by Connolly, stuck it to the gleaming surface of the vehicle's side panels. She'd voted Green at the last election and this action represented her very own protest against gas guzzlers, her somewhat skewed contribution to a greener environment.

Patricia Dean opened the door, asked for identification and took care matching their faces to the photographic images provided.

Connolly studied her while she examined their IDs. She wore a pair of slim-tailored trousers and a wide cropped top in winter white. Striking woman. Put Connolly in mind of one of those mannequins that inhabit the high street fashion house windows. The flushed cheeks might have been the result of exposure to the frost or, more likely, an overgenerous application of rouge. Her hair was fashioned into an earlobe-length chic bob and her face, though attractive, was defined by a series of sharp, chiselled angles and a pair of symmetrical coral lips. Her best feature by far, a pair of large blue-green eyes, added to the overall impression of contrived allure.

Satisfied with the IDs, Patricia indicated that they should cross the threshold. The two detectives, following her perfumed wake, passed a grand staircase before entering a plush living room that wouldn't look out of place in a five-star hotel penthouse. She gestured them to an ochre three-seater wingback sofa, where a cat slept contentedly, curled up inside an open Louis Vuitton shoe box. 'You can sit down beside Mindy,' she offered.

They did.

'Something to drink?' she asked, gliding decorously across a pure wool carpet to a well-stocked drinks cabinet.

'Sorry,' Connolly said, 'not while on duty.'

'Ditto,' McFadden added, giving Connolly a sideways glance.

'Well, you'll pardon me if I have a little pick-me-up.'

It occurred to Connolly that Patricia Dean had already made one or two excursions to the drinks cabinet before their arrival. In the past, dealing with Dom Sutton's various crimes and misdemeanours, he'd come across the felon's partner. She'd been a top fashion model when she'd first hooked up with Sutton. Their romance had been well documented in the tabloid press, their every appearance at concerts, opera first nights, charity dos and celeb bashes caught on camera and featured large on the gossip columns. They'd produced a child, Jenny, who was now eleven. Since giving up the catwalk, she'd landed a weekly spot on morning television, reviewing the latest fashion trends and commenting on the social scene. At thirty-seven, she still had the ability to turn heads when entering a room.

As soon as she'd fixed herself a cocktail she turned to Connolly and McFadden and raised her glass. 'Cheers', she said. 'Now tell me, to what do I owe the pleasure?'

Connolly could tell from her speech that

he'd been right: she'd had a tipple or two before their arrival. 'We're trying to establish the whereabouts of your husband,' he said. 'We know he hasn't resided here since his release and were wondering if you could tell us where he is at present?'

'Why?' she asked, holding the glass in one hand while the other fiddled with a decorative brooch that hung from a slim silver chain round her neck. 'Why do you want to find him?'

Connolly was prepared for the question and had given some thought as to how much information he should divulge. Because of the seriousness of the investigation, there was little to be gained by holding back. 'Two men, Scott Mansfield and John-Joe Moody, have met with unexplained deaths recently. Both men knew your husband.'

'Knew him?' she said, smiling. 'Not in a biblical way, I trust?'

'No, no, not at all. I was — '

'Just joking! Whatever else you might say about him, he's straight as a pencil when it comes to sex . . . and has the lead to prove it. So, what was his connection to these two men?'

'They once played together in a band; they called themselves *Con Spirito*. Ever heard Dom mention it?'

'Not that I recall. Never knew he played in a band; might explain where Jenny gets her musical ability from. And what, you think someone is knocking off the band?'

'It's a possibility. Why someone should go after a bunch of ex-musicians, we don't know. Fact is, we've no hard evidence to conclusively prove they're being targeted but, in the absence of more solid evidence, we're pursuing that line of enquiry.'

'And what? You think Dominic is in danger?' Patricia asked.

Connolly was amused to hear Dom being referred to as Dominic, a name he felt sure no one apart from Patricia and Dom's own mother would ever use. 'Well, yes,' he admitted, 'we'd like the opportunity to talk to Dominic, let him know what's going down, see whether or not he can shed any light on his time with *Con Spirito*. We really do need to talk to him.'

'You're not the only one,' Patricia said with a laugh that showed every sign of drink intake. 'I don't know where he is, and it's doing my head in. I'm scared. That's why I let you in. I'm scared for Jenny. I know something's going on . . . something . . . I don't know.'

There was an awkward silence. McFadden spoke for the first time. 'Where's Jenny now?' she asked.

Patricia shook her head slowly and moved towards a French window that looked on to a large patio area with a water feature. 'I dropped Jenny off at school,' she said, her voice breaking. 'I'm scared out of my wits for her. Where is her father, you ask, huh? You think I don't want to know where he is? We're in fear for our lives, being followed . . . being watched, someone trying to get at us . . . maybe get at Dominic through us, I really don't know what the hell's going on here.'

'Have you seen who's following you?' Connolly asked, intrigued by the unexpected twist, wondering if what he is hearing tied in with the investigation.

'Haven't actually seen anybody, in the physical sense, if you follow me, but I'm not imagining it. Someone is watching every time I go to the television studio . . . when I go shopping. I sensed it when I picked up Jenny from her piano lessons yesterday.'

'Could it be Dom?' McFadden asked.

'Christ, no!' Patricia said, her eyes flashing with annoyance. 'Dominic is a lot of things, some of them thoroughly unpleasant, but he loves Jenny, loves me too . . . least I know he *did*, not so sure any more. But one thing's for sure, he'd never frighten Jenny. Never! There's got to be a good reason why he hasn't contacted us. It's driving me nuts. I'm

230

stuck here in this oversized doll's house, supposed to be happy, supposed to be grateful for my surroundings. Let me tell you, I don't give a shit about all this. They're just Dominic's creature comforts, his Italian marble fireplaces, his Waterford crystal chandeliers, his Spanish flagstone, his Brazilian mahogany kitchens. It's just meaningless junk, worth frig-all when you're living in fear, scared shitless all the time.'

'Have you thought about getting away from here?' McFadden asked. 'You must have some relations or friends you could go to . . . until we find out if there is a threat to yourself and Jenny.'

'Yeah, yeah, yeah, of course I've thought of that but it's not practical. I've got my television spot to get to and I don't want to take Jenny away from school. In any case, it's probably safer here than anywhere else.'

'How do you make that out?' Connolly asked.

'Dominic, in one of his mad flights of fancy, had some firm from London install a state-of-the-art security system and CCTV. We've got automatic security lights, motion detectors in the house and the devil knows what else; the place is a regular Fort Knox. Not sure if it's to keep people out or keep me in. He showed me how to operate the system so at least I'm secure once I've activated it. Going outside the place, that's the bit that scares me. The thought that Jenny might be exposed to danger while at school or piano lessons is a constant worry. I thought Dominic might be hiding away from you lot, but he would've confided in me if that were the case, so I have to figure it's something more serious. I've read about the murders you mentioned; I've seen the television news, and now you're telling me . . . shit, you're telling me Dominic might be linked to the victims. This is freaking me out.'

'Can't say for sure if it's connected,' Connolly said, trying to offer a crumb of comfort, 'but I would advise you and Jenny to take extra care. I'm going to give you a telephone number, a direct line to our Incident Centre. If you spot anything suspicious or feel an immediate threat, please ring. If Dom gets in touch, tell him to contact me . . . it'll be for his own good. Tell Jenny to be extra careful and to stay in the company of friends when she's not with you. In the meantime, we'll keep looking for Dom. We'll let you know if we have any luck tracking him down.'

31

November's early twilight cast a sombre mantle on the city as Emma returned from the funeral home in Bray, the gloom in accord with the harrowing day she'd experienced. Bidding a final goodbye to one of the finest gentlemen she'd ever known had shaken her more than she would have thought possible, the task not made easier by the presence of her ex. 'Dad loved you, Emma, you know that, don't you?' Vinny had said through tears, holding her hand tightly. 'Near broke his heart when you . . . when we . . . separated.'

Emma hadn't replied. She'd felt bad enough about Ciarán's death without taking on the guilt trip Vinny attempted to lay on her. She'd wanted to run screaming from the place, get away, away from him, away from death, as soon as decency permitted. Vinny had other ideas. He saw to it that her agony was protracted, insisting she meet all his and Ciarán's friends, neighbours, aunts, uncles, cousins, their children, most of whom she hadn't seen since the day she'd married him. After an eternity, she'd escaped and made her way from Bray, back to the city, back home to the apartment.

She felt tired. Her two days in London, followed by Ciarán's death, had knocked her for six. She'd been looking forward to getting back with Connolly, back to his arms, but worried too, fretful lest he still felt miffed about her recent activities. Her worries dissipated as soon as she opened the door. He rushed to greet her, taking her in his arms, swinging her about in an arc and kissing her passionately as he did so. 'What's brought this on?' she asked when he'd finally set her down.

'Will you marry me?' His first words to her, simple and direct. The big question tripping off his tongue. Swept off her feet, in every sense of the word, Emma was incapable of speaking. That was when Connolly went into Jane Austen mode, going down on one knee, producing a ring box and taking hold of her hand. 'You can be the most infuriating woman on the planet,' he said, 'but God, I've missed you. Not having you around has uncluttered my brain and allowed me to sort out a few priorities.'

Tears welled as she pulled him to his feet and kissed him tenderly. The kiss would have gone on forever except that Emma needed to breathe. 'Yes, I'll marry you, Jim Connolly.

I'll be honoured to be your wife.' She wiped her eyes and put the ring on her finger. Beautiful. An eighteen-carat gold and single-stone marquise-cut diamond. Perfect fit. She swallowed hard, struck by its sophisticated design, striving to block out a memory from another life when another man had honoured her in similar fashion. Her moist eyes a testament to joy, but recollections of her first failed marriage were also present in the tears. 'Can't think why you took so long to ask me.'

'Hey, don't you dare,' Connolly said, 'I've brought up the subject a thousand times and every time you've poured cold water — '

'Yeah, yeah, I know, that's true, but like they say, it's a woman's privilege to change her mind, right? Married? This is . . . I don't know . . . getting married to *you* seems sort of right just *now*, but of course, there's no knowing how I'll feel tomorrow. Only kidding, Jim, this has been quite a day of highs and lows but this, well, this is mind blowing! I've never felt so good about anything.'

To celebrate, they decided to eat out.

A taxi took them to Enniskerry, to the Ritz-Carlton in Powerscourt Estate, Gordon Ramsey's first restaurant in Ireland. Extravagant, yes, but it didn't bother them, the occasion called for something special. So special that it prompted Emma to suspend her low-carb and minuscule sugar diet. They had both been to the Powerscourt Estate before but this was their first time to visit the crescent-shaped building that housed the restaurant.

Before descending the sweeping brass-railed staircase to the lower-floor dining area, they sat, holding hands, on a large sofa in the Sugar Loaf lounge. Inevitably, conversation got around to what they'd got up to in the past two days. Emma was concerned that she might have to break a confidence with Oonagh Kavanagh but, as it turned out, her conscience was eased. Connolly's investigations had thrown up certain information that let her off the hook.

Scotland Yard, cooperating with their Irish counterparts, had tracked down the whereabouts of Owen Kavanagh and his brother Cecil Charles. They established that Charles was currently in Ireland, his exact location unknown. Connolly's team had been successful in locating Oonagh Kavanagh's hideaway. They had talked to some of her work colleagues in the Department of Social Welfare, discovered that she was staying with a fellow worker named Peggy Maloney. Connolly was scheduled to talk to her in the morning.

With restraints lifted, Emma felt comfortable disclosing her findings. She described her encounter with Cecil Charles and Owen Kavanagh, relating the strange circumstances that had led to her meeting with Oonagh Kavanagh and how it had, in turn, led her to London. Connolly listened, unable to mask his astonishment, no doubt a little irked as well. The exchange of information continued as they sat down to enjoy their meal. They'd both gone for the salad of king crab, followed by fillet of Atlantic halibut for Emma, chargrilled steak for Connolly. Both had pear and Amaretti cheesecake to round things off, the whole gastronomic treat washed down with a bottle of Trimbach riesling.

Chef Ramsey did not make an appearance and no one was heard to utter the F word or throw a tantrum, at least not in their presence. They thoroughly enjoyed the exceptional food, embracing the sense of occasion and the joy of each other's company as they lingered over liqueurs and coffees, enthralled by the glitz and glamour of their surroundings. For Emma, rediscovering the delights of sharing good food with Connolly was in itself a miraculous development, allowing her to banish the barrier she'd allowed to build up in that regard. She wanted the magical feeling of utter contentment to last forever, the giddy joy of love for the man beside her overwhelming her senses, creating a fixed idiotic smile on her face as she gazed dreamily into his eyes.

'What?' he asked, trying to decipher the expression.

'You . . . you and me . . . feels so good, so right.'

'More coffee?'

'My cup runneth over.' she said, her voice breathless with emotion.

Connolly laughed, reached for her hand, squeezed. 'I'll call for a taxi.'

'Yes, please, let's get home, let's — '

As Connolly reached for his mobile, it bleeped. A glance at the incoming number let him know the worst. 'No-ooo! I don't believe this,' he said, 'it's the shop . . . told them not to ring me unless . . . sorry, got to take it.' He identified himself, then listened in silence for several seconds, his expression turning to one of alarm. 'I'll be there within the hour,' he said, before cutting the connection.

'What?' Emma said. 'What . . . what?'

'Worst possible news! We've got another death on our hands,' he said with an angry grimace.

32

Nothing could have prepared Emma for what confronted her. The body had been secured to the centre of the giant clock above the reception area of HIT-TIME STUDIOS. The image would inhabit her consciousness for the rest of her life; the bloodcurdling moment rocking her body with the intensity of a mule's kick to the solar plexus.

The clock's aluminium hands had been ripped from their central pivot and used in conjunction with nails and stays to brace and secure Gibney to the clock's face. The sweep second hand coiled around his neck in a stranglehold clasp, the minute hand bearing most of the weight, cutting deeply into the flesh on the lower ribcage. Gibney's extended arms, pulled wide, crucifixion style, were secured by six-inch nails, driven through the wrists. The smaller hour hand had been employed as a bracket across his ankles, its bent extremities fixed to the clock's face with more nails. The dead man's face, partially obscured by the bent sweep second hand, had distorted into a grotesque, angry snarl, fragments of torn paper and his wrap-around

Ray Bans protruding from his mouth.

Streaks and spatters of blood slid down the clock but it was the body's genital area that represented the epicentre of the horror: a black-red hollowed cavity framed by shredded flesh. Hacked innards shed intestinal matter from the raw-edged depression, partially obscuring the numbers, five, six and seven.

The midnight hour had been but a few strokes away when the taxi dropped Connolly and Emma outside the recording studio. Leaving the Ritz-Carlton, Connolly had availed of a passing taxi, rather than delay waiting for a pool car to arrive from the garda depot. Emma could tell from his expression that he wished her to wait for another taxi. The look in her eye had let him know with no uncertainty that she wasn't going to be fobbed off.

For Connolly, duty beckoned. The same could be said for Emma. As a reporter she was not about to let the opportunity of landing an exclusive scoop pass; neither Bob Crosby nor Willie Thompson were going to sideline her on this one. She would be strong, resolute, take charge, create her own conditions of engagement. No more little miss nice guy. Time had come to prove her worth.

For Connolly, the constraints and demands

were of a different order. He had the unenviable job of dealing with an ever more demanding public, offering succour to victims' loved ones, and providing authoritative leadership to his team. Gibney's murder required action best undertaken at a remove from the prying eyes of the press.

'Can't allow you to come in,' Connolly had insisted, getting out of the taxi. 'Take this cab back to the apartment.'

'No, I'm getting out,' she'd replied, opening her door, 'I need to pee badly, can't wait. All that red wine, you know, gotta go — '

'Damn it, Emma, the Super is here. You know what that means. He'll have a fit — '

'We're wasting time. I'm going in, OK? I'll try to make myself scarce. Your boss won't even know I'm there.'

Once inside, diverse groups made up of masked anonymous white suits, sombre-faced personnel from police HQ and senior HIT-TIME STUDIOS staff moved about nervously. No media of any tint or stratum had been in evidence, a factor that pleased Emma. Everyone appeared busy, preoccupied with the sight confronting them, engrossed in procedures to record every vestige of information to be gleaned from the grizzly scene. Technicians were hurriedly attempting to block off a large window that faced the street, their aim to ensure that panic would be avoided in the morning should citizens get sight of the sickening display.

Emma attempted to make herself inconspicuous, anxious to deflect attention from her presence, fearful that Superintendent Smith should set eyes on her. She was overdressed for the situation, still wearing the high heels and evening dress she'd spent so much time choosing for the restaurant. Fortunately, she'd had the good sense to take a winter coat with her, knowing it would be cold in Wicklow, the same coat she now pulled closely around herself as a shield to hide her inappropriate apparel.

She sidled up to the technicians, hoping to blend seamlessly with the activity but the subterfuge was never going to fool anybody.

Smith spotted her.

Emma spotted him spotting her.

His conversation with Connolly halted in mid flow as he beckoned DS Bridie McFadden to his side. He appeared to be mentally stomping his foot, gesticulating with both hands, emphasizing some point he wanted to impress on McFadden. Emma didn't need to read sign language to know his gestures signalled the command to have her removed.

Bridie McFadden approached Emma with purpose in her stride. Both women had met on a few occasions in the company of Connolly and they'd got along fine. However, right now, the expression on the detective's face telegraphed what was coming. 'Emma,' she said, 'I'm going to have to ask you to leave the building.'

'I understand,' Emma replied, moving towards the exit, 'Might have been better if I hadn't come in the first place; most horrendous sight I've ever seen.'

'Yeah, it's not pretty,' Bridie agreed, 'Almost puked myself . . . and I thought I'd seen it all.'

'Makes you wonder what sort of individual would do the likes of this.'

'Yeah, the world gets a bit crazier every minute.'

Outside the studio, Emma used her mobile to call a taxi. She planned to contact Crosby on her way to the apartment. He'd probably be in bed, but that didn't matter; what she'd just witnessed would play big on the front page of the *Post* in the morning. With a bit of luck, the other daily papers wouldn't pick up on the story until it was too late for them to run with the story. Even if they made it, they wouldn't carry a first-hand account, not like the one she was about to write. Her long experience in the business let her know what to include and what to hold back. She would try not to step on Connolly's toes, try not to get him into trouble, but if her reporting made life difficult for him, he would have to come to terms with the fact that his wife-to-be had a job to do, just like he had.

33

Patricia Dean and daughter Jenny were in bed when the break-in occurred. Jenny remained asleep but Patricia, who'd been sleeping badly since the fuss over her partner's jail release, heard a sound downstairs. Dominic had phoned her the day after his release and told her in a hurried conversation that he couldn't make it home until certain matters were resolved. She'd asked what the 'certain matters' were but he'd refused to elaborate, except to say he was talking *life and death*, and that she'd need to watch over Jenny like a hawk until he showed up. This information, she'd failed to share with the detectives, happy to allow them to believe she'd had no contact. Dominic had not been in touch with her since.

Right now, she tried to convince herself that he was the one who'd created the noise downstairs. The alarm would have gone ballistic were it anyone but him. Just like Dominic, she thought, to sneak into the house in the dead of the night, frighten the bejesus out of Jenny and her.

Caught betwixt fear and excitement, she switched on the headboard light, got out of the bed and slipped into her dressing gown. She went to the window, peeped through a chink in the curtains and looked into the darkness. Screwing her eyes up to mere slits, she made out the shape of the main gates. They were open. Dominic had once told her that there was a way to bypass security, you just had to understand the system, know how to manipulate its mechanism. But if that was what he'd done, it made no sense; Dominic didn't need to bypass the system, he'd been the one to set the code. He'd based it on his date of birth.

She'd never bothered to change the settings. Panic shot through her. Her first thought was for Jenny; she must go to her room, wake her and get her to lock the door.

She hadn't got as far as her own bedroom door when it burst open. A gloved hand covered her mouth with a rectangular piece of adhesive material before her scream had time to emerge. Her waist was caught in the clutch of a strong arm that dragged her bodily on to the landing. She struggled to free herself but her efforts were futile. Her thoughts concentrated on Jenny. She needed to keep the intruder busy, prevent him from going to her bedroom. Frantically, she sought to disentangle herself from the gorilla-like grip, the patch over her mouth muffling her screams. The diffused spill of light from her room prevented her getting a proper look at her attacker. Gauging from his strength, she could tell that he was big and strong. The uneven battle stopped abruptly when Patricia saw a second intruder emerge from her daughter's room. The man dragged Jenny with him in an arm lock. An adhesive patch had been placed over the child's mouth. Her eyes were filled with abject terror.

The sight of Jenny, wearing nothing more than a long T-shirt and panties, being manhandled by a balaclava-wearing man, drained what energy remained to her. She tried to suppress the fear, needing to figure out what was happening; it was important to do nothing to endanger Jenny. The man holding Patricia pivoted her around. They were now face to face. Did little good. He too, was wearing a balaclava.

'OK, listen up,' the man said, his baritone voice articulating every syllable as though attempting to disguise his normal voice. 'You and the little princess have nothing to fear provided you do as you're told. My interest lies with your old man. You two are my way of getting to him. I need to know where he's hanging out. I'm not sure how much he cares about you, Patricia, but I'm reliably informed he loves his little girl here to distraction. That better be true because we intend doing some horse trading: he surrenders himself to me in exchange for you two. So I want you to get dressed and come with us. Try anything smart or make some dumb move, I'll have no hesitation in killing you, understand? Nod if you understand.'

Patricia nodded. She watched as Jenny did likewise. Knowing it was Dominic they wanted, not Jenny or herself, she felt marginally less terrified. She would not pull any stupid moves, nothing that might endanger their lives, but she would avail of any worthwhile opportunity for escape, should it present itself.

34

Smith cleared his throat, glared at the assembled media who'd gathered for the mid-morning press briefing. Like Connolly, who sat next to him, the Super had had little sleep the previous night. There wasn't nearly enough room to accommodate the huge media scrum jostling for position, waiting for proceedings to get under way. Chief Press Officer, Tom McDowell, looking more harassed than usual, introduced the speakers to the press, his voice an octave higher than normal. Approaching retirement, McDowell had been responsible for organizing the event and had underestimated the media interest. Sky News was carrying the news conference live and, like the home-based stations, had to have their crews, cameras and lights accommodated.

Smith read from notes, giving a sanitized account of Alan Gibney's murder, talking up the extra resources and personnel being committed to the case, before handing over to Connolly. Looking as though he'd rather be anywhere else, Connolly fleshed out details of the crime, careful to avoid elaborating on the more gruesome aspects, aware of the furore the killings had created among the public and how it had monopolized all the papers, radio and television. Once again, the killer, or killers, had left their signature in the form of torn sheet music fragments, something Connolly still withheld from the public. Morning chat shows had cleared their prepared schedules to deal exclusively with the murders. Phone lines and the text messaging service to the shows were jammed, listeners registering their disgust, demanding a more concerted effort from the police, denouncing drugs, drinks, sex, gays, pole dancing, lap dancing, politicians, fat cats, Bono, bankers, lawyers, the media and, especially, the church. One complainant blamed computer games, demanding that they be banned and the death penalty reinstated for the inventors.

In answer to a question from the Sky reporter, Connolly confirmed for the first time publicly that Gibney's murder was linked to that of Mansfield and Moody. This brought an avalanche of questions. Do you have a prime suspect? Is this drug related? Have the police got enough resources? Why not call in the army? Each contributor drowned out the other, the combined mob-like intensity forcing McDowell to intervene in an attempt to bring order to proceedings. A measure of calm restored, Connolly answered as many questions as possible, adding little that wasn't already in the public domain. The conference was brought to an end by McDowell promising to hold further briefings as soon as there were new developments to report.

Fifteen minutes later, after a post-conference meeting with Smith, Connolly was making his way to meet the team in the Branigan Suite when DS Mike Dorsett asked him if he could have a word in private. Of all the people involved with the case, Dorsett had worked longest with Connolly and had, over time, become his most trusted team player. The two men had developed a rapport, a friendship that was genuine, although they seldom if ever met socially. This was down to a set of personalities which couldn't be more different. Dorsett lacked Connolly's social graces but this negative aspect was compensated for by his sense of loyalty and his canny insights into the criminal mind.

'Want to run something by you before I'm called to brief the team . . . if that's OK with you?'

'Of course, Mike, what's on your mind?'

'I interviewed Oonagh Kavanagh this morning, like you asked me to.'

251

'Yeah, sorry about that. I'd intended doing it myself but with all the flak flying around, well . . . '

'No, no, that's OK, I didn't mind at all. It's just that, well, it appears that she's been dealing with Emma Boylan for some time, telling her things that could've been helpful to the investigation.'

Connolly said nothing, just nodded for Dorsett to continue, having a fair idea of what he was about to hear but dreading it at the same time.

'Look, I know how it is with you and Emma, so I wondered how much of what I've learned should be included when I speak in front of the others.' Dorsett looked every bit as awkward as Connolly felt, the hard lines on his long, chiselled face more pronounced than ever, his eyes struggling to hold direct contact with Connolly's.

Connolly tried hard to hide his unease, said, 'What did Ms Kavanagh have to say?'

'She showed a letter to Emma that had been written by her father, a letter that makes reference to Scott Mansfield, John-Joe Moody, Alan Gibney . . . and Dom Sutton. According to Oonagh, all four of them are accused of hounding Trevor Kavanagh to death. Apparently, they accused him of raping his house-help lady, and threatened to inform the authorities.

This letter had been addressed to Oonagh and her brothers but the mother kept it from them. It was only after the mother's death that the siblings got sight of it. We know for sure that both Kavanagh brothers come from a classical music background. This factor, I would contend, ties in directly with the music score fragments we've retrieved from the bodies, gives any one of the siblings, or all of them, a motive to hit back at the four men, working in concert perhaps.

'Oonagh insists that her brothers had nothing to do with the murders but she feared they would be seen as prime suspects. She contacted Emma, asked her to talk to them before we did, wanting her to establish beyond doubt that they had no involvement. Emma went to London, met the brothers and, apparently, gave them a clean bill of health.'

Connolly looked every bit as embarrassed as he felt. He hadn't planned for details of Emma's London adventure to surface quite so soon, and because of the previous night's hectic activity, he hadn't got around to figuring out a strategy for introducing her discoveries into evidence. The fact that Dorsett had come upon the information before he'd had a chance to put the record straight gave him little choice but to level with

253

his friend. 'Emma talked to me last night before the Alan Gibney murder. It was the first chance she'd had to tell me about the trip. Her account ties in with what Oonagh Kavanagh has told you. It puts me in a rather delicate position — my relationship with Emma and all that — so I was hoping I could find a way to introduce what she uncovered into evidence without bringing her name into it.'

'Well, yes, I think that's understandable. Oonagh made it a condition that Emma should not speak to anyone before agreeing to show her the letter and fill her in on the background.'

'Damn!' Connolly said, glancing at his watch, 'we've got to park this for the moment; they're waiting for us in the Incident Room. Can you do me a big favour, Mike?'

'Of course, whatever — '

'When you brief the team on this, I'd like you to omit Emma's name. I need to talk to her again, as soon as the meeting's over, nail down a few specifics, get her to come in here, have her make a formal statement . . . all official, like, but, well, not just yet . . . if that's OK with you?'

'Of course; that's why I mentioned it in the first place.'

35

The Incident Board, now running out of space, had been updated to include details of the latest killing. The graphic depiction of three murders with connecting criss-cross lines looked like a throwback to the bad old days in Northern Ireland when hard-line Republicans and Loyalists did this sort of thing to each other on a regular basis. If the current murders had been sectarian in nature, it might be easier to discern a pattern or reason for the slaying but, apart from the fact that the victims once shared a mutual interest in music, Connolly couldn't say with any certainty who, or what, lay behind the carnage. He'd only managed to get away from the Gibney crime scene at 2.00 a.m. and had been back in the station by 7.45 a.m.

Dead eyes looked at Connolly from the victim's photographic images on the white-boards. Ignoring them, he began by introducing the new personnel to the team — six detectives borrowed from vice, fraud and drugs divisions. He promised extra uniforms and clerical staff as soon as arrangements could be made. 'We know,' he said, as soon as the new crew had made themselves known, 'that we called at HIT-TIME STUDIOS every hour on the hour as arranged, and that Gibney was under constant surveillance . . . and we know, sadly, we screwed up, our precautions were inadequate. Gibney let us know that he'd be working late last night and according to the uniforms, everything appeared normal when they checked in at 10.00 p.m. One hour later they found the body nailed to the clock; that's when the proverbial hit the proverbial. We now have three dead bodies and no results. If we don't come up with something substantial soon, like in the next twenty-four hours, Gibney won't be the only one to have his hide nailed to a wall.'

'Wasn't a lot we could do while forensic were in situ,' a detective named Mick Devlin offered. 'Best we could do was contact personnel from the nearby businesses and roust them from their beds.'

'That must've been fun,' Connolly said.

Devlin got to his feet, said, 'Yeah, they just loved us.' Youngest and best-looking of Connolly's expanded team, he stuck his hands into his trousers pockets while talking, thrusting his hips forward, macho style, the pose making him appear somewhat righteous and cocksure of himself. Connolly had only worked once with Devlin in the past and had been impressed by the young man's work ethic. 'Glad you were able to persuade them to return to their premises and hand over their CCTV tapes. Any results?'

'So far, we've looked at two tapes that cover the hour that Gibney got done,' Devlin said. 'There's a side door into the studio which isn't covered by the footage but we're hopeful that that section of the building will be in shot on the CCTV we've yet to examine. We did see a car, a silver Mazda 6, pull to a stop ten minutes after the squad car's 10.00 p.m. visit. A man got out and walked towards a side door that's out of shot and returned to the Mazda quarter of an hour later.'

'Did you get the number plate, the man's identity?' Connolly asked.

'Hard to tell. Picture quality is piss-poor. Shadows everywhere. The IT guys are working on the number plate and trying to get a lift from the driver's face. Should get back to me in an hour or so.'

'Good, we need that plate. The face would be better still, but it can't be our killer; what was done to Gibney took longer than fifteen minutes.'

Connolly called on DS Bridie McFadden next.

She looked like she'd been up all night as

she made her way to the Incident Board, a Styrofoam-filled cup of coffee in hand. 'For starters,' she began, 'there's been a serious development this morning. Because of Gibney's murder, I decided to have Dom Sutton's house checked out. Given that Sutton is the only member of *Con Spirito* still breathing, it occurred to me that his partner, Patricia Dean, and daughter, Jenny, might be in danger. Looks like I was right. While we were busy with the Gibney killing, uniforms found Sutton's place empty, the alarm system disconnected and the front gate open . . . nobody home. So, we've no idea where Dom Sutton is, and now we don't know what's become of Patricia Dean or her daughter.'

The muscles in Connolly's jaw tensed. 'Dammit, we don't need this,' he said. 'You've set up all the usual procedures to trace — '

'Of course,' McFadden snapped, with obvious irritation.

'I didn't mean to imply you hadn't . . . ' Connolly paused momentarily, sighed. 'Look, OK, all right, we're all a bit uptight. Sorry Bridie. This thing is getting to all of us. I know you have it under control.'

McFadden nodded, tried for a smile, knowing it was lack of sleep made her crotchety. Detective Sergeant Mike Dorsett was next up to the whiteboard. He gave the team an account of his meeting with Oonagh Kavanagh, making no mention of Emma Boylan's involvement. He finished by telling them that Fintan Kavanagh was better known in music circles as Cecil Charles. 'I understand from Oonagh that he is in this country at the moment and that she met him briefly yesterday. She says he's here to discuss aspects of the show with the various designers, theatre managements, actors' equity, promoters and the like.'

'Do we know where he's staying?' Connolly asked.

''Fraid not. According to the sister, Cecil Charles doesn't want anyone bothering him. All we know for sure is that he's using a hired car to get around. I'm following up on that, checking out the city's hotels. We need to grab him before he skips the country. Right now, he's the nearest thing we have to a prime suspect.'

Connolly wound up the meeting by dividing up the orders and assigning the extra set of detectives to their new duties.

36

While Mike Dorsett ran the exchange he'd had with Oonagh Kavanagh by the crime team, the lady in question was on the phone to Emma Boylan. Emma had already put in several hours writing a difficult follow-up piece on the Gibney murder and doing research in the *Post*'s archives. A large sign proclaimed the area a phone-free zone but Emma had neglected to switch her mobile off, its irritating ring tone shattering the quiet. 'Hello,' Emma said in best hushed library-speak. A pause preceded a breathless voice that identified itself as belonging to Oonagh. She told Emma she'd been inter-viewed by DS Mike Dorsett and had told the detective everything.

'Everything?' Emma queried. 'What do you mean: *everything*?'

'Father's history, the whole saga,' she said, hesitantly. 'Told him about the letter . . . how it affected me . . . my brothers. Hope I haven't caused trouble for you, Emma, but, well, I let slip that I'd taken you into my confidence.'

'That's OK,' Emma said, feeling guilty,

knowing she'd already given a brief outline of the story to Connolly. At least now she didn't have to lie to Oonagh. 'To be honest, I think we've reached the stage where we can't hold back the details any longer . . . not if we don't want to be charged with obstructing the law.'

'Yes, I can see that, Emma. I just want you to speak the truth and not let my family's involvement get distorted or knocked out of shape by people who don't know the full story. I'm relying on you to see that Fintan and Owen don't become the whipping boys.'

'I'll do the right thing,' Emma said, choosing her words carefully, unable to offer a more positive assurance. Even as she closed the line, Emma knew Oonagh's revelations to Mike Dorsett would generate repercussions. Connolly would be annoyed that her involvement had become public knowledge at this juncture, annoyed that she hadn't levelled with him in the first place. People had been killed and she'd put her journalistic instincts ahead of the one person best placed to catch the murderer. In an instant she saw things with a new clarity, realizing that client privilege and all that malarkey didn't adequately cover the current situation, not when people were being nailed up like hunting trophies. She twisted the ring round her finger, the one Connolly had given her less than twenty-four hours earlier, and shuddered.

Shut away in the archives, insulated from the noise and frenetic activity of the main work areas, the germ of an idea began to seep into her consciousness. The archives room in the *Post* building saw little activity these days because the vast bulk of material had been transferred to computer, the files now accounting for all editions of the paper going back twelve years. Earlier editions remained stored in hard copy and needed to be extracted from their cases, one by one. What Emma needed went back eighteen years; she wanted to know about the events that had snuffed out Trevor Kavanagh's life, to find out whether or not the professor had engineered the fatality himself or whether other forces, apart from the consumption of alcohol were at play.

Since talking to the Kavanagh brothers in London she'd spent many hours trying to think outside the box. On the face of it, they looked good as the villains; they had motive.

And what of Oonagh?

Was she the little miss snow-white she appeared to be? Doubtful. There had to be a question in regard to her bona fides. Could she be playing some sort of double-bluff game, appearing to be the one concerned about her brothers, while in reality . . . no, that didn't make sense, besides, Emma couldn't see Oonagh being that devious. But she did have the same motive as her brothers. Emma's gut instinct, having met the three siblings, told her they were innocent. Could be wrong, of course; she'd been wrong in the past — quite frequently as it happened — but her instincts had for the most part steered her right. Conclusion: on the bases that her instincts were right — and the siblings were innocent — she needed to come up with an alternative strategy, get her act together rapidly.

That same gut instinct was telling her that the killings were tied into the boozy party in Trevor Kavanagh's house, tied into the so-called rape of Lynda O'Regan. Accused of the rape, the professor had written the letter, got tanked up and went out and got himself killed. He saw his life in imminent danger but the words he'd written did not imply, at least not in so many words, that he himself would necessarily be the author of his own demise. What if he believed there was someone, or some thing, threatening his life? He might not have been sure, might just have suspected, and so, refrained from mentioning it in the letter.

Emma was determined to shake this

particular tree until something came tumbling down. She'd put a call through to Norma and Tomás Lee in Ann Arbour, USA. On that first occasion when she'd called the Michigan number, a house-sitter named Cindy had informed her that both Norma and Tomás Lee were in Ireland but this time Norma answered. Emma explained that she'd telephoned before and launched into the reason for the call when Norma cut her off abruptly.

'Yeah, I know who you are, know what you want. Cindy passed on your message when I called home from Ireland. I gotta tell you, Ms Boylan, you ruined a wonderful vacation for me and Tomás while we were over there. Let me tell you something; I came here to the States a long time ago to get away from all that kinda shit goin' down back then . . . when I was a student.'

Listening to Norma speak, Emma wondered how a person who'd been born and reared in Dublin could have acquired such a heavily accented American twang. She was about to interrupt, calm things down, but Norma was in full flight, sounding as though she'd been waiting for this opportunity to give vent to her feelings for some time.

'After eighteen long years, I s'posed my past would be history, yeah, the slate wiped

264

clean, be allowed to see the friends I left behind, visit places I remembered as a girl. And what happened? I'll tell you what happened, shit happened, yeah? I was only five days in the country when you called my home here in the States, wanting to rake up all that old garbage again. Well, let me tell you, Ms Boylan, I ain't going there again, no way, so I spoke to Tomás and I said, Tomás, let's get the hell outta Ireland, and that's exactly what we did. And that's all I have to say to you so please do not contact me again.'

Before Emma could respond, the connection went dead. Emma held the phone away from her ear and grimaced. 'Gee thanks, Norma, been a blast knowing y'all.' At least, some good had come out of the call: *I think it's safe to rule out Norma Somers as a suspect.* The fact that Norma and her husband were in Michigan would have made it almost impossible for them to have been three thousand miles away in the HIT-TIME STUDIOS the night before.

Lynda O'Regan, the woman named by the musicians as the rape victim in their accusation against Trevor Kavanagh, was dead and, as Emma knew only too well, dead people tell no tales. Kavanagh's death meant that Lynda never filed charges and that, in turn, meant Emma had no records to fall back on, no contemporaneous accounts to check out. However, the possibility that Lynda had some family or friends willing to shed light on events from the past might be worth investigating.

As these thoughts flitted through her mind, she finally found the article she'd been looking for; it was dated eighteen years earlier and referred to the traffic accident that killed Trevor Kavanagh. A black-and-white photograph of the vehicles involved in the collision spread across four columns but the accompanying text was vague, omitting the names of all drivers except Kavanagh. Emma looked through the papers issued on the following days and found Kavanagh's obituary. It outlined in glowing detail the music professor's career but added nothing to the sum of knowledge she'd already gleaned. Reading through the obituary, her mobile bleeped again. This time it was Connolly.

There was a discernible note of weariness in his voice, maybe exasperation even, but definitely not hostility. 'I'm tied up here big time,' he explained, 'but I need us to get together soon as possible. A few things have come up, to do with what you told me last evening. Please don't fight me on this, Emma. I'd like you to come to the station, make a statement.'

'I'm not going to fight you, Jim. It might be the best thing all round. Oonagh Kavanagh was on to me, told me she'd been quizzed by Dorsett.'

'Oh, well, then you know!' Connolly said, surprised. 'Good! I'm under pressure at this end; the world and his wife are screaming for results, nothing new there, sez you. But look, Emma, I don't want to take advantage of our relationship, especially not now, but I need your cooperation on this one; I want every last detail of what you've got on the Kavanagh brothers. We're going to track them down, talk to them, but we're running out of time and need to speed things up, and so far you're the only one who has spoken to them.'

'Yes, that's true . . . I'll do whatever I can to help.'

'Well then, I'd like to know what you make of this: a CCTV camera outside Alan Gibney's recording studio shows pictures of a hired car arriving, and leaving, during the hour the murder was committed. We've since established that the person who hired that car was none other than Cecil Charles.'

Emma's intake of breath was audible. 'Shit,' she said. 'You sure about that? I mean, it couldn't be — '

'Sure as sure can be, except — '

'Except what?'

'We've no proof that Charles is the driver. We're expecting to get a cleaned-up image of the person behind the wheel from the CCTV footage and, as you've so recently seen Charles, you could tell us if it's him.'

'I'm on my way.'

37

Sweat blurred his vision, making it difficult to concentrate. Cecil Charles cursed the heavy traffic and his own unfamiliarity with the recent road and roundabout changes that had so distorted his once native city. He needed to connect with a flight scheduled to depart within the hour, determined to flee the country with all possible haste. He no longer recognized the suburbs as he drove through Drumcondra, Whitehall, Santry, places he'd known intimately as a teenager, places where he'd once been happy. He wiped sweat from his eyes, weaving his way in and out of traffic lanes, cursing the trucks, buses and motorists impeding his progress.

On the Santry roundabout, a complex junction that entwined the M50, the M1 and the N32 into a circular free-for-all, a black Hyundai Terracan 4WD crowded his space. 'Watch where you're going, dickhead,' he yelled at the darkened windows of the SUV. *Jesus, they still haven't learned to drive in this country.* He floored the accelerator, avoided contact. But, after he'd exited the roundabout, the 4WD continued to infringe.

What's the problem with this guy? There was room for the Terracan to pass, room to switch lanes, but the intimidatory tactics continued. In a moment of enlightenment, Charles knew he was dealing with something more serious than a case of bad driving; this had to be connected to his reason for fleeing the country. And the black Terracan, he'd seen it before. Recently. The smoked glass hid the occupant but he had a good idea who sat behind the wheel.

Charles wrestled with gear stick, brakes and accelerator, pulling the Mazda 6 away from the threat. Within inches of colliding with other road users, he yelled at them to get the fuck out of the way. Didn't stop the 4WD from hitting him. First impact caught his back bumper, just a quick jab but the shudder registered through the steering wheel. Side by side now, the bigger vehicle threatened to propel him across the line, into the next lane. Pumping the accelerator, he manoeuvred the Mazda forward just in time to avoid disaster. *Jesus, the bastard wants to kill me.* He escaped. How, he didn't know, but somehow he'd extracted himself from the danger, managing to put another car between him and the Hyundai Terracan.

With one eye on the rear-view mirror, one on the road, he noticed the word AIRPORT stencilled prominently on the surface of the lane to his left. Ahead of him, the roundabout that allowed access to the airport was coming up fast, too fast, but he was in the wrong lane, the word BELFAST stencilled every few yards in front of him. *Got to switch lanes.* Traffic on either side of him ignored his frantic signalling. No one gave way. The space ahead was now too short to execute the manoeuvre. In panic, he barged in, ignoring the cacophony of angry horns accompanying the move. He'd almost made it when the black Terracan materialized out of nowhere.

Crushing impact. Ear-splitting noise. The steering wheel wrenched from his hands. His head jerked sideways. The Mazda, no longer earth bound. Cecil Charles felt himself being propelled into the pathway of the oncoming traffic on the Belfast lane. Frantically grabbing the wheel, trying to regain control, he watched in horror as the articulated truck bore down on him. There was a blinding flash, then nothing.

38

Determined to follow proper procedures, as set down by the book, Connolly put question after question to his new fiancée. Accompanied by McFadden, he sat across from Emma in the No.1 interview room. No rancour in evidence, at least not on the surface. Serious questions from them. Straight answers from her. The room was spartan, the bilious green walls and twin fluorescent tubes creating an atmosphere of institutional indifference. An almost imperceptible layer of dust covered the laminated mock-timber table that separated them. A hi-tech tape recorder and video camera were in evidence but Emma noted that no move, at least none that she could discern, had been made to activate them. McFadden had secured coffees and a packet of plain biscuits for the meeting, the goodwill gesture failing to defrost the atmosphere. While waiting for the enhanced CCTV images from the camera outside Gibney's recording studio to arrive, Connolly and McFadden had Emma repeat, verbatim, all conversations she'd had with the Kavanaghs.

'As we speak,' Connolly said, after she'd

finished her account, 'Cecil Charles is in intensive care in St Vincent's; he's unconscious, broken neck, multiple fractures, fifty-fifty chance of survival. We've put round-the-clock surveillance on him until we find out what exactly is going on. Until this happened, I liked him for the murders, but now someone's tried to take *him* out.'

'How did it happen?' Emma asked.

McFadden answered. 'He was forced into the path of an articulated truck at the airport's main entry junction. Witnesses saw his car being rammed by a four-wheel-drive.'

'The airport?' Emma said. 'Was he — '

'Had a reservation to fly to London,' Connolly said. 'Someone went to an awful lot of trouble to stop him making the flight. I need to know who that someone is.'

'Does this mean Cecil Charles is in the clear?' Emma asked.

'Not exactly,' Connolly said. 'We're checking to see what other flights he may have taken to and from the country in the past few months; we need to see if there's a pattern that ties him in with the dates of the murders. When, and *if*, he regains consciousness, he's got a hell of a lot of explaining to do. Like, for instance, what was his car doing at Gibney's recording studio? Was he the driver? However you look at it, it's safe to assume he is involved in some way with the murder. So, until we talk to him, all bets are off. And now, with the disappearance of Dom Sutton's partner and daughter, well, we've got a whole new set of problems.'

Connolly stopped talking and stared at Emma, concern on his face. 'Emma, you've held back on information which would have helped our investigation. I need to know if there's anything else you're not telling us; this is way more important than any story you're working on for the *Post*. Three people are dead; could be Dom Sutton's partner and child next; Sutton's own life is probably in danger. And it's not beyond the bounds of possibility that Dom Sutton himself is the culprit in all this; makes about as much sense as anything else. So, I'll ask you one more time, do you have anything to say to us that could help?'

Emma felt a need to make amends for having held back earlier. 'This incident at the airport exit,' she said, 'there's something eerily familiar about it, a bit like history repeating itself.'

McFadden looked enquiringly at Emma, said, 'I don't follow?'

'OK, let me explain. Earlier today I unearthed reports of a traffic incident that took place eighteen years ago. According to

Oonagh Kavanagh, her father brought about the mishap on purpose. I've read the letter, and yes, her father appears to predict his own death, but I don't believe it's a suicide note in the strict meaning of that term. It could be interpreted that he feared for his life, believing that someone was out to get him. I think it might be useful to dig up the office files on that fatal accident, find out what exactly happened.'

'But surely,' McFadden said, scepticism in her voice, 'whoever handled the investigation at the time would have gone into all that?'

'They should have, yes, but did they? According to the coroner's report Trevor Kavanagh had twice the legal amount of alcohol in his blood, enough to chalk the crash up to drunken driver. It's possible the incident was not entirely of Kavanagh's making, that someone else engineered the crash, the intention being to make it look as though alcohol was responsible. And now, eighteen years later, we have Kavanagh's son, Cecil Charles, caught up in an eerily similar scenario, only this time there are two differences: one, we know for sure the crash *was* engineered and two, the victim has survived.'

'You don't think that's stretching credulity a bit?' Connolly asked.

'No, no I don't,' Emma replied, sounding sure of herself, 'I think the two incidents could hold the key to the murders. I have a feeling — OK, call it a hunch if you like — that the same driver who pushed Cecil Charles into the way of a bloody great truck could be the same driver who caused Trevor Kavanagh's death.'

Emma's pronouncement was met with questioning looks from both detectives. Connolly was about to say something when DS Mike Dorsett ambled into the interview room. 'Got the CCTV prints,' he said, handing several 10″ × 8″ prints to Connolly. Connolly shuffled through them before selecting one and passing it to Emma. 'Here's a pretty clear head shot of the driver, recognize him?'

'That's Cecil Charles,' she said straight off.

'So, what the blazes was he doing at the recording studio if he wasn't Gibney's killer?' McFadden asked, taking one of the prints from Connolly.

'If we had the answer to that,' Connolly said, 'our case would be solved.'

39

Patricia Dean felt proud of Jenny. The eleven-year-old was being so brave, determined not to cry, at least not in front of her. This was undoubtedly the most harrowing experience ever to visit the child. Wasn't exactly a bed of roses for her either; being roused from sleep and manhandled by the masked intruders represented her worst nightmare. They'd been allowed to get into their daytime clothes — watched by their captors — blindfolded and shunted at knife point into the back of a car, a high vehicle that she guessed to be a four-wheel-drive. She had no idea where they'd been taken but after what felt like twenty-five minutes duration, the journey ended abruptly.

Still blindfolded, they were pulled from the vehicle and ushered through a series of doors. The men gripping her and Jenny's arms barely spoke except to indicate steps up, steps down, or similar admonitions. Being blindfolded, she relied on her other senses to help establish her environment. They'd finally arrived in what felt like a small enclosed space and were made to sit on hard chairs, at which point their blindfolds had been removed. Their captors still wore balaclavas.

Only now did Patricia see the location, a small windowless room, little more than a cubicle with a row of steel filing cabinets and no other furniture save the chairs Jenny and she sat on. A narrow grill set above the door appeared to be the only form of ventilation. The taller of the two men, the one giving the orders, handed her a mobile.

'Call Dom Sutton.'

'I don't have his number.'

'Oh yes you do! Don't make this more difficult for yourself than it already is. Call him!'

'Told you, I don't have his number.'

The masked man shook his head, turned his back on her and moved to face Jenny. Without warning, he slapped Jenny's face, the force enough to knock her off the chair. Mother and child screamed in unison.

'You bastard,' Patricia shouted, leaping from her chair, moving to help her daughter. The tall man stopped her, forcibly pushing her backwards, his hands digging into her stomach, pressing her back down into her chair.

'That didn't have to happen,' he said. 'That was down to you, yeah? So, I'm going to ask you again to get dialling . . . you refuse, I'll slap her again. It's your call, Patricia, in every sense of the word, but bear this in mind, I'll keep hitting her until you do as you're told.'

'OK, all right, just don't touch her again.'

'Fine! I don't want to hurt the kid,' he said, helping Jenny back to the chair. 'See, no need for rough stuff, no need at all.'

Jenny's eyes sought her mother, her fingers kneading the side of her face.

'Right!' the masked man said, 'now, make the call.'

'The number I have automatically transfers to voice mail.'

'He's probably using it as a screen but he'll still get the message. Tell him that the person he's running from is holding you. If he wants to see his daughter alive again, tell him he needs to talk to me.' The man handed Patricia a piece of paper. 'Give him this number to call back.'

'If I do it,' Patricia said, 'you must set us free after that.'

'I don't have to do anything, OK? But if you do as you're told and cause no problems, I'll let you go . . . *when* Dom rings back.'

Patricia pressed the digits on the mobile, got through to Dom's answer phone, delivered the message as instructed and finished by giving the number he needed to call back. 'What do we do now?' she asked her captor.

'We wait,' he said, 'we just wait.'

40

It had been their first proper chance to experience the fruits of their engagement, a whole night spent together between the sheets. Pushing aside the external pressures buffeting their lives, they'd given each other the kind of comfort and devotion denied them of late. Sheer indulgence, emotional fulfilment. Both felt spent after their rapturous hi-jinks but the afterglow still enlivened their spirits and sleep escaped.

Connolly was first to allow the real world back into play. Emma, snuggling like a baby in his embrace, protested; she didn't want extraneous thoughts to interrupt. But her resolve to shut out shop talk didn't last. Without wanting to, she found herself discussing the various aspects of the case. Connolly talked about his plans to examine the road traffic reports on the eighteen-year-old accident that claimed Trevor Kavanagh's life.

'Could be,' he said, 'that some of those old records could give us the names of the occupants of all vehicles caught up in the incident.'

'You think I'm right, don't you?' Emma said. 'You think there's a link between that incident and the recent crash at the airport?'

'Could be,' Connolly conceded. 'I need to get hold of all available CCTV footage on the airport roundabout area to give me an accurate picture of what happened there; might give us a name for whoever is orchestrating all this mayhem.'

'What about Cecil Charles . . . suspect or victim?'

'Good question! Right now, I'm taking no chances; I've got two uniforms guarding him in the hospital; can't let any harm come to him, not now.'

'You still don't know why he visited Gibney's recording studio?'

'Not yet, but I'm keeping an open mind.'

'You haven't a clue, you mean, right?'

'Wouldn't say that,' Connolly said, pretending to be hurt by the remark. 'I've got a few theories but unlike you lot in the media, a policeman's theories aren't worth diddly squat without proof. For the moment I'm keeping my feelings in regard to Charles's involvement in Alan Gibney's murder to myself . . . lest I find my deliberations quoted on the front page of tomorrow's *Post*.'

'Very funny! Don't flatter yourself,' Emma said, rubbing her nose against his. 'I regard all conversations conducted between the sheets as sacrosanct.'

'Can I hold you to that?'

'You can hold me to whatever you like, big boy,' Emma teased.

'Oh, you wanton trollop,' Connolly said, gently kneading stray tresses of her hair. 'Seriously though, that was quite an adventure you had with the Kavanagh brothers in London. Bob Crosby must be very pleased, yeah?'

'Depends on how the story pans out. I'm meeting him in the morning to suss out where we go with it. He will decide how much we use.'

'Why? Is there a problem?'

'Well, now, you should know what Crosby's like, you two being such buddy-buddies.'

'Worried about litigation, is he?'

'Yeah, right. There could be ramifications for the *Post* if the paper is seen to imply that Cecil Charles has been involved in murder . . . should it turn out he's innocent.'

Connolly was enjoying this. 'What you mean is: Crosby can't decide whether to shit or get off the pot. He doesn't want the *Post* to pull its punches if it turns out that the man's guilty.'

'That's it in a nutshell! That's why he's anxious to discuss it with me before adopting a position on the issue.'

'I assume you're going to run with the story about Patricia Dean and her daughter?'

'Well, yes. Sutton's name is already in the public domain and Willie Thompson is feverishly following up on it, making damn sure that I don't muscle in. The fool's got notions above his station, thinks he's God's gift to journalism, thinks this story will do for him what *In Cold Blood* did for Truman Capote. So it's going to get out, like it or not. I think Dom Sutton is protecting — '

Connolly pressed a finger to Emma's lips. 'Shhh,' he said. 'Neither of us will be in any shape to do our jobs if we don't get some sleep.'

Emma smiled as she moved her body above his, straddling him like an eager young jockey. 'I'm not ready for sleep just yet.'

41

Five hours had elapsed in the claustrophobic room. No word from Dominic. Patricia and Jenny Dean's freedom depended on a response. Every twenty minutes or so the two masked men took turns to check on them. Jenny lay on the floor in a sleeping bag that had been provided by the smaller of the two men. Patricia wanted to climb in beside her but remained on the chair, alert to everything. It had been some time since she'd asked to go to the toilet, an excuse to see what sort of environment existed outside their cubicle. The ruse hadn't worked. The smaller man had blindfolded her before leading her to a toilet, warning that if she pulled any funny business, Jenny would 'get it'.

Her watch told her it was just past 6.00 a.m., daylight just a few hours away. *What the hell's keeping Dominic?* She got up from the chair, stretched, paced up and down, up and down, a caged animal, confined to the narrow space next to the sleeping bag. Jenny appeared to be sleeping, though how anyone could sleep under such circumstances was beyond her. The even rhythm of the child's breathing should have provided comfort but served instead to exacerbate her worries. She refused to contemplate anything bad happening to Jenny. For the most part, she'd brought her up on her own. Dominic was usually locked up or away on one or other of his projects for the best part of his daughter's life.

'I need answers,' Patricia said out loud, pressing her palms against her cheeks. 'I need answers, and I need them now.' She stopped pacing, rushed towards the door and pounded on it with her fists. Within seconds, it opened. 'What's with the racket?' the tall captor asked, pushing her back, locking the door behind him. He was the one in charge, the one giving the orders. The smaller man remained outside.

'What's Dominic done?' Patricia asked. 'What's he done that you should hold us here like this?'

'Took something from me that's irreplaceable; time he made reparation.'

'Look . . . maybe there's a way I can . . . well, make it up to you.'

'Shame on you, woman. I do not desire intimacy with — '

'Whoa! Bloody hell, I wasn't offering *that*. What do you take me for? As if! I meant money. I can get hold of money . . . a lot of money; you just tell me what — '

'Haven't been listening, have you? What Dom took from me is *irreplaceable*. You could offer me sex, love and comfort . . . and all his ill-gotten gains . . . wouldn't make the slightest difference.'

'OK, all right, have it your way. It's just that I'm having trouble taking you seriously with your face covered; why don't you remove the mask, discuss this like a responsible adult?'

'Mask stays put . . . makes me invisible . . . the way I like it; besides, I couldn't let you live if I removed it. We don't want that, do we?'

'You're so full of shit,' she said, sounding braver than she felt. 'I'd still like to know what Dominic's supposed to have done?'

'Well, seeing as how he hasn't got back to us, I think maybe you deserve an explanation.' He picked up the chair that Jenny had sat on earlier and placed it in front of Patricia's. 'Sit,' he ordered, indicating her chair, 'and I'll tell you what this is about. You sure you want the kid to hear it?'

'She's heard so many stories about her father; one more or less isn't going to make a whole pile of difference.'

'Your decision,' the man said, leaning his

body forward, purposely invading her space. 'Once upon a time — isn't that how all good stories start — a young maiden toiled as a cleaner for a music professor.' The masked man spoke in the way that people do when narrating a fairy tale. 'Now, this professor had the reputation for having something of a roving eye and lost his job for doing bad things with one of his students. To survive, he was forced to teach music in his own home. His spiteful wife didn't like this arrangement at all. She hated her neighbours seeing how low they had fallen, so she flew off to London and was never seen again. This upset the professor and he began to drink heavily. His two sons had already gone out into the world to seek fame and fortune. His daughter was too caught up in her own life to look after her old papa. So, the poor man had no choice but to hire the young maiden to help with the house chores.

'Young people from all corners of the big city came to the professor to learn how to play music. And even though the professor had grown very fond of drink, he was still the best music teacher in all of the land.

'One day when the professor's drinking had got out of hand he invited four of his brightest students to join him for a drink.'

The man in the balaclava stopped talking

momentarily, appearing to think about what to say next, though it was impossible for Patricia to know what kind of expression lay behind the mask.

'Your old man was one of those four musicians,' he said after the pause, his voice reverting to normal cadence. 'Yes, Dom Sutton was there that evening, younger of course, but present in the professor's house. At first, Dom and his pals drank beer and vodka until one of them — I'm not sure which one — introduced drugs to the party. Pretty soon things got a bit out of hand. At some stage, the young cleaning lady attempted to quieten the growing boisterousness. One of the musicians — again I can't say which of them — promised they'd leave if she agreed to have one drink with them. Being naïve, she foolishly agreed. She drank a vodka and mixer, unaware that the drink had been spiked.

'The world became a darker place for her after that. She didn't regain full consciousness until the following morning. She tried to recall the previous evening's events but memory eluded her, yet she could tell that she'd been sexually assaulted. In a state of great agitation, she contacted the professor, demanded he tell her what happened. He couldn't help, claiming to have passed out on booze during the period in question. When she told him she'd been raped and intended to see a doctor and the police he became alarmed, begged her to hold off until he established what exactly happened. He contacted the young musicians, demanding they come to his house straight away. As soon as they arrived, he told them what the young woman had told him, insisting they should come clean, acknowledge what they'd done, and discuss what, if any, redress they might offer the victim.

'Appealing to their sense of decency, he insisted they tell him who was responsible. 'We resent being accused of raping the girl,' they told him, 'it's something we totally refute. We find it particularly offensive in view of the fact that it was *you* who sexually molested the young lady.' Well, as you can imagine the professor was flabbergasted and asked how they could stoop to telling such barefaced lies. They reminded him of his record for inappropriate behaviour towards young ladies, claiming that what he had done to his young cleaning help represented another example of his uncontrollable lustful behaviour.'

42

'So, *who* raped the woman?' Patricia Dean asked.

'The *woman* — she was just a school girl, really,' the masked man said. 'Her name was Lynda O'Regan. The professor's name was Trevor Kavanagh. Dom ever mention either name to you?'

'Can't say he did but then there's a lot of things my husband never mentioned.' What Patricia was hearing now, coupled with what she'd picked up from the detectives, made her realize how little she knew about the man she'd married, the man who'd fathered the most precious thing in her life: Jenny. 'So, who took advantage of this young woman you call Lynda?'

'If you'd asked me that at the time, I'd have said Kavanagh. It would've been the word of a disgraced, alcoholic professor against the word of four young men, all of them coming from so-called respectable backgrounds.'

'And what about . . . Lynda? I don't follow, surely she could tell — '

'She was confused, in a state of shock, didn't know how to react or what to do, didn't know who to turn to. Her family were supportive, especially her younger brother, John. They were not a well-off family, struggled financially to put her and the brother through college; John studied architecture, Lynda, music. They worked part time to help provide the additional money required for their education. Lynda trusted the professor; she couldn't bring herself to believe he was the molester. Her instincts told her that the four men were responsible but they insisted they had nothing to do with it.'

'Why didn't she go to the police, let the law decide who — '

'Wasn't that simple; apart from the financial implications of going to the authorities, she feared her action would result in Kavanagh's arrest. The professor knew it would just be a matter of time before he was questioned, knowing that when that happened his past would blow up in his face. He'd no wish to go through that again. Seeing no way out of his dilemma, he simply gave up on life. And, I suppose that would have been the end of it except, as it turned out, it marked the beginning.'

'The beginning? Beginning of what?'

'The beginning of something that's only being concluded here and now.'

'Look, I'm not sure where you're going

with this,' Patricia said, feeling as though she'd been plunged into some sort of surreal episode from a Stephen King novel, cooped up in a small room, her daughter sleeping on the floor, a man wearing a balaclava talking calmly as though it was the most natural thing in the world. She tried to visualize the features of the face hidden behind the mask. 'I don't know who you are,' she said, 'and I don't know what connects you to the story you've told me, and I don't see why you needed to kidnap Jenny and me to tell us this.'

'Hadn't intended telling you any of this,' the voice behind the balaclava said, 'but seeing as how Dom is taking his own sweet time to return the call, I thought I'd let you know why I've decided to make Dom Sutton pay for what he's done.'

'You're mad! Jesus, look around you; this whole fucking thing is crazy. Even if Dominic and his friends did what you say they did — and I agree, rape is an awful crime — you can't just take it upon yourself to go after them . . . kill them; that's sheer madness; there's no way your action can be justified —'

'If it were only rape, then, yes, I might agree, but you've only heard half the story. You'll understand when I tell you what followed.'

'I'll pass on that if you don't mind. No disrespect, but I've heard enough, I don't want — '

'Well, that's just too bad because, like they say on *Mastermind*, 'I've started, so I'll finish'. You're going to hear a whole lot more. I'll ask you to reserve judgement until you've heard just what kind of monster you've been living with.'

He waited for a response from Patricia but, getting none, continued. 'After Kavanagh's death, Lynda stayed with her family, tried to blot out all the ugly stuff. Her biggest worry was that she might be pregnant but as it turned out, she wasn't. Now, this is the point where I become a player in the drama. You see, I'd got to know Lynda during her time with the professor and we had become friends — nothing serious, a platonic relationship. I also got to know the four men during this period, not that they ever acknowledged my existence. I didn't need to wear a balaclava back then to be invisible, at least not as far as those gentlemen were concerned. I made a point of drinking in the same pub, watched and listened as they behaved in their usual cavalier way, taking the piss out of the barmen and other customers, groping the female floor staff, drinking to excess, snorting cocaine, and boasting of the women they'd had it off with. I overheard one of them tell how he'd had to deal severely with a slapper who'd refused to swallow after giving head. Another time I heard one of them admit he'd had to see a doctor because he'd picked up a dose of clap.

'My friendship with Lynda developed on to a romantic footing about a year after her traumatic experience. She was still living with her family, afraid of her own shadow, but I worked hard trying to get her to regain confidence. I coaxed her to join me on trips to the country; took her dancing, got her to accompany me to the theatre, the opera, the cinema, encouraged her to take walks in the park. My persistence paid off. She learned to trust me and to feel safe in my company. Everything was fine except for one aspect of our relationship. She was still afraid of sexual intimacy. I was prepared to be patient, knowing her history, and never once pushed her into anything she didn't feel comfortable doing.

'Eventually, I got her to agree to share a bedsit with me and it certainly helped cement the relationship. She was frustrated with her inability to partake in a full relationship and she tried hard to overcome the problem. We were probably together for a year when, with her approval, I attempted to make love. I took it ever so gently, not rushing anything, slowly, ever so slowly, venturing to visit the area that held such terror for her . . . but as soon as I touched her, she screamed out in pain. I assumed the problem was mental rather than physical, but Lynda, who seemed more upset than me, decided she needed medical advice.

'The specialist she consulted referred her on to the Sexual Assault Treatment unit in the Rotunda Hospital. It turned out that quite an amount of old damage remained from the time she'd been raped. Surgery was required to remove serious scar tissue that had formed. In the course of her treatment it was established that she had contracted chlamydia. Because the disease had been left untreated for so long, the bacteria had spread from the cervix into the fallopian tubes, which in turn led to far more serious complications. Irreversible damage had been inflicted; damage that meant Lynda would never be able to conceive.

'Well, you can just imagine how we felt about that. A few minutes ago you accused me of being mad and you might just be right; I was certainly fit for the loony bin at the time. I wanted to go after the four men there and then. Lynda was devastated but she insisted I do nothing, threatening to leave me if I took any action. Reluctantly, I agreed. We tried to put the past behind us, tried to contend with what we had. I asked her to marry me but she refused. Oh yes, she loved me all right, but somewhere, lodged in her head, she felt unclean, defiled, unworthy of the sacrament of marriage — her Catholic upbringing I suppose — and I was unable to persuade her to change her mind. I referred to her as my wife, and indeed we were husband and wife in every respect except for the certificate that would give our union official recognition. We moved to a house in Swords, had a decent garden, a golden Labrador, good neighbours, and we managed to scoot off to Tuscany for three weeks every year. She was happy, or as near to happy as it got for her. Her smile used to break my heart.

'Two and a half years ago, the uneasy peace and contrived contentment we'd created shattered. Lynda went for her biannual medical check-up, something she'd attended to religiously ever since the assault. She had no symptoms, and normally this presented no problems, but on this occasion a Pap test indicated changes in the cervix. The doctors ordered further tests: colposcopy examination, a cone biopsy and a wide range of similar procedures. Finally, with all the results in, she was given the bad news: she had cervical cancer. We were gutted, absolutely devastated, refusing to believe what we were hearing. Lynda showed a great fighting spirit, subjecting herself to all manner of treatment but the disease spread and the diagnosis remained constant.'

Patricia, listening with rapt attention, was moved by his account but she guessed where he was going with it. 'I'm sorry,' she said, 'I know it's awful when someone gets cancer — some friends of mine have died from it — but you can't blame it on what happened eighteen years ago. As far as I know, cervical cancer, after breast cancer, is the most common form of the disease in women. It's something we get or we don't get; we have no say — '

'See, that's where you're wrong, dead wrong. I read up on the causes of cervical cancer and do you know what I discovered?'

'No, I don't, but I'm sure — '

'The American Cancer Society, an organization that ought to know what they're talking about, provide a list of risk factors for cervical cancer, things like smoking, HIV infection, dietary factors, contraception, multiple pregnancies and certain hormonal drugs, a whole list that didn't apply to Lynda, right? But, these wonderful top scientists do name one other possible cause; they say chlamydia infection can be traced as a trigger capable of setting off a chain reaction that can, in certain cases, cause cervical cancer.

'Five weeks ago, Lynda died from the disease, a woman who never harmed anyone in her life, a beautiful person in every sense of the word, the one person in the whole world that I loved more than life itself. I know she would not approve of what I'm doing to avenge her death but, Jesus Christ, I owe it to myself to go after the bastards who did this to her.'

Patricia didn't need to see behind the balaclava to know the man was crying. She could understand his grief but she had little time for sympathy. Her overriding concern was for Jenny's safety. 'I think you're mistaken.' she said, quietly. 'I agree when you say Lynda would not approve. What you're doing is wrong; it won't bring Lynda back, and you'll most likely get caught.'

'Won't make any difference to my life whether I get caught or not. Without Lynda . . . well, what can I say, there is no *without Lynda*. Without her, I don't exist; I'm a dead man walking. If it weren't for this need to exact revenge, well — '

The sound of the mobile stopped him in mid sentence. He grabbed it, looked at the incoming number display, said, 'Hello Dom.'

43

Connolly arrived early in the station. Feeling drained. And not just because of his prolonged amorous encounter with Emma. No, wasn't that at all. More a question of the pressure to produce results getting to him. Three men dead. A potential suspect in hospital, unconscious, on round-the-clock watch. Dom Sutton, a potential victim, who might just be a suspect, had disappeared from the face of the earth and his wife and daughter had either been kidnapped or done a runner.

Until yesterday, he'd been reasonably sure that Trevor Kavanagh's son, the one calling himself Cecil Charles, looked good for the crimes, or at least had an involvement in the deed. Charles had visited the scene of Alan Gibney's murder but, and this was the bit that didn't add up, he hadn't stayed long enough to commit the crime. A day later, he'd been deliberately run off the road while attempting to flee the country.

More questions than answers.

Emma's suggestion that he examine the records of Trevor Kavanagh's road fatality and compare them with the one that had put Cecil Charles in hospital failed to throw up any startling revelations. Data available on the initial crash indicated that there had been no suspicion of a conspiracy to kill the professor. Each driver had been interviewed at the time and all had been declared blameless. Evidence showed Kavanagh to be driving in a reckless manner, the collision down to him alone. Alcohol in his system underlined his culpability.

Connolly had telephoned Emma with this information, not something he should have done, but he knew she was banking on there being a connection. This would save her the trouble of going down that particular route. He'd been put through to Bob Crosby's office and had had a quick word with him before being passed on to Emma. She'd been disappointed to learn that her hunch didn't fly, but it was obvious she was not alone and couldn't make any reference to their previous night's love fest.

Thoughts of what they'd got up to brought a smile to his face, a smile that surprised DS McFadden as she approached him. She knew the kind of increased pressure he'd been under these past few days and had got used to the ever-present sombre expression inhabiting his face. 'Hey, what's the joke,' she asked.

'Joke?' Connolly said, his expression back to funereal solemnity. 'Don't know what you're on about.'

'Just thought for a second I saw you smile, that's all.'

'Hmmm, yeah, well, I was . . . I was thinking about . . . oh, nothing, nothing at all. What'd you want to see me about?'

'Well, maybe I can bring another smile to that face of yours. I've just had news from St Vincent's; Cecil Charles has regained consciousness and he's going to pull through.'

'Has he spoken to anybody yet?'

'No. The doctors are keeping everyone away. But if *you* were to talk to the people in charge they might relent, let you see him.'

'Sounds like a plan. Get on the blower, find out who's in charge and tell them I'm on my way.'

44

Coming up to 8.30 a.m. and Bob Crosby was all business, coat off, sleeves rolled back, waistcoat stretched to breaking point across the expanding girth, determination writ large on his face. Because the *Post* didn't publish a Sunday edition, Saturday mornings were usually the quietest time of the week, the only time Crosby allowed himself a lie-in. Not this morning, though. He'd already spent an hour mulling over various aspects of the case with Emma, who sat across from him in his editorial office, looking apprehensive, a coffee mug cradled in her hands.

'The more I think about it,' he was saying, 'the more I'm inclined to the notion that we're within a hair's-breadth of putting this one to bed.'

'Feel the same way myself,' Emma said, 'just wish I could turn the feeling into something more tangible.' Emma usually found her one-to-one brainstorming sessions with Crosby productive. He was her mentor, the man who'd hired her a decade earlier and who had employed a carrot-and-stick approach to teach her the fundamentals of good investigative journalism. There had been many a dust-up along the way, but a trusting friendship had evolved. 'Damn it, I was so sure,' she said, putting down her mug with more force than she'd intended, coffee splashing over the rim in the process.

'Ah, yes, Connolly's call. Bit of a bummer, that; knocked your theory on the head.'

'Thought I was on to something significant but the records show the professor was drunk as a skunk and got himself killed, an accident, pure and simple. No mystery. No conspiracy. Makes me wonder if I haven't got this whole thing arseways.'

'I know one person who thinks you've got it wrong.'

'And who might that be?'

'Willie Thompson.'

'Him? Huh, got me worried there for a minute. What the hell has that little piss ant been saying?'

'It's not what he's been saying; more a question of what he's written. I just spiked an article he submitted claiming that Connolly was derelict in his duty by turning up at the Gibney crime scene with his *girlfriend* in tow — the girlfriend not named — and that 'said girlfriend' had to be removed. His article went on to suggest that Connolly had other things on his mind besides crime-fighting and ought to be removed from the investigation.'

'And you spiked it, yes?'

'Yes, it was a cheap shot, a clumsy attempt to get at you and Connolly. Besides, the investigation has moved on. This photograph, for instance,' he said, picking up the print Emma had copied from the original given to her by Mansfield's widow, 'could hold some answers. Look at them, all dead . . . apart from Dom Sutton and Oonagh Kavanagh. The common denominator linking all these people is Trevor Kavanagh, at least that's what we've believed until now, but what if . . . what if someone else in this photograph is central to what's happening.'

'Well, the one person in that photo who could probably tell us what we need to know is Lynda O'Regan. But she's dead and dead people — '

' . . . tell no tales,' Crosby said. 'That's true, but wasn't she the one the professor was accused of molesting?'

'Yes, but where does that get us?'

'Well. Just suppose she told a friend, or her family, what happened, wouldn't they want to go after the professor or *his* family?'

'Sure, they might, but for that scenario to add up it would mean someone going after Oonagh and her brothers . . . and that's not what's happening. The professor's musical

304

protégés are the ones being targeted. Why would this so-called friend, or family, want to do that . . . and why wait eighteen years?'

'When did Lynda O'Regan die?'

'I don't know. Oonagh mentioned that she was dead; I assumed it happened ages ago. Hey, why don't I ring Oonagh, ask her?'

'Go ahead.'

Emma consulted her notebook, found the number and dialled Oonagh. 'Sorry to bother you,' she said, 'but I'm hoping you can fill me in on something.'

'Of course, what is it?'

'You remember telling me about Lynda O'Regan? Well, I was wondering if you could tell me when she died?'

'Ah, poor Lynda. I always regretted that she and I didn't keep in touch but, well, what with all that happened I felt it might not be appropriate.'

'Do you know when she died?' Emma pushed.

'It was about five, maybe six weeks ago; can't be sure of the date but it can't have been any more than seven weeks at the outside.'

'Thanks Oonagh. Just one other thing: did Lynda have any close friends that you know of, a boyfriend maybe?'

'I really couldn't say. When Father

employed her, I didn't need to visit the house all that often, so I couldn't say. She was young, very pretty, quiet personality, well spoken, tallish, about 5 ft. 9 in., so I'd say she would've had no trouble in attracting the opposite sex.'

'But you never saw her with anybody, right?'

'No, apart from John, her brother. They were very close, looked out for each other. He used to drop her off at our house, pick her up sometimes. There was an older sister too but I don't recall anyone else.'

'Don't suppose you remember where this brother and sister lived?'

'Let me think for a second. Yeah, I'm nearly sure the O'Regans lived in Rathmines. Funny the way certain things stick in your mind; I remember Lynda telling me about going to see some film in the Stella in Rathmines. If memory serves me right, I'm pretty sure their house was in Charleville Road.'

'Thanks, Oonagh, thanks for your help.' Emma hung up, put on her overcoat and picked up her car keys from Crosby's desktop. 'I'm going to see if the O'Regans still live in Charleville Road.'

'Hold it a sec.' Crosby said. 'Let's look the number up in the directory? If they're still there, we can ring.' Crosby flicked through the pages, had a result within seconds. 'There's an O'Regan listed for Charleville Road,' he said, pleased with himself. 'The house is called *Teach Solais*.'

'*Teach Solais*?' Emma said. 'Isn't that Gaelic for lighthouse?'

'Well yes, but it could also mean *house of light*, maybe *sunshine*.'

'Certainly no need of a lighthouse in landlocked Rathmines. Let's ring the number, see who answers it.'

'It's not ringing,' Crosby said, after dialling, 'It's making that out-of-order sound. You'd better get over there, see if there's anyone home.'

Saturday morning traffic was lighter than usual. Emma made it to Rathmines in ten minutes flat. Parking restrictions on Charleville Road forced her to drive into the grounds of St Louis High School, blithely ignoring the PRIVATE sign as she reversed into a bay reserved for teachers.

She strode out of the school grounds and headed along Charleville Road, thinking, *don't see any sign of a lighthouse*. Minutes later she saw the nameplate *Teach Solais*. The terrace two-storey was a dirty shade of grey with small windows and a dingy little porch surrounded by faded lattice work and scraggly remnants of rosebush. Whoever had come up with the name for the house, Emma thought, surely had an overdeveloped sense of irony.

A good-looking woman, early forties, answered the door. Emma asked her if Lynda O'Regan had once lived in the house.

'Why do you want to know?' the woman asked.

'I'm with the *Post*,' Emma replied, offering the woman her business card, 'I'm writing a piece on the murders of four ex-musicians who were once tutored by Trevor Kavanagh. I've discovered that Lynda O'Regan worked part-time for the professor and I'm trying to dig up what I can about her time there.'

'I'm Ellen O'Regan,' the woman said, taking the proffered business card. 'I'm Lynda's sister. Would you like to come in?'

Emma accepted the offer and was shown into a small but comfortable sitting room. The house's interior belied the exterior and helped explain the name. A glass atrium, inserted into the roof above the central stairway, allowed light to filter into what would otherwise have been a rather dingy home. A semi-open-plan layout meant that the ground floor, including the sitting room, benefited from an abundance of light.

Ellen told Emma that she was familiar with the recent murders. 'Because of Lynda, God rest her soul, I take a keen interest in what's happened to those men. She once told me, back when she worked for the professor, that she disliked them intensely.'

'Did she say why?'

'Well, no, not at the time, but years later she told me what they did to her; I expect you know what I'm talking about?'

'I know they accused Trevor Kavanagh of raping your sister and threatened to go to the authorities.'

'Bullshit! The bastards blamed the professor for what they themselves did to her. It was them, not Kavanagh, who destroyed Lynda, so you'll forgive me if I don't shed any tears at their demise.'

'But why . . . why would Kavanagh have let them get away with it?'

'He knew no one would believe him because of his history. He'd lost his job, lost his wife, lost his self-respect. The man couldn't face another scandal; I believe he'd lost the will to live.'

'What happened to Lynda after Kavanagh's death?'

'She remained here, became withdrawn, depressed, a mental breakdown you could call it. She hid away from the world. We tried to rally round but it was a terrible time for the family. Me and John — that's my brother, he's an architect; designed and reconstructed the interior of this house for our parents when they were alive — did what we could to help Lynda. If it weren't for her boyfriend, she never would have got over it. He managed to get through to her, made her seek medical attention, got her to rejoin the human race.'

'A boyfriend, you say? Can you tell me who he was?'

'He was her saviour, saved her life. Lynda met him while working for the professor; he kept in contact with her after she'd lost her job.'

'Was he receiving tuition from Kavanagh; was he a musician?'

'No, he was a photographer, still is as far as I know. Name's Walter, he used to visit the professor's house with his father, Friedrich Schiller. They used to come to the Kavanagh house to listen to music and take photographs. That's how Lynda and Walter got to know each other.'

Emma experienced what Oprah Winfrey liked to call a 'light bulb' moment. The answers she'd sought bombarded her brain simultaneously. Ellen O'Regan continued talking but Emma's mind had gone into overdrive. She wanted to get out of the house with all possible haste, decide what she must do with what she now knew.

45

Not many limbs were left uncovered. Looked for all the world as though the Michelin Man had undergone an horrendous liposuction procedure. Intravenous morphine drips, tubes, monitors, chains and all manner of modern scientific equipment clicked, bleeped, and buzzed around the patient like an exploding alien life form. One fully extended leg, cased in a surgical splint, remained hoisted by a cord on a pulley, the other, hidden beneath a contraption resembling a covered dog house. Looking down at Cecil Charles, Connolly cloaked his astonishment, wondering how was it possible a person could withstand such punishment and still continue to breath. Half of Charles's face remained bandage-free but even that small proportion looked as though it had been subjected to a close encounter with a food grater. The part of his nose still visible was blackened and one corner of his mouth appeared to be held together with some sort of elasticized material.

Connolly identified himself by waving his ID in front of Charles's one good eye. The one good eye blinked acknowledgement.

311

Charles made no effort to speak.

'Sorry to bother you,' Connolly began, 'but I'm hoping you feel up to answering a few questions; you OK with that?'

There was movement in Charles's lips as he struggled to formulate words. 'Yes,' he said, a torturous croak. 'Yes . . . ask away.'

'Who drove the four-wheel-drive that did this?'

Again, Charles struggled to form his words. 'His name is . . . is . . . Walter Schiller.'

Connolly had a vague recollection of Emma mentioning that name but he couldn't place it. 'Who is Walter Schiller?' he asked.

'I knew . . . Walter and his father . . . the photographer . . . Friedrich back . . . back when they were friends with . . . my father.' In obvious distress, Charles took breaks between every few words, making his delivery hard to follow, even harder to listen to. 'They were photographers, yes, but . . . it was their knowledge of opera and stage settings that fascinated Father . . . fascinated me too. I've employed Walter Schiller to construct initial stage settings for all my shows. He is gifted . . . a genius . . . sees things in visual terms . . . the whole world . . . reduced to diorama dimensions. Could've earned a fortune in set design but . . . refuses to give up his photographic practice. His photos . . .

you should see them. Amazing. Like full theatrical productions . . . unbelievable constructions.'

'So, how come you and he — '

'I'm getting . . . getting to that,' Charles croaked, struggling for breath. 'I asked Walter to design a stage setting for a musical version of *Pulp Fiction*. He's been working on a concept for a few months now . . . decided to pay him a visit two days ago. He showed me sketches and a scale model . . . brilliant concept . . . but then . . . later in that evening . . . after I'd had time to consider it . . . back in my hotel, I decided I needed to tease out a few technical aspects with him. It was late . . . but I knew he worked all hours . . . drove to his place in Essex Gate. Tom, one of his assistants, told me I'd just missed him . . . said Walter had gone to see an old friend in Rathmines. Tom didn't have an address or a name for Walter's friend . . . but I guessed who it might be.'

'You guessed?' Connolly said, raising an eyebrow. 'How?'

'I've been . . . following the story of the murders. I knew these men. I knew what they'd done to Father, made it my business to discover where they hung out, what they worked at. Dom Sutton proved elusive . . . couldn't trace him . . . I found the others . . .

313

I didn't kill them . . . if that's what you're thinking, wasn't me, though God knows I wanted to. I traced Alan Gibney to the recording studio in Rathmines. When Tom told me Walter had gone to see a friend in Rathmines, I immediately thought . . . what a coincidence.'

'I don't follow,' Connolly said, 'how could you — '

'Let me explain . . . please, OK? Walter knew the musicians . . . took their photographs . . . listened to them playing . . . and, crucially, he was aware that his wife, or partner, Lynda, had been gang raped by them. Well, I found myself considering these facts and it struck me that . . . if Walter had gone to Rathmines to see an old friend, then . . . maybe . . . this so-called 'friend' might be Alan Gibney.'

Conversation halted as a nurse entered the room and began checking the readings on the various monitors. She entered the details on her clip pad, smiled pleasantly at Connolly. 'Mustn't tire Mr Charles,' she said, in a lilting Kerry accent, 'he's been through a lot and needs his rest.'

'Just a few minutes more, nurse,' Connolly told her. As soon as she left he turned to Cecil Charles. 'What happened in Rathmines?'

'I parked outside the HIT-TIME STUDIOS.

The place appeared to be in darkness. The main entrance was closed so I went to a side door . . . tried it. It was locked. I was returning to my car when . . . when I heard a banging sound . . . came from inside the building. Should've walked away . . . should've got in the car, but I was intrigued. I climbed upon a low windowsill and pressed my face against the windowpane. The glass had that frosted effect . . . couldn't see through it . . . noticed a clear section higher up. I got on my tippy-toes . . . stretched my body until I was able to peek inside.

'Couldn't believe my eyes . . . thought I was hallucinating. The lights inside were dimmed, no stronger than candlelight but I saw two men moving about . . . dressed in black . . . hard to make out what they were up to. I stayed at the window . . . got used to the dim light, saw them use step ladders to haul the body of another man on to a clock on the wall. Couldn't believe my eyes. It was like something out of a Dali or Bosch painting, except . . . except it was real. And then, when I saw the mutilation to the body I think I must have screamed . . . because the men stopped what they were doing and turned to look at me. I recognized Walter straight away . . . and even though he could only see part of my face, I knew . . . I knew he'd recognized me.'

'Wasn't it dark outside . . . how could he recognize you?'

'There was a street light . . . not too far away . . . I don't know . . .'

'Did you know who the second man was?'

'No, I had no idea . . . and I wasn't about to hang around to find out. I was in a state of shock . . . my whole body shaking, I got in my car and somehow managed to drive away. Knew for sure that Walter would come after me, knew right well what I had to do. I arranged a flight back to London. You know the rest.'

46

Emma sat in the passenger seat as Bob Crosby pulled to a stop in Essex Gate and parked on double yellows in front of Walter Schiller's photographic studio. Crosby had fetched Emma from Charleville Road after she'd failed to retrieve her car from St Louis High School; the gates had been locked while she'd been talking to Ellen O'Regan. She'd used her mobile to call Crosby, explaining her predicament, furious because she knew the school would not re-open until Monday. Being separated from her car would, under normal circumstances, have had her stomping her foot like a disobedient child, but not on this occasion. Before Crosby had a chance to bawl her out, she told him about her 'light bulb' moment. Barely containing her excitement, adrenalin racing through her like an electric charge, she finally knew who was behind the murders.

Crosby and Emma approached the double set of doors to the side of the photographic studio. They were locked but Emma pressed the bell push and held it down. She had told as much of the story as she could to Crosby in the time it took to get from Charleville Road to Essex Gate.

'Damn! No one's here,' she said.

'It's Saturday,' Crosby said with a shrug, 'What'd you expect?'

'Yeah, I know, but I *have* to get in . . . need to see what he's up to.'

'You're not suggesting we break in?' Crosby said, looking at the solicitors' offices above the studio, apprehension in his eyes, as though he'd already committed a crime.

'There's nobody in, Bob; solicitors don't work weekends.'

'You sure about that?'

'Sure I'm sure, but we've got no choice, we have to get inside,' Emma insisted, examining the perimeter of the ground floor. 'The place is like a fortress; look at the windows, they've got iron grills behind them.'

Crosby, breathing a sigh of relief, used his fingers to smooth down the scattering of grey hair that a breeze had unsettled. 'Too bad,' he said, heading towards his car. 'We'll have to return on Monday.'

'Monday's too late. Could have another dead body by then. I'm going to ring Connolly; this is too serious to — ' Emma stopped mid sentence as three cars raced towards her. Two of them were patrol cars but the lead car, unmarked, had Connolly at the wheel, Bridie McFadden riding shotgun. Connolly was as surprised to see Emma and Crosby as they were to see him.

'Just about to call you,' Emma said. 'How'd you know about this place?'

'Could ask the same of you,' he replied. 'Something else you haven't told us?'

'No, not at all,' Emma said, defensively, 'I just discovered Schiller's involvement after talking to Lynda O'Regan's sister. How'd *you* find out?'

'Cecil Charles told me,' he said, before turning to acknowledge his friend, Crosby. 'Hi, Bob. What brings you to a place like this on a cold Saturday morning?'

'You need to ask?' Crosby replied, nodding towards Emma while exchanging a knowing smile with Connolly.

'I take it there's no one here?' Connolly said.

'Well, as you can see,' Emma answered, not missing the macho interplay between the men, 'the place is locked up.'

'Not for long it isn't,' Connolly said, signalling to four uniformed officers who'd emerged from the patrol cars. 'Get this door open,' he ordered.

The double door gave way in a matter of minutes. Before the uniforms had time to dust themselves down and get their breath back, Connolly and McFadden had already entered the premises, followed closely by Emma and Crosby. 'I've been here before,' Emma informed Connolly. 'I've talked to Walter Schiller.'

'And you didn't smell a rat?'

'Didn't smell a damn thing. Most plausible fellow you could ever meet; course I'd no idea at the time that he'd lived with the woman at the centre of Trevor Kavanagh's rape accusation. He told me his wife was dead. I didn't twig, didn't ask the right questions.'

The vast area where Schiller's Christmas set stood on Emma's previous visit was vacant except for an array of lamps, lights stands, reflectors and industrial-sized rolls of coloured paper. The set had been disassembled into a series of flats that now leaned at slanted angles against the walls. Emma looked into the small office where she'd talked to Walter; everything appeared in order, including Friedrich Schiller's impressive collection of cameras. She was running her eye over the displays when she heard McFadden yell at Connolly to come see what she'd found.

Emma followed Connolly next door, a room twice the size of the reception area. Laid out like an exhibition display, the room contained several miniature scale models of theatre sets, each placed atop its own plinth, each with a postcard-sized identification plaque.

'These are beautiful,' Crosby said, 'see the detail . . . it's like looking at a film set or being in the Gate or the Abbey.'

'You're right,' Emma agreed, 'they're exquisite.' She recognized one or two of the sets from shows she'd seen in London with Vinny, back when they'd been together. Connolly drew her attention to the set he was studying. *Dance of the Vampires*, the plaque said, the model on the plinth above it, a miniature version of an overgrown cemetery, complete with Gothic church and horizontal grave stones. 'Well, it's obvious where he got his idea for killing Scott Mansfield,' Connolly remarked. 'Seems like Walter Schiller lives his life through his stage sets, a kind of fantasy land.'

'Except that people tend to end up horribly mutilated in his fantasy world,' McFadden said. 'There are a few other sets here that give me the willies just looking at them.'

Emma could see exactly what she meant. Apart from some of the better known stage productions, there were sets from shows with plaques that read: . . . *'James Joyce's The Dead', 'Carmen', 'Tristan und Isolde', 'Hill of Calvary', and 'Assassins'.*

'Looks like he's still working on this one,' Crosby said, indicating a model on a work-bench to one side of the room. A miniature American diner, complete with scale model table, chairs, jukebox, dance and stage areas, with stamp-sized posters of James Dean, Marilyn Monroe, and other icons from the 50s era, forming part of the elaborate set. 'Looks a bit like something from one of those paintings by Edward Hopper,' Crosby offered.

'No, it's not,' Emma said, 'but I think I know what it is.'

'Of course you do,' Crosby said with heavy sarcasm.

'It's *Pulp Fiction*. When I was in London I discovered that Cecil Charles and his brother Owen were working on a stage version of the film.'

'That ties in with what Charles told me,' Connolly said. 'He's known Walter Schiller from the time Walter and his father used to take photographs and listen to the music in the Kavanagh home. Cecil discovered that Walter had a special talent for set design. He's used him ever since to design and construct preliminary sets to help him sell the project to the financial backers. Charles then employs professionals to scale Walter's set concepts up to full size. He came here twice to see this set; on his second visit he missed

Schiller but followed him to Rathmines. He saw what Schiller had done to Alan Gibney and decided it was time to hot-tail it back to London.'

'And that was something Walter Schiller couldn't let happen.'

'Exactly, Emma,' Connolly said, 'which makes me fear for Dom Sutton and his wife and daughter. I had hoped that one, or all, of them might be here but it looks like we're too late, the place is empty.'

'Hey you guys,' McFadden called out, holding an open manuscript aloft in one hand. 'Take a gawk at this, will ya.'

'What is it?' Crosby asked.

'It's a musical score and it's got several pages torn out.'

'Let me see that,' Connolly said, taking it from his sergeant. '*The Rape of Lucretia* by Benjamin Britten,' he said, reading from the cover title. 'Well, at least we now know what was pushed down the men's throats. I'm not sure how much that would have helped if we'd known, but — '

Connolly was interrupted when a uniformed officer rushed into the room and beckoned him to hurry to the open studio. 'There's a noise,' the officer said, 'but we don't know where it's coming from.'

Emma and the others followed Connolly

into the main studio, all straining to hear the noise.

'Shhh,' Connolly said, putting a finger to his lips, 'be quiet for a minute, listen.' Silence followed. Just as everyone was about to resume talking, they heard a crashing sound. 'What's that?' Crosby asked. 'Sounded like it came from outside these walls.'

'It came from over behind that door,' Emma said, pointing to one of the flats that had formed part of the Christmas set. 'There's an actual door lurking behind those flats.'

The uniforms pulled the flats to one side, proving that Emma was right. Connolly tried the handle and wasn't surprised to find it locked. 'We don't know what's behind this,' he said, 'got to be careful.'

McFadden pointed to a grill above the door. 'Lift me up and I'll try to see if I can see or hear anything.'

Connolly nodded approval and directed two uniforms to hoist McFadden up until her head was level with the grill.

'Hello,' she shouted. 'I'm Detective Sergeant Bridie McFadden; if you can hear me bang on the door.'

Immediate response. Bang! Someone hit the door. They all heard it. A woman's voice, faint but discernible. 'Door's locked! Get us out. Please!'

47

Walter Schiller discarded the balaclava, wanting Dom Sutton to see his face, see the pain, the despair, the grief, the rage. Sutton attempted a defiant response, projecting the hardman visage he'd perfected in jail. A medium-sized man in good physical trim, Sutton's every pore exuded menace, his lived-in face a puzzle for those attempting to guess his age. Jail had left its mark. Scars and blemishes were scattered loosely about his shaven head, indications of the rough passage he'd endured. His eyes, little more than slits, looked sharp as black diamond.

With hardened criminals for company, men who'd raped, maimed and killed, Sutton had to use intimidatory tactics, convince them not to mess with him. It had worked for the most part, but not today, not in front of the merciless inspection of Walter Schiller. The past few hours had shaken his self-confidence, shaken it to the core.

A month earlier, John-Joe Moody had told him about Lynda O'Regan's death, warned him about Lynda's partner, Walter Schiller, claiming the man was on a vengeance trip, determined to get back at those who'd been involved in the rape. At first, he hadn't known what Moody was on about; it was only after he'd been reminded of the music lessons in Trevor Kavanagh's house and the night they'd got stoned, the night they'd each taken turns to have their way with the pretty housecleaner, that the episode came back to him. He'd never given it a second thought in the intervening years.

Hearing Moody's warning, he'd shrugged, thinking nothing would come of it. But then Moody disappeared. That gave him cause for concern. The murder of Mansfield left him in no doubt whatsoever. He went underground, attempted to find out what he could about the man Moody had told him about. Walter Schiller, he'd discovered, was unknown to his gangland friends, unknown to the police, and had no record of ever having been involved in crime or illegal activities of any kind.

The late-night panic phone call from his wife Patricia cut short his plan to get to Schiller before Schiller got to him. He'd been given little choice. *Do as we tell you or Jenny gets it* had been the photographer's mantra. Threats weren't necessary; he would never put his daughter's life in danger. She represented the one good thing in his life. He'd made a shed-load of money through his dubious business enterprises; he'd married a beautiful model, a trophy wife who in turn had married him for the luxurious lifestyle he could provide. Too late, he realized that without Jenny his existence wasn't worth a fiddler's fart.

Since Walter Schiller and John O'Regan had taken him, bound and gagged, from the photographic studio and brought him to the warehouse in Dublin's Island Bridge district, the interrogation had continued non-stop. 'You *really* don't remember me, do you?' Walter was saying. 'Back in Trevor Kavanagh's house when you, Mansfield, Moody and Gibney swanned around like spoilt, sniggering brats, you considered the rest of us unworthy of your attention. Except for Lynda O'Regan; she caught your eye, all right, didn't she? She caught all of your eyes. She was just the professor's lowly house-help, not someone from your social background or standing, but she was beautiful, young, innocent, ripe . . . everything you all lusted after . . . and that made all the difference.'

'Look,' Sutton said, 'you're right, we were a pain in the arse back then. We were young, thought the world was our playground. But you are wrong about Lynda O'Regan. We — '

Sutton's protestations ended abruptly when John O'Regan, who'd allowed Schiller do the talking until now, stepped forward and struck him across the face with his bare knuckles, drawing blood from his nose. 'Enough lies,' he said, 'we know what you did to my sister.'

'I'll handle this,' Schiller said to O'Regan, before turning his attention back to Sutton. 'What the four of you did to Lynda is beyond doubt. Some weeks before her death, she remembered exactly what happened. She'd received a heavy dose of medication and it induced a near-hypnotic state in her mind, it prompted her, involuntarily, to revisit the horrors from her past. She described how she was constrained while each of you had your way with her, how she screamed and begged you to stop, how you all laughed at her protests. She described the crude language, the filthy gestures, the smells, even the clothes you wore. Oh yes, Dom, she remembers the T-shirt you continued to wear after you'd dropped your trousers, it had a *Jesus Christ Superstar* logo on it; it was all she could see as you mounted her, grunting like a wild animal in rut, oblivious to her pain, her terror, her humiliation.

'There's something I'd like to show you, Dom,' Schiller said, producing an A4-sized envelope and extracting several 10" × 8" black-and-white photographs. 'I am an artist and I like to keep records of my work. Over the years I've created memorable images for fashion spreads that have graced some of the world's top glamour magazines; I have produced concepts for the sets used in several of the great stage shows in the West End, Broadway and throughout Europe but none gave me more satisfaction than this current project.

'This one for example,' he said, singling out one print and placing it in front of Sutton. 'This depicts your departed friend Scott Mansfield.' The image conjured up a Gothic atmosphere with Mansfield sprawled atop a gravestone, a stake protruding from his chest. 'Appropriate, don't you think?' Schiller said to Sutton, who stared at the photograph in stunned silence. 'Mansfield sucked the life out of Lynda. I had to give him an appropriate ending. Have to admit the initial idea came to my architect friend here.'

'It was through my architectural business,' O'Regan said, 'that I happened to come across Mansfield's elaborate plans to develop the St James's churchyard site.' I decided to put the information to good use, incorporate it into our quest for vengeance. It provided the perfect opportunity for me and Walter to achieve a measure of recompense for my sister's suffering. The whole Dracula nonsense was just a sideshow, a distraction for the investigators, a device to allow Walter exercise his creative faculties while giving us a little breathing space to complete the mission without undue interruption.'

'As it turned out,' Schiller said, taking up the commentary, 'we did the people of that neighbourhood a favour by focusing attention on the proposed desecration of the site.'

'You're fucking mad,' Sutton said, his voice little more than a croak. 'You're a one-hundred per cent fucking fruit cake. What you're doing — '

John O'Regan struck Sutton's face again, this time with more force than before, splitting his lips. 'You, Mr Sutton, are in no position to call anyone names so keep it buttoned, just look and listen.'

'This one,' Schiller said, placing a second print in front of Sutton, 'is how we treated your grunge friend Moody. On the spectacular scale it probably misses the wow factor but on a personal satisfaction level it achieves a certain poetic resonance. What Lynda remembered most about Moody was his suffocating body odour — it appears he was somewhat lax in the personal hygiene department. Turns out she was right. Eighteen years later, when John and I paid a visit to his sheep farm in County Meath, we discovered that he still stank to the high heavens. We packed him into his double bass case and doused him in his own sheep dip. The sad bastard needed it far more than his sheep.

'Ah yes, now we come to Alan Gibney,' Schiller said placing a third photograph on top of the others. 'He spent the longest time inflicting himself on Lynda. You and the others shouted at him not to hog the time all to himself. Didn't put Gibney off his stroke in the slightest, he continued to pound away like some kind of human piston, vocally insisting that he needed *time* — *time* to heat the meat, *time* for his knob to throb, *time* to let loose the juice. This was done to the accompaniment of hands clapping in rhythm with his thrusts, all of you chanting the word *time*, *time*, *time*, over and over again. Well, my theatrical instincts honed in on the *time* theme, so myself and John decided he should mark time on the clock above his reception desk.

'And now we come to you, Dom. You were the one who came up with the plan to make Trevor Kavanagh the fall guy. You knew how vulnerable the professor was, yet you persuaded the others to sacrifice him in order to save your own skins. You crucified the old man, sent him to an early grave, and it never cost you a second thought. That was bad enough but what you did to Lynda was the ultimate degradation. You were the one who inflicted the greatest damage on her; you were the one who, more effectively than any of the others, subjected her to a living hell, a hell that would bring about a prolonged, agonizing death years after the initial savagery had been inflicted on her.

'I gave considerable thought as to how I might devise an appropriate measure to make you understand the horror you subjected Lynda to. At first I was drawn to a biblical theme. I thought about the torment of Herod's final days, his genitals being eaten away by maggots, wondered if perhaps there might be a way to bring about a modern-day reconstruction, but with some reluctance, I rejected the idea. It didn't have the theatrical flair I desire. So, after tossing about a few more ideas, the two of us devised a *spectacular*, a setting like no other. We want the people of this great city to stare in awe at our production and wonder at what unspeakable crime you committed to have been given such a dramatic finale.'

48

Mother and daughter were traumatized. Their descriptions of what happened confused, barely coherent. Connolly, following proper procedures, insisted that they both undergo medical examinations. Patricia bitched like hell, railed against it. Exhausted, hungry and angry, she was furious that Jenny should have been subjected to such an experience and felt the need to lash out. Connolly and McFadden were the nearest to hand.

It took all the skill, patience and perseverance at Connolly's disposal to calm the woman down, get an intelligible account of what happened. Her erratic recollections helped fill in the blanks that had, until then, eluded him. Patricia hadn't known the names of either masked man but it was apparent to Connolly that Walter Schiller had been the one holding her. The other one had to be John O'Regan, Lynda's brother. This new information allowed him create an almost complete picture of Walter Schiller. For the first time since the case began he had a handle on the events that led to the killings and the motives that had driven the photographer to do what he had done. The knowledge enabled him to cross out the names of the Kavanagh siblings as suspects. It also cleared Dom Sutton but, more worryingly, it suggested the ex-con's life was in imminent danger. Patricia told him about the phone call she'd been forced to make to her husband and how she'd had to advise him to return the call or forfeit the life of his daughter. Dom Sutton had returned the call and eventually surrendered himself to the masked men.

Neither Patricia or Jenny had been allowed to see Sutton but Patricia had managed to hoist herself up to the vent above the door by levering a filing cabinet into a position against the door. She managed to overhear the odd word of conversation — not enough to make sense — but she was adamant that she recognized her husband's voice. According to her, the two captors talked to Dominic for no more than twenty minutes. There was silence after that, a silence that lasted until the arrival of Connolly and his back-up team.

After the interview, Connolly had given Patricia his mobile number in the hope that she would call him should she remember further fragments of conversation. What he'd got from her helped define the motive behind Walter Schiller and John O'Regan's murderous spree, but it didn't tell him where they had taken Dom Sutton.

It was 4.30 p.m. by the time he got back to Emma. Darkness had already spread its grimy shroud across the city, the narrow alleyways and older buildings assuming something of a Kafkaesque appearance. Nowhere more brooding than Dublin Castle. It was there, within the walls of the eighteenth-century building, ensconced in the Castle Vaults bistro, that Emma had arranged to meet Connolly.

'What a day,' Connolly said, allowing his shoulders to slump and his body sag like a bag of spuds as he collapsed on to a chair. He placed the mug of black coffee he'd been served at the counter on the table and sweetened it with two heaped spoonfuls of sugar.

'Been one heck of a day, that's for sure,' Emma agreed. 'But at least now we know who we're after.'

Connolly took a deep swig of coffee, said, 'Right, you're right, just a pity we haven't got a clue where they're hiding out.'

'I have this awful gut feeling that any moment now we'll get word that Dom Sutton's body has turned up in some bizarre murder scene.'

'God, I hope not! Right now I'm powerless to prevent something like that happening. It's like working in a vacuum. I've got the whole force on full alert but none of them know what to do or where to look . . . and the joke is: neither do I.'

'Didn't Patricia overhear snippets of conversation between Schiller and Sutton?'

'Ah, the woman's all over the place, doesn't remember half what she heard. Best I could get out of her was a few disjointed words, nothing worthwhile. I mean, there's not a lot you can do with random phrases and words like . . . *stretch* . . . *hang* . . . *kiss the ground* . . . *John Paul's children* . . . *show-time* . . . *spectacular, no rehearsal* . . . *swansong*. I have people working on it but so far, we're all at sea.'

'John Paul's children,' Emma said, 'has to refer to the Pope John Paul II. The *children* . . . can't think what that could mean.'

'We've all had a think about that one,' Connolly said. 'Back in 2006 there was a three-part television series called *The Pope's Children*; we thought it might be a reference to that so we've got someone looking at it as we speak. The programmes examined how the young people who greeted the Pope so enthusiastically on his visit to Ireland back in 1979 changed in the intervening years; they became the new middle class. Instead of bending the knee to Rome, they pledged their

336

allegiance to the Celtic Tiger, wanted to booze, eat, shag, shop, spend, play hard and earn bags of money. Which was all very fine and dandy except that, in the end, the Celtic Tiger turned rogue and the money dried up. If there's a connection in any of that to our case, damned if I see it.'

'Yeah, don't see how that ties in with Walter Schiller . . . except the current Pope is a German, and Walter's father was a German.'

'The German connection, of course,' Connolly said, keeping a straight face. 'What about the Marx Brothers and Matt Groening?'

'Very funny . . . I just thought . . . feck it, we're going around in circles.'

Connolly finished his coffee and was leaving when a call came through on his mobile. 'Yes, this is Connolly,' he said, 'who is this?' He covered the mobile, whispered to Emma, 'It's Patricia Dean.'

Emma said nothing, raised her eyebrows.

'You sure about that?' Connolly said into the phone. 'OK, thanks Patricia, could be a help. If you think of anything else, call me straight away.' He closed the connection and looked at Emma, a glint in his eyes. 'This could help. Patricia has just remembered hearing the words *Phoenix Park* being said to Dom Sutton. On its own it means diddly-squat but when you put it alongside the reference to the *Pope* — '

'Of course,' Emma said, tipping the heel of her fist against her forehead, 'The Pope visited Phoenix Park when he came to Ireland. A million people attended his Mass there. D'you think — '

'Yes, I think . . . I think that Schiller has taken Sutton to the Pope's site. I need to call HQ, get my team out there pronto.'

49

Emma knew exactly where she needed to get to. Dublin's Phoenix Park is the largest urban park in Europe with 1,760 acres of walled parkland, but that didn't faze her. Connolly, who had to check back with the station before leading his team to the park, did not allow her to accompany him. She didn't argue on this occasion. Because her car remained locked behind the gates of St Louis's High School, she'd contacted Pete Clarke, a photographer with the *Post*. He agreed to pick her up and take her to what she promised would be the biggest scoop of his life. Clarke, a gangly young man from Tipperary with carrot-red hair, had worked successfully with Emma on a few previous assignments.

It was Saturday, which meant they didn't have to bother with the evening city exodus of home-going workers. Clarke took the Strawberry Beds route and made it to the Knockmaroon Gate entrance at 7.10 p.m. in the evening. Emma couldn't help but notice the two small plastic cubes hanging from the central rear-view mirror; they were like dice without the dots and had the words — BALLS

TO PICASSO printed across them. Clarke obviously liked the visual pun because Emma could swear she'd seen the self-same cubes hanging in his previous car.

'Where to now?' he asked.

'Straight through to Furze Road and on to Chesterfield Avenue. We need to get to the Fifteen Acres site.'

'In that case I'd better take a right at the Phoenix monument.'

The park was quiet, just a few joggers happily pounding the cycle lanes, their Day-Glo track suits reflecting starkly in the beams of Clarke's headlights. Electric lighting, in the guise of antique gas lanterns, cast ghostlike effulgence on the oak, beech, pine and chestnut clumps that bordered Chesterfield Avenue. Dark skies, anchored to the treetops, were mottled by reflections of orange light spilling from the city's glow.

Passing the American Ambassador's residence, heading down the Acres Road, a herd of startled deer dashed across in front of them. Seconds later, it became clear what had spooked the animals; a cluster of bright headlight beams lit up the road, the reflected glare in Clarke's mirror temporarily blinding him. Three Garda squad cars whizzed by at great speed, sirens going full blast, blue lights flashing, and behind them, several unmarked cars going hell for leather.

Clarke and Emma watched the blue strobes and red tail lights zoom ahead of them, then suddenly break and halt. They had stopped at the junction that allowed access to the spot where the Pope had celebrated mass in the open air back in 1979. The altar had long since been removed and the site had become something of a tourist attraction. At night, the place evoked a more ungodly milieu, having gained a reputation as a pick-up spot for rent boys. Tonight, Emma could see a series of bollards blocking the entrance to the short length of road that allowed access. 'Pull in behind the cop cars,' Emma said, 'they'll think we're part of the posse.'

Clarke did as instructed, taking a sideways glance at Emma, unsure of what she was up to. They got out and edged their way on foot to where the occupants of the other cars were now grouped. Emma picked out the silhouettes of Connolly and McFadden, saw them gesticulating to those around them. All eyes stared upwards at the Papal Cross on the summit of a multi-stepped concrete platform. The towering steel structure had been erected as a monument to Pope John Paul II.

'Oh, Christ no!' Emma gasped. Like everyone else, she could see the semi-naked figure of a man being hauled upwards. Ropes, slung from the cross's transverse, tied to the man's arms, exaggeratedly extended the limbs. The body moved slowly upwards along the central post towards the arms of the great cross. The man's head slumped forward, his face hidden in dark shadow.

Emma strode towards the cluster of uniformed officers, determined to get past them in order to follow Connolly and his team. 'Hide the camera,' she whispered to Clarke, 'we've got to get up close.'

'Hey, hold it right there!' a uniform said to Emma, holding out a hand to stop her. 'Just where d'you think you're going?'

'I'm with Detective Inspector Connolly,' Emma lied confidently. 'He called me, told me to get here.'

'Oh, I see,' he said, sounding dubious, 'OK, you can pass.' He turned to Clarke, looked him up and down, said, 'That doesn't apply to you, mate, you're not getting through.'

Emma glanced back at Clarke, shrugged her shoulders, and hurried forward. She knew Clarke was resourceful enough to skirt around the site and get what he wanted with a telephoto lens. Moving quickly to the site, she could now make out the shape of the figure on the cross more clearly. Ground-mounted spotlights accentuated the body's contours, showing a black, gaping cavity where the man's genitals should have been. Blood glistened like black molasses in the artificial light. An ill-fitting T-shirt with the *Jesus Christ Superstar* logo stretched across the upper part of the body.

Activity at the base of the cross diverted Emma's eyes away from the grotesque sight. She could see Connolly, McFadden and a number of uniformed officers approach two men who were pulling on the ropes. Even in the uneven glare of light and shadows, Emma recognized Walter Schiller. She had never seen the other man before. Neither of them wore balaclavas, which struck her as odd.

Do they want to get caught?

They'd been about to secure the ropes to stays on the ground when the detectives interrupted. It was hard to hear what was being said but she was sure she heard Connolly tell the men to lower the body. She recognized Schiller's voice as he remonstrated, ranting on about how he had a duty to Lynda O'Regan, his words descending into a diatribe, words running into one another as he lambasted the musicians for destroying Trevor Kavanagh, destroying Lynda, destroying Lynda's family, blighting his life.

Connolly's voice cut through the denunciations. 'Let it down,' he ordered. 'Lower

Sutton to the ground.'

There was silence for a moment, then slowly, Schiller and the other man holding a rope levered Dom Sutton downwards. As soon as the blood-soaked body made it to the ground, Connolly had his officers arrest the two men. In the background, Emma could hear the wail of ambulances. She needed to get back to Clarke's vehicle, get away from here and write up her story. This really was a genuine exclusive. It would insure that her reportage would appear on the front pages of every paper in the coming days. So far, Connolly hadn't seen her and that was good as she had no wish to cause him embarrassment.

50

It was midday Sunday by the time Emma and Connolly got a moment to themselves. So much had happened in the hours since the dramatic events in the Phoenix Park. Because the *Post* didn't publish on Sunday, Emma had bought copies of every other newspaper available. All carried reports on the latest murder investigation developments at the time of going to press but the events at the Papal Cross had taken place too late to make it to the main issues of any of them. One story to catch Emma's eye concerned St James's churchyard and abbey. Plans to uproot the headstones and level the site had been rejected by the planning authority who, bowing to the wishes of the local residents, slapped a preservation order on the entire site. In a parallel development, Hugh Foley, the self-proclaimed carrier of the Bram Stoker flame, had prevailed on the Arts Council to provide a sizeable chunk of cash to fund Stoker's Lair. According to Foley, the money would be used to promote and develop an awareness of Bram Stoker's place in Irish literature.

Emma was relieved that Dom Sutton's murder had only managed to make a brief 'late news' sidebar on those papers available. Her story would headline the front page on Monday morning with the sort of banner treatment she liked to dream about.

She'd had long discussions with Crosby and Pete Clarke about the appropriateness of using photographs of the Papal Cross that included images of Sutton's body. Crosby had been greatly concerned, worried about giving offence, knowing that some might see the images as blasphemous. A compromise had been arrived at; they would use one of the shots Clarke had captured at some distance from the cross. It showed the Fifteen Acres site and the city lights in the background with the outline of the cross standing out in sharp relief against the orange-hued sky. A silhouette of ropes hanging from the cross's transverse added to the dramatic effect. Sutton's body was not visible.

Emma had returned to the *Post* with Clarke as soon as Schiller and O'Regan had been arrested and taken into custody. Before leaving the crime scene, she'd contacted Crosby and brought him up to speed with how events had unfolded. He'd been waiting for her and Clarke when they arrived back at the *Post*. Before Emma could tell him what had happened, Willie Thompson stormed into the room, his facial expression not unlike the proverbial boiled shite. Someone had got word to him about the breaking story. He had demanded to know why Ms Boylan — he never called her Emma — had been given the lead on what he termed, the 'crucifixion' story.

Crosby's reply had been concise. 'In a nutshell, Willie, Ms Boylan is a better reporter than you'll ever be. I took a chance by giving you lead status on this murder investigation but you lost your way, lost focus, got sidetracked on trivia. You came up short when the chips were down, penned pieces that were simply inept. You were conspicuous by your absence at the end of the chase. Emma *was* there! That's the difference! I didn't give her the lead, she went out there all by herself and worked her butt off to get it.'

'Well, in that case,' Thompson snarled, 'I'm quitting the *Post*. There's other newspapers out there who will appreciate my talent.'

'You do that, Willie.' Crosby said. 'Best of luck; you're going to need it.'

After that unpleasantness, Emma had worked on the story, finally at liberty to tell all the bits she'd been forced, until then, to hold back. At some point she would offer

Oonagh Kavanagh and her brothers the opportunity to put an account of their involvement in the case on record. Somehow, she doubted they would avail themselves of the offer, and that was fine as far as she was concerned. The next few days, she knew, would be taken up with television and radio news-based programmes, giving her firsthand account of what had happened in the lead-up to the events in the Phoenix Park. It would be a non-stop merry-go-round except there would be little merriment in what she had to talk about.

But before all that happened, she and Connolly got to close their door on the outside world, at least for a few hours. It was Sunday afternoon, and not since watching the film *Angela's Ashes* had she seen such unremitting rainfall. Going to bed seemed like the perfect option. They might have been dead on their feet but somehow or other they found enough energy to make love. In between times, they discussed the case that had taken up so much of their time in recent weeks. They talked about Walter Schiller and Lynda O'Regan's brother and wondered how the courts would deal with them when it came to the trial. They were silent for a while after that.

'All we need to know now,' Connolly said, 'is the date.'

'Could take anything up to a year; you know how long it takes the Director of Prosecutions to sort — '

'No, Emma,' Connolly interrupted, clasping her close to him, 'I'm not talking about the trial. I'm saying, all we need to know now is the date . . . the date for our wedding!'

We do hope that you have enjoyed reading this large print book.

Did you know that all of our titles are available for purchase?

We publish a wide range of high quality large print books including:
Romances, Mysteries, Classics
General Fiction
Non Fiction and Westerns

Special interest titles available in large print are:
The Little Oxford Dictionary
Music Book
Song Book
Hymn Book
Service Book

Also available from us courtesy of Oxford University Press:
Young Readers' Dictionary
(large print edition)
Young Readers' Thesaurus
(large print edition)

For further information or a free brochure, please contact us at:
Ulverscroft Large Print Books Ltd.,
The Green, Bradgate Road, Anstey,
Leicester, LE7 7FU, England.
Tel: (00 44) 0116 236 4325
Fax: (00 44) 0116 234 0205

M